High Prais(
ROBIN AND HE
by Kelly Ann Jacovson

D0752849

ROBIN AND HER MISFITS revisits a classic story about breaking the law, turning it into a poignant, exciting novel about queer love, homecomings, and hope.

FOREWORD REVIEWS

IN THIS MODERN reimagining of the legend of Robin Hood, a cast of queer girls fight to free themselves from the control of powerful crime families and their own pasts. Fast-paced action and high stakes.

KIRKUS REVIEWS

FOUND FAMILY IS a huge trope of this story . . . Compelling and heart-warming, with twists and turns, badassery, and a big sense of love.

READS WITH PRIDE

ROBIN AND HER MISFITS is another superb queer young adult retelling of a favorite classic from the marvelous Kelly Ann Jacobson. Misfits, indeed! Such stunning storytelling, with vibrant characters wholly Jacobson's own. I haven't enjoyed the trials and tribulations of a group of misfits quite as much since watching *Times Square*. You don't want to miss it.

ADDIE TSAI, author, *Unwieldy Creatures* and *Dear Twin*

THIS LIGHTNING-PACED NOVEL is addictive for any misfit who's felt lost and angry, who hankers after a little bit—okay, a whole lot—of revenge. If you're craving a dose of transgression in your reading, these queer gangster girls, and their madcap capers, are for you.

LUCY JANE BLEDSOE, author, *No Stopping Us Now* and *Tell the Rest*

ROBIN AND HER MISFITS reads like the action movie with all-female leads you always hoped for. A greasy, gritty adventure carved for those who need a massive flip in the script. This is one gang of master criminal misfits you wouldn't want to mess with. A delightfully queer troop of outliers who dare to lean into all the twists and curves.

JESSAMYN VIOLET, author, *Secret Rules to Being a Rockstar*

ROBIN
AND HER
MISFITS

ROBIN
AND HER
MISFITS

a novel

KELLY ANN JACOBSON

THREE ROOMS PRESS
New York, NY

Robin and Her Misfits
A NOVEL BY Kelly Ann Jacobson

© 2023 by Kelly Ann Jacobson

ISBN 978-1-953103-31-4 (trade paperback)
ISBN 978-1-953103-32-1 (Epub)
Library of Congress Control Number: 2022945959

TRP-102

Publication Date: April 25, 2023
First Edition

Young Adult Fiction: Ages 14+
BISAC Coding:
YAF017010 Young Adult Fiction / Fairy Tales & Folklore / Adaptations
YAF031000 Young Adult Fiction / LGBTQ+
YAF022000 Young Adult Fiction / Girls & Women
YAF058280 Young Adult Fiction / Social Themes / Activism & Social Justice

COVER DESIGN AND ILLUSTRATION:
Victoria Black: www.thevictoriablack.com

BOOK DESIGN:
KG Design International: www.katgeorges.com

DISTRIBUTED IN THE U.S. AND INTERNATIONALLY BY:
Publishers Group West: www.pgw.com

Three Rooms Press | New York, NY
www.threeroomspress.com | info@threeroomspress.com

For Heather

ROBIN
AND HER
MISFITS

PROLOGUE

AN HOUR OUTSIDE OF PHOENIX, VISITORS who know what they are looking for drive down the highway at a hundred miles an hour and then, seemingly out of nowhere, squeal to a stop. There is no sign at the turnoff, but if visitors look closely, they can see an N carved in the trunk of a desert ironwood. From the ironwood, cars follow a dusty dirt road over the mild ups and downs of hills, passing giant saguaro cacti, prickly pear cacti, Palo Verde trees, and a variety of palms. Feral, rosy-faced lovebirds nest under the palms' fronds and forage for seeds and berries. Lizards bask in the sun.

At a second N, visitors turn left and meet the blank face of a building. Nottingham, the building proclaims in austere letters. A greenhouse to their right contains tropical flowers pressed against the glass; a garden to the left is full of ripe fruits and vegetables ready for picking. Only the founders know the real secret behind this utopia.

"Well, hi there!" says a middle-aged woman in an unfamiliar southern drawl. She wears a cowboy hat over her chin-length brown hair, and her wheelchair sports a sticker that says PRIDE in rainbow letters. "Welcome to Nottingham! Y'all just make yourselves at home. If you need anything, just holler 'Skillet' and I'll help you get where you're going, you hear?"

There is a map nearby, and visitors check their cottage assignments. Behind the main building, which contains the mess hall and classrooms where the girls will take their summer classes, are ten cottages labelled A-J. Farther back, three houses take up the rest of the map space but aren't labelled. From the brochures, visitors know that the founders live there, and that they will give keynote addresses every morning after breakfast in the Daisy Chain Auditorium. Their schedules, ordering them to computer science, statistics, ethics, and biology classes every day for the next week, are safely packed in their bags.

"That's her," one girl whispers. She points her parents in the direction of a woman in hiking boots, cargo pants, and a tank top with sweat circles under her arms. Her long red hair is tied up in a ponytail stuck through the back of a baseball cap. "That's Robin. Her real name is—well, no one knows. Anyway, she's the woman who founded this whole place."

Other celebrities make their appearances. Little John stands out from the crowd with her trademark fitted blazer, and Wanda's glasses are bigger than ever as she blinks through them at their new recruits. White Rabbit scurries past them too, her cheeks berried by the burning Arizona sun. All the original members of Nottingham are there except one—who exists only as a name on the side of a building. They shake hands, make introductions, calm the girls' nerves by making silly math jokes.

Once the girls have chosen bunks and stored their trunks at the foot of them, they kiss their parents goodbye and head to the auditorium for orientation. Many of the adults will go home, but some will take Tiny Notts up on its offer of one free night at The Nott in Phoenix and turn the week into a vacation, in the meantime spending hundreds of dollars on drinks, slots, and entertainment. When they come back for their children, they will be hungover and sleep deprived, and the explanations of the differences between C, C++, Java, and some other words they don't understand, will flow around them like the water in their hotel room hot tub. *That's wonderful,* they will say, rubbing their temples. *You can tell me all about it once we get home.*

Most of these girls will grow up to be coders, engineers, CEOs of businesses.

Some of them will be thieves.

But for now, they are just energetic rabbits hopping across the grounds, or shy mule deer hiding in the shadows of cacti, or occasionally mountain lions prepared to fight for their territory in the harsh terrain of the world outside of Nottingham. They are voices rolling down the hills, and laughter echoing with the birdcalls. They are children.

Robin watches them from the window of her camper and thinks of how once, a long time ago, she and the other Misfits were children too. How they danced around the campfire in Florida and forgot their worries for a brief time. Little Notts Retreat brings them all together one week a month, but soon they will dissipate like water from a dried-up creek.

Someone knocks on her door. "Are you ready?" Skillet calls out. Robin is to give the welcome address, as she does at the start of every session.

"Just a minute." Robin grabs her notecards from the bed, where she once lay with Daisy Chain and quoted Shakespeare, and checks herself in the mirror. *Perk up*, she tells her frowning face. She must be a beacon for these girls, the kind of example that Daisy Chain would have been. *Or maybe still is*, Robin thinks, though she knows better.

"Robin?"

"Meet you in there!" she yells.

Robin listens to the sound of Skillet leaving her trailer. She loves Skillet, but she isn't in the mood for one of her pep talks. She wishes she could go to the greenhouse and work or take her bike out on the road and let the dust fly. She wishes she could be alone. She is like a mountain lion, preferring to hunt by herself from dawn to dusk.

How can she inspire a group of girls to work hard when she can't even inspire herself?

Still, Robin aims her feet toward the auditorium anyway. She has a duty to fulfill, and she has never shirked her responsibilities as Nottingham's leader—not back when it was just five girls who had no idea what they were doing, and not now, when it is a hundred girls who know exactly where they're headed.

Robin passes the welcome booth, where Adele—Skillet and White Rabbit's daughter—waits to check latecomers into their online system. She looks so young in her oversized Tiny Notts Retreat t-shirt and khaki shorts, but two nights ago, Skillet took her driving for the first time. "I nearly peed myself," Skillet confessed when she came over for a drink that night. "I'll tell you, that girl might be my daughter, but she has way more of White Rabbit in her."

"What's the count?" Robin calls out.

"Only missing five," Adele yells back, "and one of them called to say her flight was delayed."

Robin waves to Adele and then enters through the back door by swiping her access card. She always wonders about those few girls who never show up—about whether they just got nervous about leaving home for a week, or whether they are like Daisy Chain, barreling down a highway in the car of a stranger, running away.

If the second is true, she hopes that they find their fellow misfits soon.

Once inside, Robin pulls her shirt away from her sweating body to allow herself to cool. Then, she follows the babble of excited voices down the hall to the door marked "backstage," and then to the edge of the thick red curtain. Skillet is there waiting for her, and as soon as she sees Robin, she nods and moves to the center of the stage to give her introduction. The whole room goes quiet to listen.

"I am honored to introduce a very special guest," Skillet begins. "Many of you know her as the founder of the Tiny Notts Retreat, but Robin is so much more than that."

Robin knows the rest of the speech by heart, though every time she listens to it, she still marvels at how she could be the subject. Junior police academy failure. Then thief. Leader of thieves. Car mechanic. Thief again. Finally, founder, though she never quite feels she can take credit for what is really Daisy Chain's dream.

Skillet whistles like she's calling pigs for slop. The crowd goes silent.

But for some reason, this time, Robin doesn't move. She can't. Her memories are like the wind that whips against her cheek as she barrels down a highway at ninety, and the present, all of Nottingham, is the fading background in her rearview mirror. How can she sell the idea of doing good when Daisy Chain's disappearance was Robin's fault? How can she stand up here and proclaim she knows what's best for these girls?

How can she do anything but run away?

Skillet angles her head away from the microphone and whispers, "You comin'?"

Robin turns to her and motions for her to keep going with a roll of her hands.

"So . . . uh . . . I guess Robin can't give her speech today," Skillet begins, "but I'll do my best to replace her. And to stop myself from making any lame jokes . . . Though, really, my whole life felt like one bad joke until I found Nottingham: what do you get when you cross a queer girl, a getaway car driver, and a Southern belle? Honestly, I'm still finding out the punch line for that one, but at least I have a group of friends who have my back no matter who I decide to be."

The girls listen, enraptured. Their faces are bright in the warm auditorium lighting. Their hands are clasped in their laps.

Behind the stage, Robin feels something strong inside of her break, like the limb of a wind-whipped live oak. She starts to cry.

Skillet tells the girls about her upbringing in Georgia and the way she used to dance around their farm in rubber boots; how her father once sent her to a conversion camp with the warning that if it didn't work, he never wanted to see her face again; how after she left, she made money as a Shania Twain impersonator, singing "Man! I Feel Like a Woman" on street corners in a veil and top hat. Then she sings a few lines. The girls are mesmerized. The ones that know the song join in, belting the lyrics to the chorus, and the rest clap and holler.

Once the crowd settles down again, Skillet tells the girls about her wife, White Rabbit, and how she was given up for adoption; how she ran away from her fifth foster home with five dollars and a stolen Dell laptop; how for a long time she wished she had never been born. Without the Merry Misfits, she says, the two of them would probably still be out hustling for a few bucks. Instead, they made themselves a new home—a safe space where they could be themselves. "This is your safe space," she tells the auditorium of girls. "You might hit some obstacles along the way, but you'll do what families are *supposed* to do—support each other, so that you can all be the best versions of yourselves."

The best version of yourselves.

But what was Daisy Chain's best version? Portia? Rosalind? Viola? It's been twenty years since she disappeared, and Robin still doesn't know.

Soon Little John will go back to her casino empire with Wanda, who runs her own surveillance company, and Skillet and White Rabbit will go back to their house in Georgia. Robin will be the only one left, married, as the Misfits claim, to the earth of Arizona.

Robin's name is getting louder and louder.

"Robin?" Skillet is calling. "Robin, can you please come to the stage?"

Don't think about the past, Robin scolds, the way she used to over and over again in that Florida forest. *Focus on the road.*

But this time, all she can focus on is *her.*

PART ONE
ROBIN

CHAPTER ONE

THE ROAD AHEAD OF ROBIN WAS empty, save for one long truck plowing through the Florida humidity like a bull through a red cape. The silver letters of the company name, More4Less, were scattered in a way that made the two words look like horns, and they glinted in the early morning sun. Around the straight shot of I-10 was a wall of trees she'd been whipping past for thirty minutes—these were the way she noted the distance between her and her mark—along with the occasional rest stop.

Her cell phone rang, and she answered it with her earpiece.

"It's time for the robin to leave the nest," a distorted voice said.

"Copy that. Robin leaving the nest."

Robin leaned forward, squeezed the Yamaha's clutch lever in and out, and twisted the throttle toward her, simultaneously pressing the pedal of her motorcycle like an equestrian kicking her heels. The truck came into focus; she could read the caution sign on the back door. According to the warning, she should stay back at least two hundred feet—though of course she had no intention of doing so.

A dusty red truck swerved onto the highway at twenty miles over the speed limit and took the right lane. At the wheel was a brunette wearing a cowboy hat and aviator sunglasses, and in the passenger seat, the top of a shorter girl's head was barely visible over the door. Both driver and passenger looked at Robin, who nodded as best she was able with her head covered by her helmet.

The cowgirl accelerated.

Robin accelerated.

Like two synchronized skaters, the car and motorcycle changed places, with Robin slightly ahead.

The More4Less truck was only one hundred feet away, then fifty, then ten. Robin choked on exhaust, and then she was past the edge of the truck and at its side, riding the shoulder. The road was bumpier there, rattling her whole body. She pushed the motorcycle even faster, until she could see the driver through the window. Pudgy guy, dusty blue baseball cap, burger wrapper on the dash.

"What are you doing?" he yelled through his half-open window. His face was red and furious. "You're going to get yourself killed."

Robin's cell phone rang again, and she kept the motorcycle balanced with one hand and answered.

"Fly," the husky voice said.

Robin took a deep breath, filling her lungs with oxygen, exhaust, and humidity. Her muscles clenched and unclenched like a boxer punching his gloves together before a match. Then she swung her right leg up and secured her foot on the seat, crouched so that she had all her weight on that foot, and leapt from the motorcycle to the truck, finding a hold on the handle and balance on the step. Her own vehicle careened off the road into the trees, and she said a little prayer for her departed baby.

Wind whipped against her helmet, so she threw it off, revealing her face to the scared driver. His eyes squinted; he was probably thinking, *What's a redheaded punk doing on my truck? Is she even old enough to drive?*

This was what she intended.

She wanted him to underestimate her.

Robin reached through the window to unlock the door. She had done this so many times before that the steps—balancing her weight on the frame of the window, letting the door swing wildly open like a bull bucking her off, and then circling the door and jumping inside before it slammed closed behind her—were automatic. They were a dance, and Robin was the experienced choreographer.

The clap of the door falling into place made the driver jump. "Are you crazy?" he screamed. Then he slammed against the brakes, making them squeal. Robin got herself buckled into the passenger's seat just in time, and though her neck whipped forward toward the dirty, bug-crusted windshield, she trusted that the driver wouldn't put his own life at risk. Sure enough, the stop was abrupt—but not dangerously so.

"Are you some kind of runaway?" the driver asked. "Why didn't you just put your thumb out, like a normal kid would do?"

Robin smiled at him. "I'm not a normal kid." And she wasn't even a kid anymore—not since her eighteenth birthday a month ago—but it was better not to deal in numbers. When he gave the police report, his description of *Fifteen or sixteen, at the most?* would only add to her mystery.

"I can see that." The driver seemed to calm down at the sound of her voice, which she'd set at a purposefully charming tone. He leaned toward her a little, his belly straining against the belt. "What do you want, then, if it's not a ride?"

A little closer, Robin thought. Slowly, she unzipped her jacket pocket. The driver leaned in, continued to lean, so that she could see the redness of his sleep-deprived eyes. *Now.*

She reached into her leather jacket to the secret pocket, removed a pair of handcuffs, and in one quick snap, locked the driver's hands together. Then she leaned back, pulled her legs up onto her seat, and kicked the driver squarely in the chest, sending him out his door and into the waiting arms of Skillet and Little John.

"Oof," Skillet grunted, though she was several feet taller than Little John. "This guy weighs, like, a thousand pounds, and he's ugly as homemade sin."

Robin made a mental note to increase Skillet's morning training by thirty minutes—two more laps around camp, thirty more squats, and fifteen more push-ups. She'd also need to have a firm discussion with her about her heist attire—in this case, boot-cut blue jeans and a crop-top with fringe—though she couldn't resist smiling at one of Skillet's southern-isms. Little John, who never said much, looked at Skillet and then rolled her eyes. She had followed Robin's instructions, arriving in a sensible black turtleneck and comfortable black jeans. Her short black hair was smeared in a comb-over, which Robin knew from experience wouldn't get tussled even if a fight broke out.

"Leave Little John to watch him," Robin instructed Skillet. "You and I have work to do."

Robin removed the keys from the truck, jumped down, and circled around to the back, where Skillet had parked the red truck backwards. *Please be there. Please be there.* Then she confidently lifted the door to find boxes upon boxes of flat screen televisions.

Robin hopped up and eyeballed the measurements of one of them—53 inches by 32 inches by 7 inches—and then did a little mental math with the seven-foot compact long bed of their truck. She should have asked Little John, the math genius, to figure it out, but she couldn't bear admitting that she struggled to do even basic division. "We can fit twelve straight in," Robin finally determined. They had to be fast now, so Skillet handed down each box and Robin packed it onto their truck bed while counting down the seconds. The whole operation had to take less than five minutes—the amount of time it usually took the cops to notice what they were doing—and they only had a minute to get their butts in the truck and drive away. Thirty seconds. Ten. Before she turned away, Robin pulled off the 200 feet warning sign and threw it into the back with the TVs.

"Little John," Robin yelled out. She waited for Skillet to get out of the More4Less truck and then closed the door with a victorious crash, while Skillet got in the driver's seat of her own truck and started the engine. Robin got in the passenger's seat, and Little John hopped up onto her lap. Robin knew she would hear about this later—demeaning to short people and all of that—but for now, she focused on the work ahead. Not only did they need to out-drive the cops, but they needed to get back to their hideout undetected.

Robin's phone rang. "We're in," she said. "White Rabbit, take us down the hole."

Skillet peeled away, spinning dust behind them. Robin imagined White Rabbit hunched over her keyboard, chewing nervously on a sour straw as she hacked into the security cameras along their route and rendered them invisible. Her fingers were probably flying over the keys, clacking them like rain on a roof. Robin collected headsets from Skillet and Little John, added hers to the pile, and tossed them out the truck window so that they landed ahead of the wheels for Skillet to run over.

Everything was disposable on a job—and everyone.

CHAPTER TWO

SKILLET TURNED ONTO NOTTINGHAM ROAD, a dusty, narrow lane carved through the trees. To any other driver, the road looked like a dead end, just another false path through the maze of Florida wildlife—and that was exactly what the Merry Misfits wanted them to think. Dozens of drivers had come down this exact path and then turned, their bumpers brushing against iron plants and elephant ears and the other underbrush the Merry Misfits used to keep the wall dense and green. They knew this because they had watched each one, held their breath, exhaled when every frustrated driver sent a curse out their rolled-down windows and peeled back onto the highway. Only when this truck—or one of Skillet's previous rides—came down Nottingham Road did the "end," a gate covered weekly in new plants by the green-thumbed Daisy Chain, swing away to reveal the rest of Nottingham Road.

"Welcome home," White Rabbit yelled out, only glancing from the security cameras in her guard post long enough to wave a hand in their direction. The door to the post was open, revealing Daisy Chain, who sat in the other swivel chair in the office. She smiled dreamily and then removed a dandelion from behind her ear and tossed it to Robin.

"How romantic," said Little John with an eye roll.

"Don't be jealous, Little John," Robin said. She kissed her best friend on the cheek.

"I'm not jealous." Little John wiped her cheek with her palm. "I'm just worried that you'll get distracted."

Robin laughed as the truck came to a stop and the gate swung slowly closed behind them. Skillet left Robin and Little John to take the extra seat in the guard post next to White Rabbit, her girlfriend, so Daisy Chain ambled over to the truck and asked if they needed help.

"Can you even lift one of these boxes?" asked Little John.

Daisy Chain gave another dreamy smile. "*We are such stuff as dreams are made on.*"

Little John looked pointedly at Robin. "See what I mean. It's distracting just trying to figure out what she's saying half the time."

"Be nice, Little John," Robin scolded. She put her arm around Daisy Chain's waist and said, "I like the way you talk, Daisy."

"*This above all; to thine own self be true,*" Daisy Chain responded.

Robin still remembered the first time she had seen the girl who would become Daisy Chain sitting in front of a rest stop near Lake City braiding flowers into a crown. Her dirty blond braids were a wild haze around her blank white face; her pale fingers fidgeted the stems like an old woman worrying beads. When Robin crouched down next to her, she didn't look up from her work, and Robin realized the girl was humming to herself.

"Are you here alone?" Robin asked the girl, who dropped the flowers but didn't look up.

"*Parting is such sweet sorrow*," Daisy Chain whispered.

"*Romeo and Juliet?*" Robin thought she remembered the line from two years ago—the last time she set foot in a high school classroom.

Daisy Chain raised her wide, green eyes. They watered, and then a tear fell on the head of a daisy.

"Listen," Robin said, "me and some other runaways have a place near here. If you want, I can take you there, but I'll have to blindfold you until I know I can trust you."

The girl seemed to think the proposition over. She took up the flowers again and petted them lightly with the tips of her fingers. "*Love all, trust a few, do wrong to none*," she finally said, and though Robin wasn't sure if that was an answer or a command, Daisy Chain allowed Robin to take her yellow and orange woven bag and sling it over her shoulder. Robin wondered what was in there, clanging against her back like a percussion section; she later found out the only things Daisy Chain had packed when she left home were five sets of knitting needles, armfuls of wilted flowers, a loaf of smooshed bread, and an empty milk jug full of change that had spilled into the bottom of the sack.

Now, Daisy Chain was as unhelpful as ever, watching Little John and Robin unload the TVs as she plucked purple petals off sun-browned spear thistle and rained them on the ground.

"She's a regular Ophelia," Little John said. "If only she'd do us all a favor and—"

"Enough," Robin said sharply.

Little John huffed and then lifted one of the TVs without another word.

One set belonged to each girl, so the first five had to be carried to their various trailers via the winding path through high grass. When Robin and Little John, the first Merry Misfits, had found the foreclosed lot, rattlesnakes had hold of the land and needed to be shot dead from the steps of the rusty trailer with Little John's pistol. Once they had even had to fire the gun through an open window, a determined rattler slithering up and down the door like a branch brushing in the wind. That scratching sound still haunted Robin's nightmares, though she and Little John spent every morning patrolling the property.

With the TVs in front of their faces, Robin and Little John had to trust that they'd done a good enough job purging the property and that a resilient snake wasn't about to dash under a foot or bite an ankle. The trees were quiet today—quieter now that Little John was giving her the silent treatment—but Robin could still pick out the murmur of daily forest life. As osprey or red-shouldered hawk diving for a mouse; a woodpecker drumming its beak into a tree; two squirrels leaping from branch to branch. The path went on for about a hundred feet, where the narrow dust hit a wider roundabout.

"Just leave them inside the door," Robin reminded Little John. "White Rabbit will hook them up tonight."

Little John took a hard right toward her trailer, distinguished by its one bush and freshly swept steps, and Robin headed to the second one, where her Adirondack chairs hid beneath a tan canopy. Nottingham had changed a great deal since the early days, and the original trailer had been gutted and used for parts. Five new trailers—or rather, five new-to-them trailers stolen from rest stops—sat around the cul-de-sac like smudges in the dirt. The outsides were all painted in identical dirt brown so as not to be visible from above, but each girl had free reign to decorate the front and interior to her own tastes.

Robin slid her TV into her trailer, stepped back outside, and shut the door quickly. If there was one thing she'd learned about Florida in the past two years, it was that the mosquitos were vicious and would seize any opportunity to get inside. She hated the ringing in her ears as they circled her head, and several nights she had turned the light on and chased a single mosquito around the room for over an hour.

Already, sweat dripped from Robin's brow down her cheeks, throat, collar. She slipped off her jacket and slung it over the back of one of the Adirondack chairs, then sat in the other to take a quick breather. The chairs made up what Robin called her "Listening Corner," where the girls came to air their grievances against the other Merry Misfits or propose a job to Robin, and the two glasses on the side table between them were still sticky from the lemonade she'd drank with White Rabbit the night before.

Robin had never intended to become the leader of their band, but then again, she had not shied away from taking charge either. Thieving came naturally to her, always had, and over the years she had developed an instinct for knowing which ideas would work and which ideas would land her in the back of a police car. In the same way White Rabbit played the keyboard of her computer like an instrument or Skillet navigated her truck like a tamed horse, Robin lifted items off shelves like a magician dumping a deck of cards into an empty hat. She loved the thrill that made her heart pump faster and her hands twitch, but more than that, she loved the feeling of justice that washed over her as she "redistributed" a watch or a diamond bracelet onto a more deserving hand—though, of course, that hand usually belonged to a Misfit. After all, didn't they deserve a break after the cards they'd been dealt? Didn't they deserve to be free—even if that meant selling the watch, or bracelet, or television, or stolen car to the highest bidder to keep themselves safe?

Robin thought so.

They all did.

"You coming, Little John?" Robin called out, but there was no answer.

I guess I'll unload these myself, Robin thought, and plied her sweaty body out of the chair.

Robin dropped off the third TV inside of Skillet's Midwest-themed trailer, complete with a pair of horns on the wall and a rope lying on the couch for which purpose Robin tried hard not to imagine; she liked White Rabbit and Skillet together, but there was no denying that their relationship made the group dynamic . . . complicated. White Rabbit's TV was next, though Robin didn't see the point of adding yet another screen to a trailer already full of them. White Rabbit slept at Skillet's, so her trailer was also the security hub when she wasn't at the front post. Even her living room had so many boxes of wire, cables, and chargers that Robin couldn't find enough room to leave the TV, so she set it in the path between stacks and left to get the final set.

Of all their trailers, Daisy Chain's was the most beautiful. Pale pink walls, small watercolors framed and hung in random clusters, flowers in so many vases that the direct sunlight turned the room into a kaleidoscope. Robin had woken up there a few times after a particularly wild night, and she loved the way the light made her feel like she'd entered another dimension.

"*I would not put a thief in my mouth to steal my brains,*" said a voice behind her. Daisy Chain had come home, or she had followed Robin there, and now she stood in the doorway smiling at her own private joke. Even Robin was stumped, so Daisy Chain tilted her head thoughtfully toward the box and then said the line again.

"Oh." Robin kicked the box. "You don't want one?"

Daisy smiled a no, so Robin, now thoroughly drenched in sweat, lifted the box for the second time and carried it back to the truck, muttering all the way. The door to the guard post was shut and the shades were drawn, so she got in Skillet's truck and honked the horn. No response.

"I'm turning the truck on," she yelled.

No response, so she turned the key. The engine roared. Still no response.

"I'm depressing the clutch." Pause. "I'm putting it into first gear."

Silence. Robin thought she heard a giggle.

"Oh no, is that sound normal? What does that light mean?"

The door opened and Skillet, shoeless and shirt askew, stumbled through it. Behind her, White Rabbit had already returned to her keyboard.

"If you hurt my baby, I swear to God . . ." Skillet stopped, one boot on and the other in her raised hand, and looked at the truck.

"Can you please move your baby out of the way?" Robin asked sweetly. "I've invited a visitor."

CHAPTER THREE

THE DAY GREW HOT AND HUMID, like a bathroom with the shower temperature turned all the way up. The windows of Robin's trailer had a layer of wetness she could lick off with her finger, and her air conditioners whirred as they struggled to battle the heat beating at the roof. She waited for her buyer in short shorts and an oversized t-shirt cut and tied at the bottom to barely cover her midriff. Not exactly professional, but she and Frank were well beyond that.

Robin's cell phone rang. "Send him back," she said without waiting for an introduction.

A few minutes later, Frank's heavy fist pounded against the aluminum door.

"Come in," Robin called.

A man in a black t-shirt opened the door wide and stepped into the trailer, causing the whole thing to shake. He was the kind of man who probably had to shop in the Big & Tall section of the department store, and squeezing into the tight trailer probably felt as claustrophobic as the times Robin had ridden to a heist in a trunk. His hair was molded like a Ken doll, and the t-shirt revealed his ample biceps.

"Hey, Blake."

"Robin." Blake nodded formally—too formally for her liking, considering their history—and then stepped aside to make room for Frank, a bespectacled old man in a nondescript brown sweater, baggy khakis that fell past the tops of his shoes, a wool cap despite the heat, and orthopedic sneakers. His cane, an innocent wooden stick with a silver handle, had been used many times on unsuspecting sellers who misjudged Frank as too senile to notice a short shipment.

"Lemonade?" Robin asked. She didn't bother to get up but waved a sweaty hand toward the pitcher on the counter behind her. The trailer was set up like most houses—living room upon entry, galley kitchen, bathroom, and the master bedroom all the way in the back—but most houses probably didn't have a souvenir from every heist decorating the walls.

"New?" Frank asked, waving his cane toward the 200 feet sign.

"Sharp eye," Robin said. "From this morning."

Frank nodded at Blake, who stayed near the door as both lookout and guard. Robin felt a quick squeeze in her stomach but forced herself to appear calm.

"Why don't you tell me what's troubling you, Frank?" she said. She decided to get up and pour the lemonade after all—something to do with her hands—so she retrieved handfuls of ice from the freezer for each solo cup and filled them almost to the brim.

"I'm not the only one with a sharp eye," said Frank.

"You taught me well." She handed him the glass. "So, what's up?" Her mind went to the knife sheathed and loosely sewn into the throw pillow behind her, the pistol secured under her kitchen table, the garrote lying in her glove compartment. She sat back down in her recliner.

Her fingers tapped her cup. She tried not to stare too long at Blake.

Frank took a big gulp of lemonade. "There's a bounty on your head."

Robin laughed. "There's always a bounty on my head."

"Not like this." Frank didn't smile. "Half a mill for information that leads to your capture."

Robin suddenly felt like she couldn't swallow. "Half a mill? That's ridiculous."

"That's what I thought, too." Frank put his lemonade down on the end table next to his recliner. "Then I did a little digging. Turns out my little Robin bird has some secrets she's kept from Uncle Frank—and from her little Misfits too. Or should I call you—"

"Don't." Robin tried to take a deep breath. If Blake came for her, she would need to be fast. Her gaze went to his holster. He was quick, but she was quicker—assuming she could get a gun in her hands in enough time to fire. How many times had they shot bottles down in the yard behind Uncle Frank's warehouse?

"Give me one reason not to do it," Uncle Frank said. He was pleading with her, which meant there was still hope.

"One reason?" She had to stall, give herself time to think. She didn't have a million dollars—she didn't even have half a million between all her buried safes. "I can give you several. But the best one?" *Think, Robin. What does Uncle Frank want more than anything?* "I'll do that job you wanted."

Uncle Frank tilted his head slightly, which meant he was thinking something over. "Tempting offer," he mused.

"More than tempting. That job alone would bring in over two mill, easy. And besides," she moved her voice into its most appealing notes, "you couldn't really turn me in, could you? Your little Robin."

Uncle Frank shook his head, but at least he was smiling. "You are good, I'll give you that." Then he nodded. "I guess not. Bring me what you promised, and I'll make sure that no one else finds out about this little haven of yours. Do we have ourselves a deal?"

Robin put her hand out, and Uncle Frank took it between his two dry palms and squeezed. Then he stood up, with the help of the armchair, and turned to go.

"Oh, and Robin?" Uncle Frank asked.

"Yes?" For some reason, Robin's gaze went to Uncle Frank's cane. As if in slow motion, she registered the twist of his wrist, the almost inaudible click, the tensing of his right arm.

"No one can know we were ever here. Understood?"

Robin tried to take another deep breath, but her lungs felt squeezed by her ribs. She fought down her panic. This was not just about her—if she was captured, what would happen to the Merry Misfits?

"Understood," she managed to say.

With agility unmatched by his appearance, Uncle Frank swung the cane up onto his left forearm and pushed. The blade at the end went into Blake's chest, piercing through his heart like a skewer through a piece of raw meat. Robin held back a scream. Blake sunk to the floor of the trailer, shaking the whole room.

"I'll contact you soon," Uncle Frank called behind his shoulder. A second later, he was gone.

Robin sunk to her knees. She crawled over to Blake, who gazed somewhere over her right shoulder as blood pooled underneath him. "Oh my god, oh my god," she said as she removed her shirt and pressed it to his chest. "Blake, can you hear me? Blake?"

"Robin," he whispered. This was Blake, her brother, her friend. "I'm sorry."

"What are you sorry for?" she said through tears. Then she realized that Uncle Frank had probably been right— Blake would have sold his own mother out for a half-million dollars if she weren't already dead. "It's okay, Blake. It's okay."

He closed his eyes, and then he shut down a little more with every breath. Finally, even his chest didn't move.

"No, no, no." Robin fumbled for the cell phone in her pocket, tried to dial Little John's number, and ended up resting the phone on the ground because her hands were shaking so badly.

"Little John?" she asked when her best friend answered.

"Yes?" Little John asked with attitude, but then she must have realized something was wrong because her voice changed. "What happened? Are you okay?"

"Come to my trailer right now," Robin said. She went to rub her nose with her sleeve but then realized there was blood on it. "And don't tell anyone else."

* * *

DON'T TELL ANYONE ELSE, BLAKE HAD written at the end of the note Robin found on her pillow. The only other line— *Basement, 1:00 A.M.*—was an invitation Robin understood without needing to be told. Uncle Frank's School for Misunderstood Youth, as the twenty kids living in one of Frank's abandoned buildings fondly called themselves, had already trained them in "the arts"—picking pockets, shoplifting, and convincing naïve passersby that they were homeless—but Frank's night school required a summons.

Robin was so excited that she couldn't sleep, so she counted the cracks in the ceiling, then the marker lines on the peeling wallpaper. The building had once housed a preschool on the top floor, where Robin and Little John, who was then called Tiny Tim, slept on the floor on piles of miniature sleeping bags. She was tempted to get up and read, but then Little John would wake up too and ask what was wrong.

Robin never lied to Little John.

She did hide things from her, though. For example, the books; when she knew no one else was home, Robin would page through the books with bites taken out of the pages and remember reading them for the first time on her mother's knee. Every word brought the scene of ginger snaps, the biscuits her mother kept stocked in the glass jar on the counter, and the feeling of her mother's warm sweaters against Robin's back. One night, she had tried to include Little John in her walk down memory lane, but her friend had said "You think my mom put down the bottle long enough to read me a book?" and turned away. The only book Little John liked was *Robin Hood*, which was how Robin had gotten the idea to rechristen her. Robin herself had already been called Robin, not because she did heroic acts but because of the way her chest turned red when she picked a pocket—her "tell."

Robin's cell phone, swiped from a woman buying a hot dog from a street vendor, now told her one hour, thirty minutes, ten minutes. She felt in the dark for her pants and a spare t-shirt—one she didn't mind getting bloody—and tiptoed past Little John and out the door.

The hallway was quiet and completely dark until Robin turned on her cell phone flashlight, which she muted with the bottom of her t-shirt, since one of Uncle Frank's strictest rules was no lights after sundown. If the cops came creeping around, who knew what would happen to them, Uncle Frank warned. For the most part, he had their best interest in mind—"I'm no child slaver," he always said—and he even paid them for the products they acquired. When one of them wanted to fly the nest, Uncle Frank let them, if they promised to keep their mouths shut and seemed convincing as they did it.

Only twice had Robin seen what happened when Uncle Frank didn't believe them.

The building had an elevator, but Robin didn't want to risk the ding. The stairwell smelled like urine left over from the true homeless residents who'd lived there before—the kind of smell that no amount of mopping ever removed. She took the steps down two at a time, her muscles strong from the daily runs Uncle Frank encouraged so that his kids could outrun the cops—*"If you're light on your feet, you'll beat the police"*—and in a few minutes she felt the air cool as she reached the basement level. Behind the door, Robin heard murmurs and the sound of a fist hitting a bag.

Finally, she thought, and swung the door open.

The basement had been converted into an enormous boxing ring. Unlike a traditional ring, however, this one had large structures inside, behind which a fighter could duck or surprise an opponent with a punch. The goal of night school was to teach kids how to fight in the real world, not like the glamorous wrestlers they watched on TV. Blake stood in the center with his back to Robin as he gave the kids outside the ring a lecture. When the door shut behind her, everyone turned to see who'd gotten the latest call.

"Welcome to the big leagues," Blake teased. He wiped at his forehead with a rag and then slung it around his neck.

"Thanks," said Robin. She jogged over to the group and fell into line. Only from that position could she spot Uncle Frank, who sat on a folding chair in the shadows with his hands and chin resting on his cane as he quietly observed his protégées.

"As I was saying, tonight we learn about distractions. Think of the way you overturn something in order to pick a pocket or wait for the cashier to help a customer before walking out the door of the store. If you can draw the eye of your opponent elsewhere, you'll have a better chance of getting the first blow—and for you runts, the first blow is crucial. Alright, pair up, you know the drill."

Everyone else found partners, leaving Robin as the odd one out.

"Robin, you're with me," Blake ordered. He indicated with a wave that she should join him in the middle of the ring.

Nervous, she did as she was told. When she had first come to the school, she and Blake had hooked up a few times, but Robin had cut things off as soon as she realized she wanted to make it all the way to Uncle Frank's inner circle. Blake was hired help, and Robin wanted to be the one doing the hiring. *If we're honest with ourselves*, she'd told him instead, *then we have to admit this can't go anywhere*. When two people were as secretive about their pasts as Blake and Robin, there wasn't anything to talk about.

She hoped, as Blake threw the rag down at his feet and put up his fists, that he wasn't still holding a grudge.

"I'm going to throw a right hook," Blake warned, "then a left, then a head-butt. At some point during that sequence, you need to find a way to distract me."

"Does taking my shirt off count?" Robin asked.

Blake's cheeks turned red, and he looked down. Before he even realized she'd moved, Robin swung her right fist. She would have made impact with a different opponent, but Blake was too good; even with the delay, he still managed to grab her wrist and twist her arm behind her back.

"You're lucky Uncle Frank sees something in you," Blake whispered in her ear. "I certainly don't."

Definitely still holding grudge.

Robin kicked backward, forcing Blake to release her. She turned quickly and evaluated her opponent looking for weaknesses. She'd already used herself; even Blake wouldn't fall for that trick twice.

Wait.

The rag.

Robin took a running start and then slid like a baseball player going for home. Her pants slid up, and she felt the floor rub the skin on her leg in a way that would probably leave an angry welt. No matter—her adrenaline was too high to let a little pain stop her. She grabbed the rag in her hand, jumped up, and, using the rag as a hold, leapt onto Blake's back.

"What the—?" he yelled. He bucked like a furious bull, but she gripped his back even harder with her knees. He managed to hit her a few times in the sides, but not hard— he wasn't flexible enough to get his arm all the way around his barrel-like chest. Out of the corner of her eye, Robin saw Uncle Frank stand up.

Finally, Blake bent down and threw her by sending her over his head. Her back hit the ground hard, and before she could roll, his fist found her face. Pain, like nothing she had ever felt before. She wondered if Blake might kill her, but before she could find out, something small and dark sailed over her. An angel? A devil? Blake fell backward, fighting off his new nemesis, and Robin rolled over and crawled toward the ropes around the ring.

"Enough," Uncle Frank said. Though he did not yell, everyone froze.

Robin collapsed against the ropes and looked back, where Blake had Little John by one leg. Robin's best friend wriggled like a worm on a hook, oblivious to the beginnings of a black eye.

"Correct me if I'm wrong," Uncle Frank said as he approached, "but I don't believe you were invited to this soiree, Little John."

"No, Sir, I wasn't."

"And again," he said, his voice dropping as got closer, "tell me if I'm mistaken, but you are already on probation for coming up short this month, are you not?"

Robin hadn't known about the coming up short part, and she wondered why Little John hadn't told her so they could run a few extra shifts together. Pride?

"So please, if you can, give me one reason not to throw you out on the street tonight for this insubordination."

Robin struggled to get up, using the ropes for support. She didn't know what would happen next, but she knew that if Frank kicked Little John out, she would follow her.

"Robin and I are a team," Little John said. She didn't look afraid; in fact, she looked furious. "Where she goes,

I go. We might as well train together because we'll always be together."

"Are you sure about that?" Frank asked. "It's a nice sentiment, but we all know you're harboring a crush on your little bird. What if you change your mind?"

"We're a team," Little John said again. She crossed her arms, which looked so ridiculous upside-down that Uncle Frank laughed. "And besides, I'm your niece."

Uncle Frank laughed again. "Indeed, you are—that's why I expect more of you." He turned around and hobbled away, calling back, "Alright, Blake, you can put her down."

As soon as she was back on her feet, Little John kicked Blake in the shin.

* * *

LITTLE JOHN KICKED BLAKE LIGHTLY, AS though she couldn't believe he was really dead. When she'd first arrived, Robin had pulled her into the trailer and covered her mouth to muffle her scream; eventually, when she'd adjusted to the sight in front of her, Little John went over to the corpse and Robin had sunk back into her recliner.

"That's Uncle Frank for you," Little John said, giving Blake another kick.

"I just don't understand," Robin said. She felt like she was going to throw up.

"*Everyone's expendable.* Isn't that what Uncle Frank always used to say?"

So that's where Robin had gotten the phrase from. She sunk her head down into her lap and tried to take a few deep breaths. Little John didn't seem to notice her panic; then again, wasn't that why Robin had called her?

"I get that Uncle Frank didn't mind killing his body-guard," Little John mused, "but what made him do it?"

Robin couldn't think straight. Should she tell her best friend her suspicions about who had put the bounty on her head? But then again, she didn't know for certain whether they were true, and speaking them might jeopardize the precious peace she'd found at Nottingham. Even thinking them . . .

"No clue," Robin said so convincingly that she almost believed her own words. "But what do we do with the body?"

Little John lightly kicked Blake again. She was taking too much pleasure out of this moment, but Robin didn't have the will to stop her. Besides, Blake had tormented Little John for years, from calling her everything from Dead Eyes to dyke, and they had been fierce rivals for Uncle Frank's limited attention.

"We bury him," Little John decided. She turned away, a cat bored with its mouse. "Tonight."

CHAPTER FOUR

THE BODY WAS HEAVY, SO HEAVY that Robin and Little John had to drag it most of the way into the woods. Wrapped in Robin's bedsheet, Blake was a mummy without its sarcophagus. Robin thought of the way he'd used his own sheet to wrap around his waist in the morning, and the way his arms, now bound to his sides, had once picked her up and thrown her over his shoulder. Her eyes teared, but she couldn't let go of her grip under his armpits, so she used her shoulder and sleeve to wipe her eyes. Little John, six feet behind her with Blake's feet, didn't notice.

Branches stabbed at her arms. Roots tripped up her feet, almost toppling their whole train. Every crack of a footstep sent her heart racing. How would they explain this to the other girls?

"You're sure Uncle Frank didn't give a reason?" Little John whispered suddenly. With the weight of Frank's decision between them, it was no wonder the situation had caught her attention again.

"I'm sure," Robin whispered back.

They reached the far end of the forest and put Blake down on the ground. Little John had picked the location during the afternoon, and now they lifted the shovels she'd left there and began to dig. Little John kept going on about the optimal grave depth—*six feet, which is 72 inches, which is 182.88 centimeters*—while Robin thought of the way Blake had chastised her during weight training for putting her knees down during push-ups when she thought he wasn't looking, and the way she would get him back later, in his room, by tickling him in the sensitive place below his chin that only she knew about.

"—which is 1,828.8 millimeters, which is 1,828,800 microns, which is—"

"Little John. Please stop counting."

The hole grew into a mouth, and when they couldn't see the bottom, Robin and Little John rolled the body into it. The thump made Robin's empty stomach clutch.

"Nighty-night Blake," Little John said, and shoveled some dirt onto his feet.

Filling the hole took less than half the time, though by then Robin's arms ached. She felt weak, like she had the flu, but when they finished, the last thing she wanted to do was go home.

"The girls have a bonfire going," Little John said. Strange how she could be so oblivious one minute and then read Robin's mind the next.

"Alright," Robin said.

They left their shovels at the edge of the woods and followed the smell of smoke. The bonfire was on the other side of Nottingham, away from the trailers, a hole with a circle of stones inside of which the girls had built yet another teepee of tinder and kindling with fuel logs like railroad tracks around the bumpy terrain. There were five stumps for the

Misfits, along with a stump for a hypothetical guest they had never invited to stay. Who could they guarantee would keep their mouth shut? And even if the girls met someone, they were under strict orders not to bring her back to Nottingham. No wonder White Rabbit and Skillet had made things easier on themselves and partnered up.

Currently, White Rabbit was sitting on Skillet's lap. Daisy Chain danced around the fire like a demon. Frank must have paid the girls and taken the extra televisions on his way out, because they each held their celebration flasks, which they only drank out of after a job well done.

"Here." Daisy Chain handed Robin her flask.

"Thanks." Robin took a long swig. Little John scowled and stalked to her stump, where she begrudgingly accepted a s'more from White Rabbit.

"Say the line, Robin!" Skillet called out, the word line sounding closer to *layne.*

Robin sighed. Then, with a fake smile, she raised the flask. "Steal from the rich—"

"—give to ourselves!" they yelled. Then they cheered, and for a moment, Robin felt better. Blake was just a sad memory—someone she had glamorized in her guilt.

These girls were her real family.

* * *

IN HER DREAM THAT NIGHT, BLAKE barked orders over her as she pushed her body up and down over a fire. She felt like a human shawarma, slowly roasting to death. *Lower!*, he commanded. When she looked up to plead with him, Blake had become Little John, who stepped onto Robin's back so that her arms shook, and the air pressed out of her lungs.

Lower, Little John said, *All the way down to hell.* Suddenly Robin was in the pit they'd dug for Blake, and instead of Little John on her chest, a sheet tightened around her like a constrictor. *Guess I'll get that bounty after all,* Uncle Frank's voice said, and then the three of them began digging dirt into Robin's grave.

"Robin?"

She woke up in an unfamiliar bed. Or rather, it was familiar, she realized on closer inspection—just not her own. Daisy Chain hovered over her, hair tickling Robin's face, and when Robin sat up, Daisy Chain pressed the cool back of her hand to Robin's forehead.

"I'm fine," Robin said, ducking away.

"Be wary then; best safety lies in fear."

"I said I'm fine." Robin got out of bed and pulled on her t-shirt. "Just a bad dream, that's all."

Daisy Chain shrugged and lay back in bed.

As Robin stepped out of Daisy Chain's trailer into the sunlight, she blinked a few times to adjust her eyes. When she checked her cell phone, she had three missed calls from Little John and a text: *When you get through practicing Shakespeare, come over. Uncle Frank sent us a job.*

Skillet's trailer door was open, and judging by the smell, she and White Rabbit were cooking breakfast. Though Little John's text had sounded urgent, Robin's stomach grumbled, so she diverted to the left and climbed the steps into the trailer without knocking. White Rabbit was stretched out on Skillet's couch surfing through channels on the new TV.

"Morning," Skillet called out without looking up from the stove.

"Morning," Robin said.

Skillet was making something in her namesake. Robin went over and stood beside her, head against Skillet's muscular arm, and watched as Skillet added one skillet of potatoes into a second skillet filled with cooked sausage, bell peppers, onion, and mushrooms. She tipped in some seasoning and sauce, including her trademark maple syrup, and ended with four eggs cracked into the corners and cooked with a lid on top until they turned opaque.

"You look like you could use a hot meal," Skillet said as she handed Robin a full plate.

"More than anything."

Little John entered the trailer carrying her clipboard, and, after shaking her head at the sight in front of her, joined Robin by the stove. "How did I know I'd find you here?"

"Because you knew she worked up an appetite last night?" White Rabbit teased.

Little John chucked her clipboard back at White Rabbit, who caught it with one hand and put it under her legs. "So childish," Little John grumbled. Skillet handed Little John another plate, and after Little John retrieved her clipboard using intense poking to White Rabbit's midsection, the two girls carried their food over to Robin's trailer, where they could talk in peace. As general and colonel, they usually vetted jobs first before taking their proposals to the group for a vote. Sometimes they even made executive decisions for small jobs—but only when they came with big cuts. Or, in this case, when they came from a man who had their leader in his debt.

"Talk to me," Robin said between mouths full of juicy sausage.

"It's an easy job," Little John said. She referred to her clipboard. "One truck, the usual roads. Andy said there's just one mark, a box of watches."

"Interesting." Robin thought as she chewed through soft potato. "I wonder what's really in there." She also wondered whether this was the job she'd promised Frank, but from what she knew, that job was supposed to involve the military. Maybe there were codes scratched in the metal?

"Diamonds? Passwords? Who cares, as long as we get paid."

"True." Robin skewered another potato but didn't put it in her mouth. "How come Frank didn't call himself?"

"Andy said he's travelling."

"Course he is." Leave it to Uncle Frank to murder someone in cold blood and then take a vacation. Robin thought of Blake, of the way his chest had spilled blood like a tipped milk carton, and felt like she was going to be sick. "Whatever. Take the job."

"Only catch is it's this afterno—"

"I said take the job," Robin said, and stood up abruptly. Her plate overturned into the dirt, but she didn't pick it up. "We leave in two hours."

After entrusting Little John to break the news, Robin hurried to her trailer. As soon as she shut the door, she ran to the bathroom and threw up her breakfast. She tried not to think what the tomatoes looked like floating in the bowl. Blake's face swam into view, but she flushed it away with an angry slurp. *Think of the job. Think of the job.*

After her stomach settled, Robin turned on the shower and let it run hot, hotter, scalding. The tiny bathroom steamed, hiding first her hair, then the circles under her eyes, then her skinny shoulders, then her chest. She rubbed a finger against the mirror where she knew her tattoo to be—an *epigaea repens*, or "trailing arbutus," with broad green leaves and white flowers creeping over one shoulder—and remembered the way the tattoo needle buzzed against her skin until it burned. She'd chosen the wildflower not because it reminded her of home—although it did—but because the trailing arbutus was a flower found among the cover of fallen leaves in spring, the same way Robin had been discovered by Uncle Frank among the refuse in the back alleys of Boston and brought to join his crew.

Robin turned away from the mirror and stepped into the shower, not bothering to close the door behind her. So what if she got water on the floor? So what if the moisture from the air grew a little mold on the wall? Blake was dead. Nothing mattered but that.

The spray from the showerhead landed on her face.

She thought of the night Uncle Frank had found her in the alley.

A rainy night. Cold. Robin had only been away from home two nights, but already she smelled like the ripest version of herself. Her hair felt greasy against her scalp. Her hands were clammy in her gloves. She had begged on the street the first day while she got her bearings, but the second day, she had found ways to pick up groceries from the bodegas and the refrigerators in pharmacies, a new hat from an understaffed department store, and even a pack of cigarettes from a gas station while the attendant unplugged the toilet she'd clogged just minutes before. Not that Robin smoked, but she knew most homeless kids did, and she figured she could bribe them for information about where to spend the night.

"Hey Kid."

Robin had turned around. An old man in a long brown coat stood with both hands on his cane. Next to him, a body-builder in a black windbreaker watched the road behind them uneasily. When she looked closely at his face, however, she realized he was no more than eighteen, if that.

"I'm no kid," Robin had said, though she was, just sixteen and until two days ago a sophomore in high school.

"Sure, you're not." The old man winked at the body-builder. "Whatever else you are, you're a skilled thief, and I could use someone like you in my crew. That is, if you're not determined to die in this alley."

Robin wondered how he knew about her.

"You stole my watch," the man said without further prompting. He stretched his arm out, revealing a naked wrist. "Just a few minutes ago, in Quincy Market."

She felt in her pocket for the Rolex. In her hand the watch felt heavy—but not heavy enough.

"Here." Robin threw the watch, and the bodybuilder caught it with one hand. "It's a fake, anyway."

The old man laughed. He stretched out his other arm, the right, revealing another Rolex. This was a real one, judging from the way the diamonds glistened.

"Smart." Robin was beginning to have an appreciation for this man's street sense. Besides, she was cold and lonely, and what could be worse than being homeless, anyway? "What does your crew do?"

"What you do," he said. "But much, much bigger."

What she did. What she had always done, even when her dad had threatened to kick her out of the house, when he had called her a dirty-no-good-thief, when he had locked her in her room as though a little metal knob could contain her. She didn't want to stop stealing; she couldn't.

The old man caught her attention again when he took a few steps, the cane adding a light tap that accompanied his pace. When Robin didn't follow him, he looked backward over his shoulder. "Come on, then."

She shrugged and picked up her bag, a light backpack easy to throw on when she needed to run from the police or an angry shopkeeper. She'd stolen it too, and off a kid no less, but he'd been irresponsibly swinging it around outside the Institute of Contemporary Art. The way she saw it, someone else was bound to steal it if she didn't swipe it first. All it had taken was a mustard-topped pretzel to his Ralph Lauren half-zip and swish, the bag was hers.

"So where's this crew you mentioned?" Robin asked.

"A bit of a drive." The old man pointed to a car, black with tinted windows. "Do you trust me?"

"Not in the slightest."

The old man laughed again, and Robin followed him across the street to the car. Right before she slid onto the leather seat, she had looked back—not to escape, but to view the bodybuilder, who had opened and held the door.

His mouth, which had been a straight line during their entire conversation, finally turned up in a slight smile.

CHAPTER FIVE

ROBIN WOULD NEED A NEW RIDE, so after she dressed, she and Skillet took a trip to the crew's mechanic. Through her aviators, the road cut through an amber forest, and the sky turned a muddied blue. She kept quiet—her throat was still hoarse from getting sick, and besides, she and Skillet never had much to say to each other—so Skillet turned the radio to a country channel and cranked the volume. The Forgotten Coast, less glamorously known as the Armpit of Florida, often felt more like an extension of Georgia than a sister to the fun cities or retirement communities of the East Coast. Southern twang, Southern cuisine, Southern hospitality—all wonderful things unless you were a runaway trying your best to fit in.

"Boiled peanut?" Skillet asked. She took a lidless can from the cup holder and held it out to Robin.

"Gross." Even the nutty scent turned her stomach. "How can you eat those?"

Skillet plucked a peanut from the can with two fingers and plopped it into her mouth like a bird eating a slimy worm. "Delicious."

Robin's throat clenched.

Fine Fixers was a dump, just the garage, two gas pumps, and a convenience store that sold stale trail mix and water bottles. But the owner, Mikey, kept a secret stash in a second garage behind the first. When they pulled into an unmarked parking spot and got out, the girls followed the sound of pop music to the first garage, where the blasting radio competed with a drill. The floors were a stained gray-brown, but Mikey kept them meticulously swept; the workbench tilted to one side, but the tools on top were organized in labeled bins.

Robin crouched down and looked under the dented fender of a Subaru Impreza. Mikey lay on his back on a Craftsman creeper, grease on his uniform and wrench resting on his chest, singing along to the music in a terrible attempt at a feminine voice.

"Hey, Mikey," she yelled.

Mikey startled, hit his head on the front mount, and cursed. "Can't you ever call first?"

"Nope." She waited while he pushed himself from underneath the car. First came the black work boots, then the loose blue pants, next the matching top with middle-aged pudge straining the bottom buttons, and finally, Mikey's bald, red head. What he lacked on top, he made up for in a thick black mustache, currently even bushier than the last time Robin had seen him.

"Starred in any pornos lately?" she asked as she gave him a hand up.

"Ha. Ha." Mikey wiped his forehead with a once-white towel from the workbench. "*Not* crashed any bikes lately?"

"Course not." Robin boosted herself up so that she was sitting on the only clean part of the bench. "That's why I have you."

"You do not have me," Mikey blustered. He looked back at his employee, a quiet guy named Alvin, but Alvin either hadn't noticed their presence or pretended not to. Smart man, Robin thought, and made a mental note to consider him for future work. "I don't want any part of your teenage shenanigans."

"Oh really?" Robin pulled a gold chain from her hidden pocket and dangled it. "Guess I'll keep this, then?"

Mikey's eyes followed the chain like a hypnotized patient. Through the top of his shirt, Robin spotted the glint of several similar chains around his neck and smiled. Vain people were the easiest to manipulate.

"Fine." Mikey snatched the chain out of her hand. "But this is the last time."

Mikey led them to the second garage, the one only he could open, and unlocked the three deadbolts keeping the door shut. The lights came on automatically, revealing Mikey's substantial collection of motorcycles displayed in clean lines of alternating 60° angles. Most of them were Yamahas, with a few Suzukis, and one Ducati. Robin slid her sunglasses down the bridge of her nose to see more clearly.

"What did you think of the Tracer 900 GT?" Mikey asked despite his claimed disinterest.

"Nice," said Robin as she adjusted and readjusted the mirror of a Zuma 125, then continued down the line, "but I'm not touring the West coast, Mikey. I need more sport. More speed. More . . ." She halted at a black and red Aprilia RSV4 that hadn't been there before and put her hand on the front fairing of the racer like a master on the head of a dog. " . . . like this."

"No. Absolutely not." Mikey slapped the top of her hand. "That baby was a gift from my wife."

"You don't have a wife," Robin said.

"How do you know?" Mikey stuttered.

Robin held up her left hand. "No ring. And besides, if you had a wife, she wouldn't let you spend all your money on a garage full of unridden motorcycles."

"True. But I do have a girlfriend."

"Sure, you do," Robin said, and swung her leg over the seat of the RSV4.

Skillet stood next to Robin as she turned on the engine. "That's a beautiful sound," Skillet said over the purr. "But may I ask, for the millionth time, what's the point in riding a bike like this if you're just going to trash it?"

Robin pursed her lips, not because of Skillet's comment but because she'd only brought $5,000 in her backpack. The Aprilia was worth at least $15,000.

"The point," she said loudly, annoyed at the way Skillet always questioned her but also at her lack of funds, "is that I can."

But she couldn't, at least not today. Robin patted the fuel tank like the neck of a prized horse and whispered, "I'll be back for you, baby." Then she threw Mikey her backpack and said, with a detached wave, "I'll take the Nighthawk—with a full tank of gas this time."

"Coming right up," Mikey said, eyes on the money in his hands.

The Nighthawk was comfortable and easy for Robin to ride, like bolting training wheels onto a kid's bicycle. As soon as Robin pulled onto I-10, she raced ahead of Skillet, letting the wind whip the worries right out of her. Instead of Blake's face, she imagined her first bike—not a Nighthawk, but a different Honda CB, also black and chrome, with a throttle that often stuck instead of snapping back into place. A "suicide throttle," aptly named considering how recklessly Robin risked her life every time she took her bike for a ride—and how little she cared if it failed. Back then she had been living at home and parking the bike at a friend's house, only riding it on days when she skipped school, or her dad worked the night shift.

Back then she had called the girls she let ride on the back her "friends."

Don't think about the past, Robin scolded. Her father and those girls all knew a different Robin—a Robin who was buried in the Florida forest somewhere between Blake's grave and the safes full of cash the Merry Misfits kept for a rainy day. *Focus on the road.*

Robin upped the bike's rpms and then snapped the front of the Nighthawk up into a wheelie.

When Robin got back to Nottingham, Little John was waiting at the open gate. She sat on a hard black suitcase full of supplies—mostly ways to pick locks, which were Little John's specialty—and didn't get up when Robin slipped the back tire over the ground, creating a cloud of dust. She took of her helmet and enjoyed the feeling of fresh air on her hot scalp, even going so far as to toss her hair like a girl in a shampoo commercial.

"So dramatic," Little John said in a bored tone.

"Where's Skillet?" White Rabbit called out from the guard post. She didn't look up from her computer, though she did Robin the courtesy of taking her headphones off to hear the answer. "She called me to tell me to leave the gate open, but I haven't heard anything since."

"No clue. I guess I lost her," Robin said, feigning innocence. But right at that moment, the red truck zoomed through the gate, past Robin, and down the road ahead.

"She's going to do a burnout," White Rabbit said, eyes still straight ahead.

The truck's wheels spun, producing the mother of all burnout smoke. Skillet drifted to a stop less than two feet from the trees on the other side of the driveway and then beeped, indicating that she wasn't going to bother to get out—Little John and Robin could come to her.

"Girl's got style," Little John said, following the compliment with a whistle between her teeth.

"Style?" Robin said. "But you just told me I was being dramatic."

"So?" Little John snapped her men's Ray-Bans so that the arms popped into place and slid them on her face. "You were."

Little John dropped her suitcase in the truck bed with a metallic thump, set up the ramp, and then circled around to open the door. Country music again, and this time louder and twangier than before. Robin eased the motorcycle up the ramp onto the truck bed, parking it there and then chaining the wheels to the side of the bed as an extra precaution. The key went down into her shirt, where her secret purse dangled around her neck.

"Can you turn that off?" Robin yelled over the fiddle and banjo.

"What?" Skillet yelled back, though she could obviously hear her.

"I said—"

"What?"

Little John slid onto the hump between the driver's and passenger's side of the bench and buckled her seatbelt. She mumbled something to herself, and Robin picked up the words "childish" and "I'm too old for this" as she got into the passenger's side and closed the door.

Skillet started the truck again and eased the front bumper to within inches of the gate, where White Rabbit had finally emerged from her burrow long enough to give Skillet a goodbye kiss. Luckily, their parting tradition was a quick peck on the cheek, so for once the other girls didn't have to watch them share saliva.

White Rabbit straightened up and raised her fist. "Steal from the rich—"

"—give to ourselves!" the three girls in the truck finished.

White Rabbit opened the gate. As they drove through, Robin looked back in the side view mirror to see Daisy Chain dancing in a circle like a drugged-out hippie at a concert. From her pockets she pulled petals, which she rained on the dusty road beneath her feet. Her hair flowed around and around like the cascading greenery of a weeping willow.

"Should we be worried about her?" Little John asked, suddenly close to Robin's ear. She had leaned against her to follow her gaze.

"No more than usual," said Robin.

Little John snorted a little laugh. When Robin had first brought Daisy Chain to Nottingham, Little John had taken one look at the strange fairy creature and determined, "Nope. Absolutely not."

"Little John!" Robin had scolded, though Daisy Chain hadn't seemed to hear her. She was too busy setting out her items on a wool blanket like a witch preparing for a séance.

"What?" Little John waived her hand at the evidence. "She's straight up cuckoo. What are her skills? Knitting sweaters?"

"I'm sure she has lots of skills," Robin lied.

"Yeah, like catching the eye of a robin." Little John folded her arms and planted her feet firmly on the ground, as she always did when she was about to make a pronouncement. "This little stray kitten needs to go back to her alley. Do you know how much our odds of capture go up with her in our crew? Let me walk you through my calculations—"

"Please don't."

Daisy Chain brushed off her pants and then her hands, as though satisfied with her work. Then she noticed Little John for the first time. "*O beware, my lord, of jealousy,*" Daisy Chain said softly as she approached them. Her head tilted from side to side, like an animal examining a potential threat. "*It is the green-eyed monster which doth mock the meat it feeds on.*"

Little John's mouth fell open. "Did she just call me lord?"

"And a jealous lord at that." Robin raised her eyebrows. "Is she wrong?"

Little John had stormed away then, muttering to herself all the way until she disappeared into the woods. Since that day, she had barely spoken to Daisy Chain, let alone allowed her on any missions.

Considering her constant quoting and dazed demeanor, Robin couldn't exactly make a case for her either.

CHAPTER SIX

SKILLET WOVE BETWEEN CARS TO THE tune of "I Walk the Line." Her lips mouthed the words, but her full concentration seemed to be on the black truck in the right lane ahead of them. The truck had showed up fifteen minutes late, sliding in front of them onto I-10 like a bison ambling into a herd, and again, Robin couldn't help feeling that something wasn't quite right. The afternoon clouds threatening rain weren't helping, and sure enough, a few drops hit the windshield and slid, leaving comet tails and dotted lines in their wakes.

"Traffic will make a clean mount difficult," warned White Rabbit through the speaker phone, "but you're coming up to an exit that looks pretty empty. One gas station, a few cars, but otherwise, lots of room to work."

"Copy that," said Robin. She hung up and then turned to Little John. "You don't happen to—"

"—have a very bad feeling about this?" Little John let her lip turn up on one side—her version of a smile. "Every time we leave Nottingham."

Without a specific reason, Robin couldn't justify turning around. Uncle Frank wanted this job done, and as he would be keen on reminding her, she owed him one. She clenched her fists, took a deep breath, and then slid the glass behind her head over so that she could climb through the open window.

The Nighthawk waited like a racehorse in its starting stall, and Robin, its jockey, suited up in her gloves and helmet. The wind whipped her hair into her face, so she tied the thick mass back with a rubber band. Still, the ponytail lifted in the wind, like a kite on a short string, so she tucked it into the back of her shirt until she got moving.

"Be free," she whispered to the Nighthawk as she unlocked the chains. She liked to think of her bikes this way, like animals or even people, and she mourned their losses in the same way. Once she kicked up the stand, she prepared the bike for car dismount. "Ready, Baby?"

The Nighthawk seemed to rev in response.

Robin raised her hand, and on cue, Skillet hit the brakes. The cars behind her honked and then cut into the left lane, leaving the road clear behind the truck's dusty fender. Robin urged the Nighthawk backward, managing to keep her seat during the jump, and hit the pavement with a jolt. Skillet's truck, which had slowed to about fifteen miles an hour, sped up again.

Robin's cell phone rang, and she answered with her earpiece.

"Nice job," said White Rabbit. "Now hurry up or you're going to miss your chance."

Robin sped ahead, passing Skillet and catching up with the black truck in under a minute. The exit sign appeared, and then the impending ramp.

Robin veered behind the black truck and popped a wheelie. Balancing the front of the bike on the bumper, she paused for a moment to prepare for her jump. *Eyes on the prize*, she thought, zeroing in on the two vertical bars. Then she jumped up onto the seat and spring-boarded through the air, untethered by anything, as close to a real hawk as a human could be. Then the bars were in her hands, and the bike was falling behind her, and she was bound to the earth again.

"Knock knock," she said as she banged on the door with her fist.

The truck braked hard. Robin, prepared for the stop, flexed her muscles to keep herself from hitting the door with her head. The exit came up on their right, and like a puppet on strings, the driver followed the path to which the Merry Misfits had guided him. Exit, shoulder, full stop. Skillet's truck came to an abrupt stop behind them.

"Need help?" Skillet called out. Robin, still perched on the back of the truck, could only imagine the driver walking the length of the vehicle to check on his load.

"Don't think so," said the driver. "Something came loose is all."

"Suit yourself," Skillet said. She indicated with her left turn signal, as if she was preparing to leave—Robin's cue.

The driver rounded the corner, and Robin flew again, this time into his chest so that he fell backward onto the road. She protected the back of his head by wrapping her arm around it, and her padded jacket softened what could have been a deadly blow. The Merry Misfits robbed and stole, but they didn't spill blood—at least when they could help it.

"What the—," yelled the surprised driver. His face was so close that she could smell the onions and ham on his breath.

"You're welcome," said Robin. She cuffed him and then stood up. He was young, twenty at the most, with a mop of scruffy blond hair and mayo on his cheek. She found his baseball cap, which had come off in the fray, and put it back onto his head. Poor guy—probably new to the gig and about to get fired for losing his first delivery.

"Robin," said Little John sharply, and Robin shook her head. She was going soft, or maybe Blake's death had just shaken something loose in her that she needed to repair. *The mind is a machine,* she thought, then wondered where she'd heard the saying before. Uncle Frank? Her father?

Skillet retrieved a sledgehammer from Little John's case in the bed of her truck and then, like a railroad builder, swung the flat metal head against the door until it broke open. The space behind the door was dark, and when Robin climbed up, she noticed the air was surprisingly cool. What kind of shipment required air conditioning?

Using her cell phone light, Robin guided Skillet and Little John all the way back until they found the box marked with a white circle.

"Wait." Robin stopped abruptly. "Something's wrong."

The box was larger than Robin had expected—too large. And no company would put the word "watches" in bright red letters on the box in place of their logo. Were those air holes?

"Run!" Robin called out as the box burst open, revealing a black helmet, mask, bullet proof vest, and two holsters from which the officer removed two guns and aimed them at Skillet and Little John's heads.

"Freeze, or your crew splatters," the officer said. A woman's voice—young, maybe in her early twenties—with a twinge of Boston lurking in her soft r's. On closer inspection, the vest did have a telltale curve on the top half, and the woman's pants flared slightly at the hips before falling around her legs.

Robin put her hands up. "What do you want?" Her face stayed forward as her eyes roamed the truck looking for an escape. Some of the smaller boxes could serve as weapons thrown at her assailant's head; a chain on the ground could swing around her neck. But with a gun in play, could Robin really stop her finger before it pulled the trigger?

"What do I want?" The woman laughed. Then she pushed off her helmet, revealing a familiar freckled round nose and bob of brown curls. "I want you."

Robin shone the light into the woman's face. "Shaina?" Robin stepped forward, forgetting all about her crew, but Shaina shook her head.

"Stay back." Shaina waved the gun in Little John's direction. "You know I'll do it."

Robin stepped back mechanically as her mind raced. Her enthusiasm evaporated. She and Shaina had grown up together, back before Robin ran away, and if she was looking for Robin then that meant—

An engine idled next to the truck and then stopped. Gravel crunched under boots, and Robin estimated five men, maybe six, were coming to back Shaina up. "Secure their hands," Shaina ordered, and someone took Robin's raised arms and forced them behind her back. Pain shot up her hands, forearms, elbows. Something tightened around her wrists, and when she strained slightly, she felt cold handcuffs dig into her skin.

"Can't we talk about this?" she asked Shaina as someone dragged her backward.

"Talk?" Shaina called out as Robin's guard pulled her out of the truck and carried her to the van. "There will be plenty of time to talk where you're going."

Going. The word echoed in Robin's head as the guards closed the door with a final thump.

"Got a plan?" Little John whispered.

Robin leaned back against the worn fabric of the seat and closed her eyes. "Working on it," she said.

In a minute, her mind slipped home.

* * *

"YOU'RE GOING TO GET EVERYONE KILLED. Is that what you want?"

Officer Ramirez paced on the opposite side of the metal table between them. Robin's hands were palm down on the table, chilled like a nose pressed against a frosted glass, and she did not move them, even when her nose itched. If she moved—if she even twitched—she might lose control completely.

"They were wrong," she said through gritted teeth. "Those kids had nothing, and they just—

"—stole from a small business owner and almost got themselves killed in the process?" Officer Ramirez slammed his hands down on the table, sending vibrations under her skin. "How many times do I have to tell you the same thing? We're police officers, Samantha. Returning stolen stuff is what we do."

"That doesn't make it right." Robin was hot, or maybe it was the collar of her uniform, buttoned up to her neck per protocol, that made her feel suffocated. She looked past Officer Ramirez to the blank wall in front of her, and then turned her head slightly so that she could stare through the observation mirror. How many times had she been on the other side, wondering what was going through the mind of a handcuffed suspect? *Don't let him in,* she thought, and went back to staring into space without blinking. Officer Ramirez was the best interrogator in the precinct, but Robin was an even better secret keeper—if she didn't move.

Officer Ramirez took a deep breath. "You're not a police officer, Samantha." He scraped the chair back and then sat down heavily, stomach pushing the table toward her. Then he took of his hat and wrung it in his hands. "You're a junior police academy student. You're here to *learn,* not go out on cases. How did you even hear about this, anyway?"

Robin pursed her lips. She would never tell him about the radio she kept in her closet, hidden behind a wall of empty tampon boxes. She would never tell him about how she and Shaina kept bikes at their friend Ricardo's house, along with extra uniforms in gear bags Robin had lifted from the locker room a few weeks ago.

She would never tell him anything.

"Samantha . . ." Without his hat, Officer Ramirez looked old. He had streaks of gray at his temples, and a bald patch starting at the back. ". . . I . . ."

"What is it, Dad?"

He put his hat back on. "I have to take you home."

"Okay." She relaxed her shoulders a little bit. "Just let me tell Officer Anders that—"

"No." He straightened his shoulders—the sign that he meant business. She could almost see him becoming another man, father into officer, and she realized that she'd finally messed up for the last time. "I mean . . . for good."

For good. Over. The past four years at the academy were a thrown stone sunk to the bottom of a pond. All those nights when she stayed up late to study protocols; all those weekends spent training with Shaina. Robin blinked, finally wetting her dry eyes.

"Unless you can tell us how you knew about the case . . . ?" he ventured. "Or maybe who helped you steal the file?"

He had almost tricked her. *Kick them down, then offer a hand to lift them back up.* Classic.

"We need that file, Samantha. We need the evidence, or else we can't bring justice to—"

"Save your breath, because I'll never tell you anything." Robin crossed her arms. "Obviously you can't prove I did it, so will you let me out of here? Or should I get a ride home myself?"

* * *

ROBIN, LITTLE JOHN, AND SKILLET HUDDLED in the back row shoulder-to-shoulder, and their guards took the middle seats and front. The backs of their heads, topped with cop caps, looked like a shelf of toy soldiers. They started the engine again and tore off, blaring their sirens, though there was not a single other vehicle in sight. Robin leaned into Little John, who kept her upright with her shoulder.

"We're screwed," Skillet breathed, eyes on their guards. Her hands twitched nervously in her lap, and her eyes were frantic. All the Merry Misfits had nightmares about police raids, but especially Skillet, who wouldn't ever say much except that the Constitution wasn't the only thing the police liked to uphold.

"No question." Little John propped Robin back up. "Who was that girl, Robin?"

Robin looked out the window. They were taking the girls west, that much she knew, though in a minute they turned off

I-10 and onto a back road she'd never seen before, nonde-script in its nothingness. Occasionally a trailer or a dilapidated house with peeling paint and old farming tools grown rusted in the yard interrupted the blank green scenery.

"Let's just say we've met before," Robin said, "and that our parting was . . . not ideal."

Little John rolled her eyes. "Great. We go two years without a single incident, and then your ex shows up and it's sirens and handcuffs all around—"

"Hey! Quiet back there!" one of the guards in the middle seat yelled.

Little John leaned over so that her elbow was on Robin's thigh, and she could lean up to whisper in her ear. "Just tell me this much: Are they really with the police? Or is this all a show?"

Robin sunk back into the cheap plastic cushion of the backseat and rested her head. She was suddenly tired, more tired than she had ever been. Her stomach clutched like a fist, empty from her morning purge. "They're as real as they come," she said, and closed her eyes.

Skillet cursed under her breath.

After a few more minutes, the van took a right at the first stop sign and came to a halt in front of an abandoned lot that had once been a farm judging by a roofless chicken coop and a barn with no door or panes in the windows. The engine stopped, but no one got out. "Let them out," a voice said over the radio.

"Copy that." One of the guards opened the sliding door and then returned to his position. "Get out."

None of the girls moved.

"I said get out," the officer repeated.

"No offense, dude," Robin said, unable to keep her mouth shut, "but we know better than to trust—"

"GET OUT."

The girls did as they were told, though Robin stepped backward out of the van to keep her eyes trained on the officers. One twitch of a hand, one reach for a gun, and she would do her best to take at least one of them with her, weapon or not. But no one moved, and as soon Skillet stepped out, the officer slammed the door shut.

"Is this some kind of mind game?" Little John asked.

The van started up again and raced away.

"Well, if it is, it's working." Skillet sunk her hands onto her knees and took a few deep breaths. Her arms and legs were shaking. "I'm scared out of my mind."

"It's okay." Robin put her arm around her. "If they wanted us dead, we'd be dead. Right?"

She turned back to the barn and gave the building her full attention. Something about the curve of the door seemed so familiar, and the rusted weathervane with a ship on top, and the burned-out grass making patterns across the yard, and yes, absolutely, she had been here before. Back then, the place had been old but tended; back then, her great-grandmother had hung laundry on the same line that was now broken and swished like a cat's tail in the wind.

"If it isn't Robin and her band of Merry Misfits."

Robin's father slipped out of the shadow of the barn. He dropped a lit cigarette on the ground and stubbed it out with a quick turn of his boot—*So he's smoking again*, Robin thought—and then walked over to them. He wore his standard casual attire, a blue t-shirt and baggy jeans held up by a struggling brown belt, and what remained of his hair was buzzed short. Considering this was a man who'd once told her that cleanliness was part of the job, his stubble told her everything she needed to know about how he'd been since she disappeared.

"Hi, Dad."

"Dad?" Little John stepped away from her. "Are you serious?"

"Oh, come on, Little John." Robin rolled her eyes. "Don't tell me you don't have secrets."

Little John didn't say anything. Of course, she had secrets; they all did. Wasn't that what had brought them all to Nottingham in the first place?

"You've got me," Robin said to her father. Then she put her hands up. "If I go home willingly, will you let my friends go?"

Her father's laugh rattled in his chest. She thought of the way he used to chain smoke after her mother died, the cup on the back porch spewing ash until the wind blew it away.

"You think I want you to come home after everything you've done?" her father said. He coughed twice, the sound dry and pained. "I'm not here because I want Samantha Ramirez . . . I'm here because I want Robin. Unofficially, of course."

A job. She should have known the minute she recognized Shaina that Boston officers would never have an assignment in Florida.

"You must be really desperate," Little John said.

"You have no idea." Her father ran a hand over his stubble and then dropped it to his side. His thumb and pointer finger twitched, missing a cigarette between them. "One of our men got taken, and BPD has all the evidence they need to assume he's dead." He shook his head. "I don't buy it. Even still, I would never have come here if Shaina hadn't convinced me. She said you would do the right thing . . . or that if you didn't, she would—"

"Make me?" Robin nodded. "Sounds like her."

"And who, exactly, are these kidnappers?" asked Skillet, who seemed to have calmed down enough to be curious.

Robin's dad laughed again. God, she hated that sound. How many times had she hidden his packs of cigarettes or burned them in the backyard? How many times had she told him that she couldn't lose another parent?

You left him, just like Mom did. What did you expect?

"You've probably heard of them," he said. "Frank's School for Misunderstood Youth?"

As if she'd inhaled her father's smoke, Robin struggled to get a deep breath. "Uncle Frank?" she said. "We might as well dig our own graves."

"I thought you might recognize the name," her father said. He pulled out a pack and lit another cigarette with a book of matches; Robin wondered what had happened to his dark blue lighter, the one he'd had for as long as she could remember. "That's exactly why we need you."

Robin and Little John looked at each other, their time at the school and Blake's death passing between them in one glance. This was why Uncle Frank had killed the only person who knew how to find Nottingham, and just as he'd planned, the girls had been too shaken by the murder to see the truth. Robin clenched her fists. Her fear had made her foolish; she would need to be smarter now if she hoped to save Nottingham.

Starting with the part of the story her father wasn't telling her.

"Going after Frank is a death sentence," whispered Little John, as if she could read Robin's mind, but Robin had moved on from Frank and was now fitting the pieces of her father's plan together.

"Oh. You're good." The last piece had fallen into place, and Robin looked at her father, unsure whether she should be furious or impressed. "Shaina has White Rabbit and Daisy Chain, doesn't she?"

"It's such a shame." Her father smiled, but grimly. "You would have made a great officer."

CHAPTER SEVEN

WHAT DAD WANTS IS IMPOSSIBLE, ROBIN thought as she dug the toe of her shoe into the remains of a layer of hay where the pigs used to revel in muddy glory. She could still feel their wiry hairs, and beneath the thistle, thick skin the color of her own. Uncle Frank was like those pigs—he reveled in his treasure, including the safes he kept throughout the school, his warehouses, his private yacht—and he had taken incredible precautions to keep his possessions in his pen. Hostages were even more valuable, which meant they were even more closely guarded.

Yet, if breaking into Uncle Frank's was so impossible, why was she already planning her way in? The layout of the building had spread in front of her like a virtual reality, and Robin chess-pieced her way through the floors, up the sides, in through the top. Her spatial instinct was what had made her such a good cop-in-training—and an even better thief.

"Your dad wasn't lying," said Little John as she came to sit next to Robin on the metal fence. "Skillet's talking with White Rabbit on Shaina's phone."

For a while, neither of them said anything else. Robin flipped up a few muddy leaves with the toe of her boot, revealing worms and ants and the occasional pill bug balled up in fear, and tried to think of a way to express herself. How could she even begin to explain away the years of omissions? The many ways she had misled her best friend simply because she didn't want to talk about where she'd come from?

"I get it, you know," said Little John finally. "You can spare yourself the energy of an explanation."

"But—"

"I said I get it, Robin." Little John shifted on the fence and then stood up, as though her legs couldn't stay still anymore. "When the truth gets complicated, it's easier to just let people think what they want. Sure, those lies might build and build until it's impossible to ever knock them down, but what other choice do we have, right? Right?"

"Right . . ." Robin looked at her friend. "But are we still talking about me?"

"Definitely not." Little John sighed and sat back down. Almost angrily, she grumbled, "I'm in love with Daisy Chain."

"What?" Robin yelled a little too loudly. "Daisy Chain? The girl you can't stand? But all this time—"

"I know, I know. You thought I was in love with you." Little John smoothed her comb-over, even though every hair was already slicked down. "Well, surprise! I'm not, and I never have been." She cocked her head in thought. "Well, maybe for a few days at Uncle Frank's, but then I got to know you."

"Great." Robin tried to frown, but then she couldn't help smiling. "You and Daisy Chain . . . now that would be a weird match."

"Tell me about it. Honestly, I can't even explain it . . . I just feel connected to her." Little John finally made eye contact with her. "You're not mad?"

"Of course not. If Daisy Chain and I felt that way about each other, we would have made things official forever ago." Robin had another thought. "Wait a minute. Are you finally telling me the truth because soon it won't matter? Because you think we need to—?"

"Go after Uncle Frank?" Little John took Robin's hand. "Yeah, it is."

The girls stayed that way for a while, knowing, as only two former School students can, that breaking into Uncle Frank's was a one-way job. How many times had they seen his office door close and heard the screams of a spy from a rival gang or the whimpers of a tortured informant coming from beneath the door? As kids, they had filed these incidents away as the unexplainable actions of adults they trusted unconditionally, but now they knew the truth: No one who entered the School ever walked out, no matter what promises Uncle Frank made them. Even if they escaped, they would always be looking over their shoulder, wondering when one of Frank's blades might find its mark.

"Wait a minute." Little John turned to Robin. "Remember the time we got cornered in that back alley by those policemen?"

"How could I forget?" Robin could still see the light reflecting off their badges and in beady eyes of their sunglasses.

"I thought we were done for," Little John said with a shiver, "but then you told me, 'The only way out is through.' Remember?"

Robin did remember. And she remembered what happened afterward, when she set off a smoke bomb and sent the police officers scurrying out of the alley like rats from a docked ship. In the confusion, she and Little John had crossed the street and found shelter in a wedding dress shop owned by one of Uncle Frank's customers, who happened to also dabble in the illegal trade of the blood diamonds worn on her brides' manicured fingers. Each girl had hidden inside of the puffy skirt of a mannequin while the police searched the street and then every store on the block, and Robin remembered the way the tulle underskirt had itched her face for over an hour.

"Are you saying—?"

"Shh." Little John put her finger to her lips. "Our little secret."

"Right." Robin clenched her fists. "Let's do it. Let's go through."

* * *

"WE'LL DO IT," ROBIN TOLD HER DAD.

She'd found him in the farmhouse resting against what had once been the kitchen counter. Looters had taken all the furniture and appliances, leaving gaps in the cabinets like teeth missing from a mouth, but no one could use the laminate countertop or the shiny linoleum floor, so it remained, but had been muddied by many careless shoes.

"I knew you'd come around."

Robin looked down the hall, where she could see the same emptiness of the living room. "Why'd you let this place get so run down?"

"Couldn't bring myself to rent it out," he said. "Felt too weird letting strangers live where my parents had once lit a fire or watched *Family Ties* or . . . I don't know." He shrugged. "I just wasn't ready to let them go."

Her dad had never opened up like this, and Robin shifted her weight, uncomfortable in the intimacy of the moment. When she'd lived with him, they had been like two cars passing each other on the street, only stopping when police work gave them something to talk about. That was why, when she left the force, she had to leave him too—who were they to each other, if not fellow officers?

"We have some demands," Robin said, and instantly, his face lost all its softness. "We need Daisy Chain and Skillet to complete the job. Also, we need to be the ones to procure all the supplies, otherwise we can't guarantee that Uncle Frank won't figure out we're coming."

"So, carte blanche with no hostages as incentive?" He raised his eyebrows. "But then how do I know you'll even do the job?"

Robin had already thought about this. "You'll keep Nottingham as collateral. Once the job is done, you'll give us back our home and leave us alone—for good."

Her dad thought about this for a while as he drummed his thick fingers against the edge of the counter. Could he trust her? Did he have a choice?

"Deal." He stuck out his hand, and she shook it, savoring the way his palm surrounded hers the way his arms used to swallow up her whole upper body in a hug. "Bring me Brian McBrewen, and you'll get your precious hideout back."

"Brian McBrewen?" Robin's hand went numb. "I thought you wanted Frank?"

"Hypothetically. Eventually." Her dad removed his hand from her frozen grasp. "But for now, we just want our man back."

"But—"

"I'll be in touch," her dad said. "Probably sooner than you'd like."

* * *

WHITE RABBIT PICKED UP THE GIRLS in Skillet's truck. The techie had no driving skills—and now that she thought about it, Robin wasn't sure if she even had a license—but at least she came to an abrupt stop ten feet from the mailbox without running the post or the rest of the Merry Misfits over with the front bumper.

"Good job, Baby," Skillet yelled out as she circled the truck. She leaned in the open window and kissed White Rabbit for longer than was comfortable to watch, so Robin and Little John busied themselves with cramming into the middle seat of the truck and hooking one seatbelt securely around their paired waists.

"Are you okay?" Little John asked Robin. "You've been really quiet since you talked to your dad. Did he say something?"

"Brian McBrewen," Robin said softly as Skillet slid into the driver's seat and White Rabbit took the passenger's seat.

"Who?"

"A kid I used to know."

Used to know. The phrase didn't even begin to describe the years they'd been best friends, or the way they'd shared a secret flashlight code, or the feel of his sweaty hand in hers as she led him down to the wide creek behind their neighboring yards. Back then Brian had a temporary interdental lisp—her fault, from the time she made him ride down the stairs in a slippery sleeping bag—and at the edge of the water she'd made him say *fish*, and *swim*, and *grass*, just to hear that sweet *th* sound that only Brian made, and he'd called her *My Samantha* even though her name also had an "s" in it. That was the same day that Shaina had come splashing down the other side in her yellow rain boots, and Robin's heart had felt as flooded as the creek pouring over the sides of its bed.

Used to know.

The phrase also didn't contain the many ways that Brian had become a stranger before Robin left the academy—the ways he turned on her once he realized that she had never really been his. Robin touched her forearm, where a faded scar hid beneath the delicate hairs and golden skin made a richer hue over the past two years by the Florida sun. The scar still hurt her, though she knew that any pain she felt was somatic, just a ghost from her past haunting her the way Shaina, her dad, and Frank haunted her.

Fish. Swim. Grass.

It was Brian who'd turned her in that day she'd stolen the file. He'd been shadowing one of the cops on duty, and he'd walked into the evidence locker and found her with the manila folder in one hand and her lock pick in the other. *What are you doing?* he'd asked, and Robin had opened her mouth a few times to lie but found she couldn't bring herself to make up an excuse. *You shouldn't be here.*

If you'll just give me a chance to explain—

She had been unprepared for the assault. Brian had done little things to annoy her and Shaina over the years, like sticking a banana peel in Robin's locker on a Friday so that on Monday the mush had soaked through her uniform or swapping out Shaina's standard issue hat for a rainbow cap, but he had never done physical harm. With the force of ten years of bottled rage, Brian had grabbed her right arm and then slammed her into the shelf so hard that a box on top fell onto her head. Before she could recover, he swung her the other way, this time connecting her forearm with the sharp edge of the other shelf. Her arm throbbed, and she knew, without being able to look, that the corner had cut through the skin.

"Give up the folder," he yelled, as though that was what he cared about, and she cringed at the victory in his voice. How long had he wanted to do this? How many times had they stood opposite each other in training, and he'd held back this anger the way the police trainers held back their growling dogs?

Robin's arms were pinned, but her feet were free. She lifted her right leg and push off the first shelf, sending them both backward into the other shelf. Off balance, Brian lost his grip on her arms, and with the speed of someone who had trained her whole life, Robin had him handcuffed to the shelf's post and out of reach of her in under three seconds.

Of course, no one ever talked about how they'd found him in the evidence locker covered in her blood.

Not even Shaina.

CHAPTER EIGHT

"So, as you can see, the plan is simple . . . and very, very dangerous."

The Merry Misfits sat in a semi-circle around Robin's trailer door, onto which Robin had hung a white board covered in her barely legible scribbles. She looked up from her work to look at them—her friends, her family—and the way they nodded along with her words, as though they could even imagine the risks of a run-in with Uncle Frank, made her want to cry. She was Napoleon and they were the force about to be slaughtered at Agincourt—or no, wait, had that been Henry V? Everything Robin had ever learned in school had become like a wet letter, the sentences blurring and becoming one incoherent blot.

"So, we all join Uncle Frank's gang?" repeated Skillet.

"Right. He won't trust us at first, but we'll give him a reason . . . something about a rival gang, maybe the Pioneers, coming after us. He hates those guys."

"And once we're in . . ." Skillet looked at the board and squinted, ". . . you and Little John find Brian McBrewen while Daisy Chain and I create a distraction?"

"Exactly."

Skillet looked at White Rabbit. "What's her job?"

"Stay here and monitor the situation," said Robin. She didn't make eye contact with White Rabbit—she couldn't, or she'd give herself away. "We need someone on the outside."

No one asked any follow-up questions, and Robin was glad—she needed to rest. The day had been long, and her eyes had begun to burn, yet every time she closed them, she saw Brian McBrewen's face so close to hers she could smell the ham sandwich on his breath. They would leave the next morning, early, on a plane her dad had arranged. How willing he had been to break the rules, she thought as she removed the white board from her door and threw it down in the grass, and how desperate to get back Brian—the son he'd always wanted.

"Robin?" Daisy Chain had come up behind her, as though to enter the trailer. Today she had vines woven into a messy up-do, and the tails of the greens hung attractively down her half-naked back. She was like a wood nymph, or maybe a seer about to issue a prophesy.

"What?"

"*To fear the foe, since fear oppresseth strength, Gives in your weakness strength unto your foe,*" Daisy Chain whispered, "*And so your follies fight against yourself.*"

"I'm fine. Don't worry about me." She shut the door before Daisy Chain could speak another useless rhyme.

Robin watched the girls drift away from her trailer through a crack in the blinds. Once their voices became an incoherent babble and then a distant murmur, Robin opened the door again and walked back out. She wanted to spend the rest of the daylight walking the perimeter of Nottingham, like tracing the lines of a lover's face before a very long trip—or before leaving forever—and she wanted to do it alone. Who knew whether they would succeed at Uncle Frank's, or even if they did, whether they would ever see the grounds of Nottingham again? The other girls loved this place, but no one could ever understand the land the way Robin, who had first found the property and shot at rattlesnakes and cut down the tall grass, did. Well, maybe Little John, but she was a city girl, and Boston would always be her one true home.

Robin couldn't go North—North was where Blake was—and she couldn't go South to I-10, so she headed west by crossing behind their circle of trailers and into the woods. This area was one she rarely explored, and the path was messy, littered with sticks and rocks and fallen leaves from the previous season. The tread of her hiking boots kept her balance on the uneven terrain, but her ankles strained against the abnormal angles of her feet. She liked the way the path required all her attention—she did not want to think.

A marsh rabbit watched her unsteady approach with beady black eyes. This was peak breeding season, when marsh rabbits seemed to sprout from the ground like the dandelions they chewed, and Robin loved to watch their jaws work the thin stalks of grass, their joyous leaps into the dense underbrush, and once, on a hike to a nearby marsh, their semi-submerged advance beneath the water, ears pushed back and nose held above the surface. She loved them because even with the alligators, and owls, and hawks, and snakes, and foxes, and all the other predators who lusted for the taste of them, nothing could not slow their progress.

She loved them because they reminded her of her crew.

The marsh rabbit disappeared, leaving her alone on the path.

I hope that we prove as resourceful as you, thought Robin as she turned toward home. *I hope we survive.*

By the time she got back to Nottingham, the light had dimmed and then disappeared, leaving her to cross the clearing by the light of her cell phone. A TV glowed behind Skillet's curtain; Little John's kitchen light kept watch. Daisy Chain's trailer was completely dark, and Robin wondered if she was meditating, or sleeping, or reading lines of Shakespeare as she drank a cup of chamomile tea. She wanted to knock on the door and find out, but she fought the impulse; she and Daisy Chain were over. They had to be over.

Robin opened the door of her own trailer as quietly as possible, slipped in, and rested the door back in place but did not allow it to click all the way closed. She did not want to draw their attention; she did not want any visitors. She slipped out of her boots and left them on the steps, then did the same with her socks, her jeans, her shirt. Without brushing her teeth or washing her face, she dropped into bed and hid under the sheet. The skin of her arms, so close to her nose because she used them as a pillow, smelled like the forest.

I hope we survive, she thought again.

The weight of her crew pressed down on her. If anything happened to them . . .

Robin curled her legs up into the fetal position and closed her eyes.

To fear the foe, since fear oppresseth strength, Gives in your weakness strength unto your foe. And so your follies fight against yourself.

Breathe. Just breathe.

Her scar burned. She saw Brian's face and heard his voice. Blake was there too, calling out from the grave, telling her not to leave him. She kicked the covers off, got cold, pulled them back again.

Sleep. You need to sleep.

Somebody was in the room. Robin sat up, grabbed for the knife she kept on her nightstand, and clicked open the blade.

"*And sleep, that sometime shuts up sorrow's eye, Steal me awhile from mine own company.*"

Just Daisy Chain, her thin legs sticking out from below the oversized undershirt she wore as a nightgown. Robin knew she should tell her to leave. She knew that Little John might see her in the morning and know what had happened, that she might never forgive her. Yet she lifted the covers and let Daisy Chain in, and when Daisy Chain settled next to her, Robin pressed her face into her braids and let the smell of lavender calm her.

A minute later, she was asleep.

* * *

"RISE AND SHINE," LITTLE JOHN'S VOICE echoed through the trailer. Robin rubbed her eyes and turned over to look out the window. The sky was dark; only the chirping of birds indicated the impending morning. Daisy Chain slept soundly through the noise, her small inhalations like those of a baby or a small animal—a marsh rabbit, perhaps—and her hands clasped in front of her, as if in prayer.

"I am in so much trouble," Robin muttered.

Daisy Chain stirred but did not open her eyes. Robin slid out from underneath the sheet and into the long flannel shirt she used as a robe. When she got to the door, Little

John looked up from the bottom of the steps with what Robin hoped was amusement.

"I take it you're not alone?" she asked. "I already tried Daisy's trailer. By the way, we need to convince her to start locking up her stuff. What if we get robbed?"

"Little John, I didn't mean—"

Little John put up a hand. "I get it. Trust me. Habits take a long time to break."

So, they were still best friends; so this thing between her and Daisy Chain would not change that. Robin took a deep breath.

"Get the others," she said, her voice again sounding like the leader she was. "We leave in ten."

After Little John left to wake Skillet and White Rabbit, Robin went back to the bedroom and sat down on the edge. Daisy Chain looked so beautiful lying there, like a princess who had fallen asleep in the woods, and Robin suddenly wished she could protect her from what was about to happen. She wished that she had never stopped at that rest stop near Lake City, or recognized that quote from *Romeo and Juliet*, or . . . But she could no more change Daisy Chain's fate than that of any other crewmember. They knew the risks, and still, they followed her.

"It's time to go," Robin whispered, and Daisy Chain finally opened her eyes. "Remember, you can bring one backpack, so choose your items carefully. We may not be back for a while."

Daisy Chain sat up and held Robin's hand. Robin waited for the perfect Shakespeare quote, the lines that might sum up their departure, but Daisy Chain just squeezed and then let go. *She's scared*, Robin thought. And she should be.

When she was alone, Robin put on her usual pair of dark jeans and a black t-shirt and then moved around with her empty backpack to see if anything stuck out as essential. Nothing in the bedroom; nothing in the kitchen. The living room was bare save for a few thrift store prints hung on the walls, their prices still marked on yellow stickers, and she certainly wasn't going to pack a photograph of a crane swallowing a fish or a painting of a young girl walking up a hill.

At the very front of the trailer, Robin stopped at the sofa and pulled up the left cushion, then reached her hand into the crack between the edge and the fold-out bed. Her fingers brushed velvet, and then she removed the small pouch and replaced the cushion. Robin dumped out the locket and silver chain that had been her mother's into her palm, feeling its coldness and thinking, *How fitting.* Inside the engraved circle were two pictures, one of Robin as a baby and one of her father, though Robin did not open the clasp to check whether the images remained. Instead, she slipped the chain over her neck and hid the locket beneath her shirt, where it cooled the skin over her heart.

The necklace had once been a symbol of love; now, it was a symbol of all the ways that her family had failed her.

These girls, her crew, were the only ones that mattered.

CHAPTER NINE

THE MORNING SKY WAS SOMBER. OVER the tree line, gray clouds revealed only a hint of hazy yellow. A woodpecker landed on White Rabbit's trailer, pecked curiously, and moved on.

The girls were gone, gathered down at the truck, and as Robin approached, they went quiet. Daisy Chain looked different in all-black clothes that, on further inspection, were Little John's. Skillet also wore black, including a cowboy hat and boots. Robin felt like they were at a funeral for something . . . But what were they mourning? Nottingham? Their reign as the best highway robbers in Florida? Each other? Did they feel, as Robin did, that they were standing on the edge of a great abyss, and that, if they didn't look down, they might go on pretending to be anywhere else?

"Ready?" she asked, and everyone nodded. *And what if we don't all come out? And what if this is my fault? And what if . . . ?* She made her voice as steady as possible. "Then let's get this done so we can come home."

Home. The word seemed to blossom over them, over the trees and the gray sky, over all of Florida, and inside of them, too, calming their fears. They had made this home, and they would return to it—all of them.

"For Nottingham," agreed Skillet.

"For Nottingham," they all cheered.

They climbed into the truck, pressing shoulder to shoulder and with Little John on Robin's lap. For once, Little John didn't make any snide comments or shoot any glares in her direction. White Rabbit took her place in the guard post and opened the gate, and then she somberly raised her hand and rubbed her fingers together as though holding a coin.

"Steal from the rich," she yelled.

The girls raised their hands and did the same. "Give to ourselves!"

But this has never been about the money, Robin thought as they drove down the road and out onto the highway, cutting in front of a slow Prius that soon disappeared in the distance behind them. She felt like she might cry. When she had looked back in the side view mirror, White Rabbit caught her gaze and did the money symbol again. Never about the money—and yet all about it, too. Money had bought Nottingham. Money had bought bribes. Money had bought trucks, and motorcycles, and tech gear.

And money had bought freedom.

Skillet brought the truck to 90, and Robin rolled down the window and took a deep breath of humid Florida air.

* * *

At UFlyU Private Jets, Skillet parked the truck in a long-term parking spot. "Strip it," Robin reminded them, and the girls pulled off the fake plates, gathered up the unpaid tickets, and even wiped the steering wheel of prints. Skillet cried as she closed the door, and Robin wondered if this was the longest she had ever owned a single vehicle. Even without this job, they would have had to retire the truck—Everything was disposable—and Robin reminded her of this as she put her arm around her friend's waist, unable to reach all the way to her shoulder.

Since they were flying out of a private facility based outside Tallahassee International Airport, there was no security checkpoint or even a guard. Their pilot, an older man with white hair and a fake tan, waited for them inside the entranceway and let them straight through the lounge to their plane. He said something about the technical aspects of the plane, but Robin barely registered his game show host-voice after she spotted Shaina waiting on the steps leading up to the aircraft.

"What are you doing here?" Robin asked, even less politely than she'd intended.

"Someone has to keep an eye on you."

Robin scowled. Still, she couldn't help admiring Shaina in her civilian clothes, especially the swishy red pants that reminded Robin of snow days and cocoa and the feeling of snow melting down her back after Shaina or Brian dumped a fistful down her shirt. Strange, to feel that chill in the middle of a Florida spring. She shivered.

"You alright?" Shaina asked.

Robin looked at her sideways. Was that actual concern in her voice, or was Shaina that good of an actor? Was seducing Robin part of her assignment, and if so, to what purpose?

"Fine," Robin said, "as long as you stay away from me." She shouldered past Shaina as she passed her on the steps, leaving the pilot and the other girls to catch up.

The interior of the plane was the nicest room the Merry Misfits had been in since . . . well, since leaving home. The plane had black carpets with the shimmer of a diamond pattern cut into the weave, chrome metal accents, and luxury seats. The leather, after the crunchy plastic and hard wood of their trailers, caused Robin and the other Misfits to sigh as they sank into the buttery cushions. There were just enough seats for the five girls, including Shaina, not including the sofa where they could lounge after reaching the proper altitude.

"Is there an in-flight movie?" asked Skillet as she reclined her chair.

"No," answered Shaina, who was reading an emergency manual from the pocket of her seat.

"What about drink service?" asked Little John.

"No."

"*Good company, good wine, good welcome can make good people?*" asked Daisy Chain.

Shaina looked up. "Was that a question?"

"She wants to know if you serve alcohol," interpreted Little John.

"Alcohol?" Shaina's voice went up. "You aren't even twenty-one, and I'm a police officer!"

"*Do you think because you are virtuous, that there shall be no more cakes and—*"

Little John put her hand over Daisy Chain's mouth to stifle whatever sassy Shakespeare quote she had pulled from her hat. Robin would never forget the time she and Skillet had got into an argument, the one relying on southern sayings like *That girl's all hat and no cattle,* the other eventually reducing them all to laughter with lines such as *Away, you starveling, you elf-skin, you dried neat's-tongue, bull's-pizzle, you stock-fish!* That one was from *Henry IV;* Robin had looked it up.

Now, she settled back into her chair and zoned out as the plane ascended and then levelled, like a submarine emerging into the air. The mild turbulence of the troposphere—as the pilot explained it, the layer that contained Earth's weather—gave in to the stratosphere. The wings of their white, midsized jet made Robin feel like a heron riding a thermal—though, as she watched the Merry Misfits banter with Shaina, she wondered if perhaps she was the heron, and they were the fish about the slide down her throat. Shaina had a way with people, a sly winning over that had made her as popular as Robin's bluntness had made her unpopular. Her old friend would make a good captain one day, Robin decided, or even a chief of police.

"You okay?" Little John asked. She had gotten out of her seat and come over to Robin's seat; now she searched Robin's eyes, probably sensing a secret and following it the way a bloodhound follows a scent.

"Yeah," Robin said through a fake yawn. "I'm just tired."

For the rest of the flight, she feigned sleep. The chatter and then laughter of the girls around her was like the screeches and trills of a belted kingfisher, though the undercurrent of Shaina's manipulation was much less visible than the kingfisher's bright blue feathers. How quickly she could put herself among them, appealing to their interests and even their fears—like Iago in *Othello*, thought Robin, before realizing that she had spent way too much time with Daisy Chain.

After they landed, Robin stayed quiet on their mostly empty shuttle; and then in their private car driven by a man in a suit and sunglasses; and then in the unmarked van where they talked over their mission with another officer on

Shaina's secret team, all crammed together into the space mostly used for transporting prisoners. Robin couldn't see Boston—couldn't see anything but the once-white van wall—but she knew exactly where they were as they moved through the city, from static whoosh of the tunnel to the salty wharf to the kids squealing at the entrance of the zoo. She knew them as smells and sounds, and she knew them as marks. Absentminded parents chasing toddlers in red panda backpacks. Tourists in ugly sneakers, loose t-shirts, bright visors, and even fanny packs—or tourists who look like Bostonians, if not for the way they keep checking the map on their phone, glancing at street signs, or crossing and then re-crossing the street. They were almost as good as the drunk professionals ambling down Boylston Street in converted office wear.

When Robin looked back now, the memories of her and Little John prowling the city were fuzzy. She felt like a ghost of herself, a walking dead girl. She felt Uncle Frank's presence like a shadow looming over her. She saw him in the buildings she knew sat between South Boston and Mattapan—which they all called Murderpan—and in the brick facades and the shops slid into their first floors like drawers and the graffiti signed with familiar tags. Her mood was infectious—or perhaps the realness of Mattapan itself called for silence—and one by one, the other Merry Misfits sunk into the same malaise. Even Shaina, previously so charming, said in a nervous whisper, "Are you ready?"

None of the girls responded.

Robin went over the plan again, if only to fill the silence. Go in through the side entrance and charm the guard. Go up to Uncle Frank's office. Threaten him at gunpoint. Retrieve the prisoner. No matter what, they needed to stick together, even if it meant letting Uncle Frank escape in the meantime.

Silence.

The van dropped them off at the corner of Morton Street and Blue Hill Ave. Like the prisoners they were, each girl filed out and stood blinking in the bright light. "Good luck," Shaina said, and then closed the back door with an ominous slam.

Robin took a deep breath. She smelled marijuana, and the natural gas emitted from the tiny leaks in the underground pipelines.

The van sped off.

Robin's panic mingled with the air and choked her. She clutched at her throat. She focused her eyes on the neon yellow sign in front of her, Cash Checks Here, and remembered the flowers of the swamp-dwelling beggar-ticks.

The van turned at the corner.

Robin closed her eyes and pretended she was back in the woods of Nottingham. With intense effort, she exhaled.

When she opened her eyes, the Merry Misfits were alone.

CHAPTER TEN

UNCLE FRANK'S SCHOOL FOR MISUNDERSTOOD YOUTH had once been a very successful insurance business—minus the preschool, which had been a strange appendage hidden on the top floor. The façade was just another brick face with some shuttered windows and others broken, the gaps under the jagged glass like missing teeth. The railing of the steps bent backward, like ears pulled away from the head. The door was a metal sheet with no handle. An outsider would look at the building and think, *No way in.*

Robin and Little John knew better.

They led the girls around the side to an alley, which was puddled with what might have been urine and sprinkled with empty food wrappers and crushed cans. Daisy Chain covered her nose with her loose sleeve, and Skillet brought her hat down in front of her face. They passed the dumpster that no garbage truck ever picked up, and the bent metal chair from Uncle Frank's office, which Blake had dragged out in the rain to wash off the blood. At the end of the alley was another door, this one wood, and without knocking, Robin pushed it open and stepped inside.

The room was dark.

Someone cleared their throat.

"Who are you?" they asked. The voice was almost a whisper. Robin remembered when she had been on door duty, how she had kept a gong she'd found at a thrift store so that she could ring it and startle the other kids.

"I'm a girl who has killed no men that didn't deserve killing," Robin said.

The voice laughed. The lights came on, flickered twice, and stuck. They were in the dining hall, where Frank's kids ate three meals a day. Not square meals, of course, not even remotely healthy, but they ate, which was more than could be said of them before Frank had pulled them off the street.

"Nice quote." A boy in a baseball cap and Bermuda shorts sat perched on one of the end tables to their right, from which point he could watch the security camera monitors on the wall and just reach the lights. "Paul Castellano?"

"Mickey Cohen."

The boy nodded. Everyone at Frank's School knew the greats, had heard Frank quote these same men so many times that their words became mantras, secret passwords, like tattoos for other gangs.

"You a graduate?" he asked.

"Something like that. Is Uncle Frank around?"

The boy led them up in the elevator, which looked like at any moment it might snap its cords like a guitar played too hard and send them plummeting down, down, down. Robin had always hated this elevator, but now, with the numbers on the buttons half erased, a panel missing from the wall, and a cracked mirror, she wondered if her fears had just become logical conclusions. The creaking sounds and jolts were not helping.

"All that lives must die," muttered Daisy Chain.

They got off at the fourth floor. This hallway was cleaner than the others, and only contained two rooms, both of which were Frank's. On their right, his living quarters, where no kid ever entered; at the end of the hallway, his office, where kids brought his visitors but left them at the door to enter at their own risk. They had seen the warped metal chair. They had heard the screams. Once, Turtle, another kid who lived at Frank's when Robin and Little John were new, had been called up; instead of getting beaten, however, Uncle Frank apparently gave Turtle a Rolex and told him to keep up the good work.

That Rolex—or the potential for Uncle Frank's approval— was why so many kids stayed at the school. They had left their parents, but that didn't mean that secretly, under the layers of sass and stealth and thievery, they didn't ache for the attention Uncle Frank could provide. Even now, Robin felt a strange quickening of her heart, not just in fear but from the pleasant feeling of coming back to a place that had meant so much to her.

"Stay alert," whispered Little John.

"Always," said Robin.

The boy knocked three times on the door, waited ten seconds, and then knocked twice.

"Come in," said Uncle Frank.

The boy swung the door open, but he did not enter. Robin remembered those days—she remembered, again, the blood on the metal chair—and she nodded to him as she walked past him and into the office. Immediately, she scanned the room, starting with Uncle Frank at his desk and moving down, across, forward. Wooden desk with manila envelopes, laptop, wide screen, stapler, hole puncher, old fashioned calculator. A new version of Blake, this one shorter and wider but still in the same black t-shirt. A fish tank with two red-tailed sharks.

"Robin." Uncle Frank rose. "I thought you vowed never to set foot in Boston again?"

Robin wondered whether Uncle Frank knew that the fish would eventually fight and even eat each other—maybe he was counting on it.

"I guess I changed my mind," she said.

Robin watched the fish. Was it her imagination, or were they circling each other?

"And if it isn't my niece," said Uncle Frank. He found his cane and circled the desk to get a better look at the other girls. "What have you brought me? This doesn't look like the package I asked you to steal."

He knows, realized Robin, for no other reason than the fish and maybe the tone of his voice. She had spent years learning to read the notes of his words, the pauses, the emphasis on certain syllables. *Someone tipped him off.*

"Some new kids to brainwash," said Robin in her best attempt at a lighthearted tease. Her eyes went back to the fish, the desk, Blake 2.0. He had a gun holstered at his hip. Probably another in his boot, or at least a knife. A pair of handcuffs hung from the other side of his belt. "A little peace offering. This is Skillet and Daisy Chain—you know them as my former crew from Nottingham."

"Former?" Uncle Frank stopped and tapped his chain on the floor thoughtfully. "What happened?"

His eyes found hers and held her gaze. *He's reading me*, thought Robin. *Just like I'm reading him. I wonder how long we're going to play this game.*

"The usual power struggle," she said. Fish, gun, desk, gun, fish. "Had to kill one girl, and then the rest fell in line. I think it might have been instigated by the Pioneers."

"Oh yes." Uncle Frank turned and paced back to his desk. "Deception by those you love the most. I know all about that."

This was Robin's moment. She thought back to White Rabbit, and the way she had bent to tie her shoelaces. *Now or never.* In one clean motion, she tucked, felt for the handle of the gun, rolled, and then simultaneously stood up and aimed at Uncle Frank's head. She got lucky—the new guy didn't have Blake's reflexes—and Skillet had read her motions quickly enough to hit his forearm and throw the gun to the opposite wall. Little John retrieved it and aimed at Blake 2.0.

"You wouldn't kill your Uncle Frank, would you?" Frank asked softly.

Would she? Robin didn't know. The gun was cool and ready in her hand, like the keys of a new bike. It wanted to go off.

"Hands up," she said, buying time, and besides, she didn't want him rummaging in his drawers. As soon as she saw his palms, she leaned over the desk—gun still aimed, eyes still raised—and slipped a USB into his computer's port. Then she checked her watch.

"What are you doing?" asked Little John.

"Finishing the plan," she said.

Robin could not turn to look at her best friend, but she imagined Little John's face, a mixture of confusion and annoyance at being left out. Only White Rabbit, who had made the USB, knew its purpose—and by now she would be long gone from Nottingham.

"Where's Brian?" Robin asked.

Uncle Frank snorted. "You know that guy? I'd have given him away freely. He's the most annoying prisoner I've ever had, and he doesn't know anything. Down in the basement, second closet. You'll need a knife to cut the ties. There, in the cup holder."

Robin retrieved the switchblade. "Go," she said, and threw the knife to Skillet. Little John started to argue, but then Skillet said, *Stick to the plan*. Without another word, Little John handed the gun to Daisy Chain and left the room with Skillet.

Robin handcuffed Blake 2.0 with one hand and kept her gun on Uncle Frank with the other. Then she checked her watch. Three minutes. Time was up. Robin removed the USB and slid it into her pocket.

Fireworks went off somewhere in the building—no, it was gunfire.

Someone screamed.

Robin and Daisy Chain turned toward the door. Had that been Skillet's voice? By the time they turned back around, Blake 2.0 had gotten his hands from behind his back to in front of him, pulled out the weapon Robin should have taken out of his boot, and aimed it at her.

Breathe, Robin thought, and she consciously pulled air in and out of her lungs. *Turn the gun into something manageable.*

For some reason, the front of the barrel reminded Robin of the black birdhouse Daisy Chain painted and hung in the tree behind her trailer. Maybe she wanted to believe the weapon aimed at her head was that harmless; maybe she was going insane under the threat of death. That bird house had been beautiful, albeit useless, since Daisy Chain had thoughtlessly put black netting over the whole thing to keep out the mosquitos—though what she actually said was *May heaven protect your highness from all enemies.* Then she'd slapped a bug feasting on her arm.

"Drop it," Blake 2.0 ordered, and Robin considered her options. What would happen if she dropped her gun? What if she fired? She hated the smug look on his face, like a puppy hoping to please its master. She remembered being that naïve. And wasn't she, still? She should have remembered the second gun. She should have secured him better. She should have—

A gun went off again, this time in the office.

Robin looked down.

Nothing.

No blood.

No pain.

She looked at Blake 2.0. No, he hadn't fired, and in fact seemed more confused that she was.

Finally, she looked at Uncle Frank.

A rose bloomed across his lapel.

"Daisy Chain?" Robin asked.

Daisy Chain—or, rather, the girl who had once been Daisy Chain but now appeared, with a gun in her hands, to be someone else entirely—swung her gun toward Blake 2.0. Her face was distorted. She looked furious.

"If I would shoot my own dad," Daisy Chain said to Blake 2.0, "I'd definitely shoot you. So, you can stay here and die with him, or you can run."

"You're all insane," said Blake 2.0, and then he ran from the room, the echo of a door slamming down the hall telling them they were alone.

Daisy Chain dropped the weapon, and then her knees gave out. Robin caught her before she could hit the floor. They sank together, Daisy Chain in her lap like a child, sobbing and sobbing as if she might never run out of tears. Robin didn't understand what was going on—Could Uncle Frank really be Daisy Chain's father? Why hadn't she ever mentioned it?—but she also knew they didn't have time to talk about it. Someone had gotten shot downstairs, and if it was a crewmember, she would need help.

"Come on," Robin urged softly. "Let's go save the Merry Misfits."

CHAPTER ELEVEN

WHEN THE ELEVATOR DOORS OPENED ON the scene in the basement, Robin wasn't even sure what she was looking at. All the doors to the closets were open. Four bodies lay on the floor. She spotted Skillet by her hat, and then Little John beside her, holding her hand. The other two bodies were men in black—Uncle Frank's men—and they were handcuffed on the ground. One of them had sustained an injury, but it looked nonlethal. Brian was nowhere to be seen.

"Are there more of them?" asked Robin. She had brought both guns with the safeties on and threw one over to Little John.

"One behind that wall." Little John motioned with her chin, since one hand held Skillet's and the other held the gun. "He's in the back of the boiler room holding Brian hostage. Skillet got the first guy with the knife and took his weapon, but there were too many of them." Little John looked at Robin in a way she never had before—doubtfully— and Robin wondered if she was reconsidering whether Robin had made the right call. "I think they hit the lower spine."

"We need to get help," Robin said. Getting Skillet safe was the only thing that mattered now. "Daisy Chain, you need to find a phone and call 9-1-1, okay? I don't care if you have to strangle that kid by the door to do it. Do you understand?"

Daisy Chain nodded numbly. Then she whispered, "*If we do meet again, why, we shall smile; If not, why then, this parting was well made.*"

"What's wrong with her?" asked Little John as Daisy Chain walked toward the door in a steady shuffle. She looked like a zombie. "And why are you trusting Little Miss Shakespeare to deliver a message?"

"It's a long story, but the short version is that she shot Uncle Frank because he's her dad." Robin should have softened the blow, but there was no time. "Stay with Skillet and put pressure on the wound; I'll go get Brian."

Little John said something else, but Robin stopped listening. As she crossed the room, she heard a different voice—Blake's voice: *You're in the big leagues now.* How strong she had felt as she pummeled him; how aware of her own weakness as he knocked her down. Yet here she was, back at Frank's School, still not having learned her lesson. She had tried to fight a giant when she was just one girl.

Five girls, she reminded herself. *The Merry Misfits are still a crew, no matter what happens.*

The boiler room was dark, save for one yellow lightbulb on in the back corner. The hisses and drips echoed off the metal machines and concrete walls, making it almost impossible to find the source of a breath or the click of a safety being pressed into place. Luckily, that also meant her opponent couldn't aim at her without sticking his face around a corner.

"Brian?" she called out. Then she closed her eyes.

"Robin?" he asked. After all this time, he still recognized her voice. *Would be sweet*, thought Robin, *if he hadn't almost killed me.* Then she reminded herself to focus. Her eyes were still closed.

"Yeah, it's me, your old pal," she said, then regretted the sarcasm in her voice. *There will be time,* she promised herself. "Don't worry, I'm here to get you. Just like that time that Shaina and I found you in that cave, remember?"

No one said anything for a few seconds. Then Brian said, "Yeah, I remember."

Robin enhanced her focus. *Pretend you're back in Nottingham,* she thought. God, it was hot in that boiler room. Almost unbearable. *It's early morning, and the birds are just starting to chirp. Find them, Robin. Identify them.*

This is what she had done every morning for two years, both because she loved being outside and because she wanted to train for a moment exactly like this one. She had the best hearing in the crew, but she wanted to be even better—almost superhuman. Now, she imagined she was sitting in the middle of a clearing, and one by one, then all at once, birdsong surrounded her. And Brian would know to keep talking.

"I suppose you think that you're going to swoop in and rescue me like the big shot you think you are," he said. His voice had gone from curious to mean.

That was how she and Shaina had found him so many years ago, when he'd broken his foot in the cave and they'd followed his voice.

"Wouldn't that show you," said Robin.

"Yeah." His voice dropped the meanness. "I guess it might." A few more seconds went by, and Robin wondered if he remembered the task. Then he started up again. "About what happened that day in the file room . . . I just thought—"

"Shut up," said a second voice.

"—I was doing my duty," continued Brian, "but it was jealousy. And in case I die—"

"I said shut up!" said the other voice, louder.

"—I just want to make sure you know—"

Robin felt a tear slide down her cheek—or maybe it was just sweat. Then she tuned out his words and focused on his voice. *Find him, Robin. Identify his location.* She picked up the sound, followed it across the room, to her left, in a small alcove she hadn't been able to see in the shadows. Brian and his captor were squeezed into the spot like squirrels into a tree hollow, and there was no way to attack without risking his life.

"—that I'm sorry."

Robin tried to think. How could she chase these squirrels out of their tree? She looked around, spotted the water heater in a smaller room to her right, and had an idea. Quickly, she put her gun down softly, removed her flannel shirt, and tied the sleeves together a few times to make a solid knot. Then she went into the other room and got on her knees next to the smooth, round bulk of the water heater. The concrete was cold, but a welcome relief after the heat of the boiler room. She removed the cover to the pilot light, shoved her shirt in, and waited for the end to light.

The flame caught the very end of a sleeve.

Run.

She got up and hurried back into the boiler room. As soon as she got her bearings, she threw the shirt against the back wall, where it bounced off the concrete and landed just close enough to the alcove to be a threat but not close enough to be put out by a stomping foot.

"What the—?" the guard's voice started to say.

Robin lifted her gun.

They came out together, Brian like a human shield in front of his smaller, armed guard. *He's just a kid*, Robin realized as she caught sight of the round, smooth face of the boy. *Just another misunderstood youth.*

But Robin understood him.

She had been him.

With the same focus as her auditory senses, she aimed for the boy's foot and fired. No one ever expected to be fired on *below* their shield, and sure enough, the bullet went clean through the boy's boot and into the concrete, chipping it in the process. The poor boy screamed, but Robin didn't care— he would live. Brian looked mostly the same, though he now had red stubble on his chin and a few cuts on his face. His uniform was a mess of rips and red stains. No lasting damage—at least not physically.

Sirens sounded in the distance.

"Robin, I—"

"Shut up," said Robin. She was trying to think, but the slide of the siren—up and down like a high-pitched recorder at the mouth of an obnoxious kid, mingled with Brian's voice—was making it impossible.

"I can help—"

"I said shut up." Robin took a deep breath. She had not saved Brian's life just to shoot him now. "Go up the back stairs and out to the street. You owe me a favor, so I'll cash it in now and request that you stall up there long enough to get us safely out of here. Okay?"

Brian nodded but didn't say anything. Good—at least he'd gotten better at listening. They both ran out of the room, their boots slapping at the concrete like two rabbits thumping the ground. Brian went to the exit sign on the right stairwell, and Robin went to Skillet on the left. Robin didn't turn around when the basement door clicked open, slammed closed. She only cared about her dying crew member; the pool of blood; and somewhere in the building, Daisy Chain.

Robin got down on her knees and took Skillet's hand out of Little John's.

"Is she going to die?" Little John asked. She suddenly seemed so much younger—like when Robin had first met her, when she was Tiny Tim and no one thought she'd ever amount to much.

"I won't let her die," promised Robin.

"Me neither," said Little John.

This was going to be hard. She took another deep breath.

"Listen to me," Robin started, and Little John knew her well enough to already start to interrupt, "I'm going to stay with Skillet and make sure she gets medical help. You need to get up to the roof and use that secret ladder on the back of the building to get to the alley. You remember?"

Little John nodded. "But I can't leave—"

"Daisy Chain is upstairs somewhere, and you need to get her out. Oh, and here." Robin pulled a few slips of paper from her pocket and removed two of them. There were four total, since White Rabbit already had hers. "One for you, and one for Daisy Chain."

"What is this?" asked Little John. The lined slips, ripped from a spare notebook in the guard post, displayed two lines of numbers.

"They're bank accounts," said Robin. She suddenly felt so tired. They were almost finished with this job—her last job—and she almost looked forward to the sparse bunk bed waiting for her in prison. She could have slept for eternity.

"Bank accounts for what?"

Robin lay down next to Skillet. Her eyes fluttered. She was so, so tired. "For all of the money we just stole from Uncle Frank."

Little John just looked at her. They didn't need to talk. Everything they could have ever said passed between them in just one glance. Then Little John put the slips of paper into her pocket and ran.

The sirens were louder now. In a minute, they would be at Uncle Frank's door. Robin stayed lying down, letting the concrete cool her sweaty back, and looked at Skillet's closed eyes. Skillet was the only one of the Merry Misfits whom Robin had actually recruited, and she would never forget watching the cowgirl in a straw hat and tassels fly past all of the men at the track. Back then, Skillet had been a small-town girl going nowhere fast; now, she was a wanted criminal about to die on the floor of an enemy she barely knew.

Everything was Robin's fault.

"What are you doing?" someone asked from across the room. Robin lifted her head. Shaina was there, at the door, with a gun in her hand. Judging by the sirens still coming closer, closer, Shaina was alone without backup.

"So, you couldn't leave me after all?" Robin laughed and put her head back down. "How sweet."

Shaina holstered her gun and ran over to Skillet. "Oh my god," she said. Then she looked at Robin. "Are you injured too?"

"Nope." Robin closed her eyes. Skillet's hand seemed colder in hers. "Just patiently awaiting my arrest. Aren't you going to cuff me?"

She heard Shaina walk around to her, but she didn't hear the hand raised before the slap. Robin's cheek stung, and she opened her eyes.

"What the heck?"

"Get up, Samantha." Shaina put her hands on her hips.

"No."

Shaina raised one hand. "Get. Up. Samantha. I'm not trying to arrest you; I'm trying to save you."

"I'm not leaving Skillet," said Robin. She wished she didn't sound like a petulant child. She would have shut her eyes again, but she wanted to watch out for incoming blows.

"Why? Because you're doing such a good job saving her life?" Shaina shook her head. "You're still exactly the same. You can't save everyone, Robin. Sometimes, you need to just focus on saving yourself."

Robin didn't say anything. The sirens were consistently loud, which meant the cars had parked outside the building. Brian could only buy them a few minutes, and Robin thought about her friends. *Please let them get out. Please, please, please.*

Shaina crouched down at Robin's side. "You won't do them any good in prison, Robin. And if she lives," her eyes went to Skillet, "then you can get her out."

She had a point.

A good point.

Only Shaina would know Samantha Ramirez well enough to trump responsibilities with more responsibilities. That part of her would never die, no matter how long she lived as Robin. Somewhere, Little John was leading Daisy Chain down the ladder and out the alley, and White Rabbit was stepping onto a bus that would take her across the country. They had stolen money in their pockets, and the men from whom Uncle Frank had taken it would eventually come looking for it.

And Skillet, if she lived, would spend the rest of her days locked in a cell.

"You'll stay with her until then?" asked Robin.

Shaina gave Robin her hand and helped her up. "I promise."

Robin took one last look at Skillet. She thought of the way her hair, now matted by blood, had whipped around her face and out the window, and how beautiful she had looked in that car, the way some riders look on a horse as they jump a fence. Focused. Calm. And yet below that, driving her forward like a switch: pure joy.

Robin turned and ran.

PART TWO
WHITE
RABBIT

To: OffroadPrincess

Subject: Are you okay???

Please respond. I am so worried about you. I love you.

* * *

To: OffroadPrincess

Subject: News

I saw the article about you in *The Boston Globe*, so at least I know that you're alive. I would kill R. for leaving you behind, but she's gone anyway, so I guess I'll never get the chance. If you wake up—WHEN you wake up— please email me back.

P.S. This account is secure, but I'm sure you already guessed that.

* * *

To: OffroadPrincess

Subject: Waiting

They talked about you on TV today. Thank god for nosey news anchors. I even saw a blurry shot of your face before the nurses pulled your curtain back. You looked so peaceful in your bed, with your hair wild on the propped-up pillows. Just like you used to sleep back in Nottingham when you had a cold. Remember how you thought going outside with wet hair would make you sick, and I had to look it up online? I believe your exact words were, "The internet doesn't know everything, Sugar Britches."

They did a segment on your childhood and interviewed your mom, by the way. They also talked to your old pastor and some counselor who claimed he worked with you at that terrible camp. Don't watch it. They sounded insane, and even the reporter looked uncomfortable.

I can't wait to talk to you about all of this.

* * *

To: OffroadPrincess

Subject: Feeding Frenzy

People seem to be standing up for you about the conversion thing, so my faith in humanity is somewhat restored.

Still no word from R. Probably for the best, since, as I previously mentioned, I'm going to kill her.

* * *

To: OffroadPrincess

Subject: Prison

I can't believe you took the blame for everything. What were you thinking??? Sure, you didn't actually admit to killing Uncle Frank, but you may as well have! S., they're going to lock you up forever for this!!! Please, please, please tell them the truth. Please.

* * *

To: ImL8ImL8
Subject: I'm alive.

* * *

To: OffroadPrincess
Subject: Code word?

* * *

To: ImL8ImL8
Subject: King Richard. Code word?

* * *

To: OffroadPrincess
Subject: Lionheart
OMG, are you okay???

* * *

To: ImL8ImL8
Subject: Slow Your Roll, Sugar Britches
1. I love you.
2. I have a contraband phone. You would be so proud of me. I traded it for the key to my truck to some girl about to get out on good behavior.
3. I'm madder than a wet hen about all this crapola on the news, but I'm glad you knew I was okay.
4. They were never going to let me out anyway.
5. I love you.

* * *

To: OffroadPrincess
Subject: AHHH!!!
YOU'RE ALIVE!!! AND YOU GOT A CONTRABAND PHONE!!! AND YOU REMEMBERED THE LOGIN INFO

AND PASSWORD!!! I AM SO, SO, SO PROUD OF YOU AND I LOVE YOU SO MUCH. AHHH!!!

* * *

To: OffroadPrincess
Subject: P.S.
What's prison like?

* * *

To: ImL8ImL8
Subject: Prison is . . .

. . . a lot like you see in the movies, only WAY more boring. The only real excitement is when one of the roosters who thinks she runs the place pecks at one of the other roosters who thinks she runs the place.

They think the sun comes up just to hear them crow, if you know what I mean.

I stay out of all that, though, and most everyone leaves me alone. Using a wheelchair has that effect on people . . . Or maybe it's that I supposedly shot a crime boss. I'm glad, because it gives me time to get used to everything—like, have I mentioned how long it takes me to use the bathroom now??

Did I tell you I named it, by the way? Bulldozer, after my first truck—R.I.P.

* * *

To: OffroadPrincess
Subject: Bulldozer

Hey, wait a minute. Wasn't Bulldozer the truck where you had your first "encounter"?

* * *

To: ImL8ImL8
Subject: Oops . . .
You're right. I reckon we'll have to rechristen it the next time I see you.

* * *

To: OffroadPrincess
Subject: New Idea
Do they still do conjugal visits?

* * *

To: ImL8ImL8
Subject: NO!
And if you step foot in this prison, I swear to God I'll make worm food out of you.
Have you heard from R. yet? I'm worried. You know how she gets . . .

* * *

To: OffroadPrincess
Subject: R.
No, and L.J. thinks she's gone for good. I emailed with her for a while, but we decided it was better if we dropped the line, at least until this all blows over. D. C. is with her. Think L.J. will finally tell her how she feels?

* * *

To: ImL8ImL8
Subject: Doubtful
L.J. won't even tell us how she likes her eggs. That girl is a vault! But ask her the square root of 169 and she grins like a possum eatin a sweet tater.

* * *

To: OffroadPrincess

Subject: ???

I swear, sometimes I have no idea what you're talking about. A sweet tater??? It's weird . . . I don't know what to do with myself now that N. is over. Should I, like, get a job or something???

* * *

To: OffroadPrincess

Subject: Officially Employed

I got a job! Turns out it's as easy as creating a fake identity and putting myself on the teaching schedule. I'm officially an adjunct professor of computer science! *crowd applause* First class on Monday!

* * *

To: ImL8ImL8

Subject: Professor W.R.

YOU as a molder of minds??? Well, that just dills my pickle! You do know that you'll actually have to TALK to the students though, right? Not just stand at the podium and type on your laptop.

Not much new in this neck of the woods. I've finally made some friends—my bunkmate Darria, who looks like R. if R. was fifty and smoked three packs a day, and our neighbor, Berenice, who looks like . . . hmm . . . remember S., R.'s friend in the force? Like her, but with more tattoos. Berenice nearabout ran me over one day on her way to breakfast, so I yelled "Son of a motherless goat!" Apparently, she has family down south, and we got to talking about farm life and how much we hate our relatives. Turns out we had a lot in common!

* * *

To: OffroadPrincess

Subject: Berenice

Your friend isn't Berenice Williamson, famed bank robber, is it??? Because if that's her, I have some questions.

Speaking of hacking, my students are protégés! I have these nerds working on a new project—something I can't talk about here, but trust me, it's cool. Of course, they think it's a simulation, but what they don't know can't hurt them.

* * *

To: ImL8ImL8

Subject: Professor W.R. II

That's great, but don't get these angels in trouble, you hear?

And yes, that's the same Berenice! She has a burner phone too of course, so I gave her your email address so you could keep in touch.

By the way, did you put all that bacon in my commissary?

* * *

To: OffroadPrincess

Subject: Maybe J

Happy birthday!!!

* * *

To: ImL8ImL8

Subject: $$$

Sugar Britches, that's enough money to burn a wet mule! I also loved the card you sent, and the way you cut out letters from a magazine like a good old-fashioned ransom note. Very clever!

You know who else sent me a card? My dad. He sounded about as nervous as a long-tailed cat in a room full of rocking chairs with the way he kept putting "um" and "so" and "well, the truth is" all over the place, but he told me that after he and mom got all that press, they got in a huge fight, and he moved out. He even apologized for sending me away!

It'll take time to forgive him, but at least it's a step.

* * *

To: OffroadPrincess

Subject: Letter

Wow, that's great! You might be the first Misfit to actually reconcile with a parent—and probably the last. We should get you some kind of award. Are you going to invite him to visit you?

Nothing new over here—just working hard on my program and running the new computer science club. Did I tell you I started that? I have a few really brilliant, dedicated members, and they're going to keep helping me with my project after the semester is over. We need to think of a better name than Computer Science Club. What do you call rabbit babies?

* * *

To: OffroadPrincess

Subject: No News Is Still News

Heard from L.J. again. She won't really tell me anything except that they're fine and running some kind of business in Maryland—I can't tell if she's a terrible communicator, or if she's afraid the feds are watching her. Maybe both?

I'll never forget that time that she and R. were arguing about how to fix the gate. L.J. wrote out a mathematical equation to figure out how to reset it and R. made some metaphor about a tree falling in the forest. Remember? And while they were yelling at each other, you took your toolbox out of the truck and tightened a few screws, and that was that.

At least she told me she has a plan to get you out. Didn't go into details, but when L.J. puts her mind to something, she does it.

* * *

To: OffroadPrincess
Subject: Victory!
My project works!!!

* * *

To: OffroadPrincess
Subject: Everything Okay?
Haven't heard from you in a few weeks, so I'm starting to get worried. I emailed Berenice, but she hasn't answered either. Let me know you're okay when you get a chance?

* * *

To: ImL8ImL8
Subject: I'm alive
Sorry, Sweet Cheeks, things went south around here for a second. Berenice got robbed, and the girl who did it said she'd been the one to get robbed, though no one on our side

believed her. Don't piss on my leg and tell me it's raining, if you know what I mean. Then all hell broke loose.

I ended up with a broken arm and a nice long stay in solitary. In the meantime, the thief got removed from the equation (at least they know it wasn't me!).

My arm still hurts like the dickens, and I feel about as useless as a steering wheel on a mule.

* * *

To: OffroadPrincess

Subject: Solitary???

If we don't get you out soon, you're going to turn into a hardened criminal!

How bad was solitary?

* * *

To: ImL8ImL8

Subject: BAD

Remember what I said about prison boredom? Take that and multiply it by 1,000. I was only in for five days, and I swear to God the walls started talking to me.

One girl had been in there for TWENTY days for attacking a security guard, if you can believe it. After that long, the lights are on but no one is home, if you know what I'm saying. I felt so bad for her.

I want to come home. L.J. is slower than a Sunday afternoon.

* * *

To: OffroadPrincess

Subject: I know.

We're working on it, I swear. I actually heard

from L.J. today, and it sounds like she has a lawyer willing to represent you. One of the best in the business. He's coming to see you next week, but by now you probably already know that.

No clue how she got him to agree to take your case, but at this point, I don't even care.

* * *

To: ImL8ImL8

Subject: Court Date

This guy is uppity, but darn it if he isn't good at his job. We're going to court! And he seems to have some evidence he thinks will get me out, though he won't tell me what it is.

The only thing I'm worried about: what about the actual shooter? There are only two people it could be, and if getting out of here means putting either of them in, I'd rather stay where I am.

Maybe he has a way to get us all out of this mess?

* * *

To: OffroadPrincess

Subject: Today

I'll be there, but don't look for me.

* * *

To: ImL8ImL8

Subject: I'm getting out!

He did it! The lawyer really did it!

Here's a list of things I want to do first when I get out:

1. Kiss you.
2. Kiss you.

3. Get a bucket of fried chicken. Doesn't need to be the best, just needs to be CRISP.
4. Kiss you again.
5. See R. and everyone else, and kiss them too, even if they don't want me to.
6. Buy a house somewhere in the south where we can live happily ever after.

That's not too much to ask, is it?

I'M GETTING OUT!!!!!!!!!!

PART THREE
LITTLE
JOHN

CHAPTER TWELVE

PLUS ONE. PLUS ONE. ZERO. MINUS one. Plus one. Zero. Divide by three decks. Index number is +4. True count lower. *Hit.*

Little John scanned the casino. A bartender rattled ice and liquid in a tumbler; a patron blew her hot breath onto cupped dice; a singer slammed two puppet hands down on the keys of a slightly flat piano. What was the index number? +4. Two guards by the table made eye contact, looked away, made eye contact again. Little John looked at the carpet, which had probably once been ruby red but was now browned like old blood.

Remember the rules, but don't set off any red flags. Don't sit out whenever they sit out; don't increase your bet too much as the game continues. Sip a drink, come with a "friend," keep your eyes moving, don't take insurance, sip again, don't split 10's, sip again, tell your "friend" something that makes him laugh.

One of the guards caught her eye again and moved, and the second followed, like two sharks on a scent. Little John held her breath. Would there be a scene? Would the singer stop with her fingers over the keys like a witch interrupted during a spell? Or would she play on, leaving the rest of the room unaware of the minor commotion at table three?

"Apprehend," Little John whispered into her mike.

She held her breath, but then she remembered that she was not the one being apprehended. The guards slid up to the table, and Little John nodded, signaling her employees to move. Eliza, Little John's first hire, leaned over to whisper in the offender's ear. He nodded and dropped his cards face-up on the table. Despite the suit he was younger than her—nineteen, at the most—and Little John wondered who had sent this boy with gelled hair and the ghost of a beard into The Nott. Or maybe he had watched a few videos on YouTube and decided to make his fortune, or even a few extra dollars to pay for a can of beans and some rice.

Little John remembered that life.

The boy allowed the guards to lead him to the door on the far side of the spacious room, and Little John could breathe easily again. They would find out a motivation, and if it wasn't a gang name, Eliza and Mike would probably send the kid on his way with a warning that his picture would be shared with every casino in town. If it was a gang name . . . Well, Little John had her ways of dealing with that problem, too.

I sound like Uncle Frank, she thought, and frowned. Ever since his death, she'd felt a kind of possession over her faculties—or, if not a possession, then at least a haunting—and even though The Nott was a hundred percent legal, Little John still looked in the mirror at three in the morning, when the carpets were vacuumed and the bar was wiped clean and the dealers were all tipped, and saw someone she didn't quite recognize.

To make herself feel better, Little John turned away from the room and to a door marked Employees Only. She fished the key from beneath her shirt by pulling up the stainless-steel ball chain and then bent down to unlock the door. In a moment, she had vanished into the dark stairwell, likely without the notice of a single reveler on the first floor, and locked the door behind her.

Little John followed the curve of the stairs around a corner and faced the many lights and bright colors of a classroom. Bold shapes danced across the empty space above a window; a timeline of women's history traced the top of a blackboard. The floor space, currently divided by clusters of four desks, made a brain teaser with its strange whirls of overlapping swirls.

A teacher's voice, recognizable with its annunciated words and patient optimism, came through the doorway on the far side of the room, and Little John trailed after it like a child after the Pied Piper.

She took in the chaos of the second classroom.

Were those . . . crabs?

"Don't be afraid!" called Daisy Chain, like a general to her troops. She had on more scarves than usual—or perhaps the scarves were so disheveled that they gained more notice. A small dream catcher dangled from one ear; she had lost the other since that morning, Little John noted, along with her shoes and socks. "A crab, a crab, my kingdom for a crab!"

Little John was pretty sure that was a Shakespeare quote— her ears perked up at kingdom, or thou, or farewell—but adapted, like a child might mishear a word from their parents and later use it in the wrong context. Little John still thought of Daisy Chain that way—like a child—and yet, she had to admit that as the Shakespeare quotes had subsided, and the lessons in the basement of The Nott had begun, her cousin had proved herself more mature than the rest of the Merry Misfits.

Then again, how could Little John know how much the other girls had grown up?

She hadn't seen them in three years.

Little John stepped carefully around the flung arms and outstretched legs of the Tiny Notts. Sand crunched under her black sneakers; a crab narrowly escaped with a quick scurry across her path. The students had made fiddler crab tanks using plastic carriers, sand mounded mostly on one side, water on the other, and a few plastic plants stuck haphazardly in the sand like umbrellas on a beach. Apparently, Daisy Chain had misjudged their ability of then getting the crabs from her container to their own new homes, and judging by the very few number of crabs in terrariums, they would be finding shells and claws around the classroom for weeks.

So much for a relaxing work break.

Little John finally got to the front of the room and whispered to Daisy Chain, "We caught another counter." She couldn't help smelling the hempy scent of her hair, or the hint of lavender that imbued her skin from her always-burning candles. *You're going to burn the apartment down*, Little John always warned during the rare hours when they both had breaks at the same time and could escape across the street—and yet she liked the smell, the way Daisy looked in the glow, the reminder of home.

Not home anymore.

Little John wondered what had become of their little circle of trailers. Had Robin's father confiscated the place? Had he left it to rot, to succumb to the vines and bugs and snakes and squirrels that came like a plague to any space left alone for too long in Florida? *The land is trying to kill us*, Little John had told Robin a million times, but Robin was like her name-sake—a part of the fabric of the forest.

Little John hated greenery.

She hated the dark spaces beneath the leaves where snakes slithered and roaches skittered.

And she especially hated crabs.

Not because of Nottingham, but because of her dad, who had spent his early mornings in Boston Public Market selling bluefish he'd had to wrestle into the cooler, weakfish swimming through Massachusetts waters in the summer, and the most desired of all: large striped bass. Little John had run the register since she was old enough to count, which in her case was three years old. By kindergarten, she could do basic multiplication.

When she thought of him now, she smelled salty spray, felt the wriggling tackle between her fingers, and heard his call of "Fish! Fresh fish!" After May 1st he'd sold blue crabs too, their metallic bodies more machine than meat—or at least that's how they'd seemed to Little John, who oversaw the dip net used to scoop them from the water. She'd had night-mares about them, their legs becoming little torpedoes that attacked her house or their claws slipping out of the ice chest to grab her by the neck. She'd been unable to forget the image of their yellow guts and gray gills scraped out by one of her father's thick fingers, and still thought of them when-ever she watched an alien movie.

Luckily, her father hadn't cooked much, so he almost never tried to make her eat one of the creatures they'd dragged up from the ocean. Sometimes, he would offer her a bit of crab soup from the grocery store's silver soup vat or one of his buddies would hand her a beer battered cod fillet, but unless she had gone more than a day without a meal, she refused anything that had once breathed. On the rare occasion when he did cook a fish on their backyard grill, beer in hand and radio crooning softly in the background, she made an exception and forced down a bite of tuna just to feel like a normal kid with a normal dad eating a normal meal together.

And then one day, like bait stuck too loosely onto a hook, he'd disappeared into the ocean.

When Little John had met Robin, she had known instantly that her best friend had a parent somewhere out there, the way she knew the difference between blue and mako sharks or the variety of Massachusetts herrings. Of course, she had not expected that parent to be an officer of the law—but everyone had their secrets.

Little John wondered, as she watched Daisy Chain pluck a fiddler crab from the ground and rehome it, what secrets lay buried beneath her braids.

"Do you need my help?" Daisy Chain asked, drifting back to the topic of conversation.

"With the counter?" Little John imagined what that help would look like. Would Daisy Chain charm him with a wave of her scarf or a jingle of her many bracelets? Then again, Daisy had killed her own father without explanation. Secrets, secrets, secrets. "I think I've got things under control."

"Good." Daisy Chain looked around the room. "*These violent delights have violent ends.*"

Little John shivered. Daisy Chain had the ability to turn the mood of a room with a single line—not just the words she chose, but the way she delivered them, like a medium passively delivering messages from the dead. There was a darkness in her—the kind of deep water that Little John tried to avoid.

A crunch sounded below them.

Weeping, a child pulled back her foot, revealing the guts and muscles of a fiddler crab.

* * *

HALF AN HOUR LATER, LITTLE JOHN met Eliza in the hallway outside her office. The guard told her they'd gotten his name—Bean—but nothing else. Apparently, he would only talk to Little John.

"To me?" Little John thought back, but she would remember a name like Bean. "Fine. I'll talk to him. You and Mike stay outside the door in case I need you, okay?"

"Okay, boss. Oh, and you should know he has a Boston accent."

The sparse room was as tidy as she'd left it, from her old-fashioned calculator with a tongue of paper lolling on the desk to her alphabetized manila folders. Bean had been ruffled a little, but nothing a little hair gel or a straightening of his tie couldn't fix. Little John didn't like her guards to hurt their guests—even guests who counted cards or stole other people's drinks—and except for one man who'd thought it would be okay to touch Vicky the waitress, they were instructed to scare but not scar. In fact, Bean seemed to be quite comfortable for a crook, seated, as he was, in Little John's swivel chair with a sweating glass of water and the candy wrappers from Little John's ceramic bowl.

About that man who had touched Vicky—well, she'd simply told Eliza to do what she thought was right. How could she have known Eliza would take his diamond-studded wedding ring and with it, his finger?

Violent ends, she thought, but still couldn't bring herself to feel bad about it.

"I heard you wanted to talk to me," said Little John. Then she sat down in the chair opposite the desk, feeling unsettled by the change in perspective. Her face, always a tightlipped and squinted purse, betrayed no additional worry—though she was worried about this boy in the suit and the whole N operation and where, out there in the world, the other Merry Misfits had skipped like stones and then landed. "So, talk."

Bean wiggled his tie lose and then removed it. Then he unbuttoned the top buttons of his shirt. Little John wanted to slap her hand on the table, but she didn't. She hated showing any emotions, especially anger. If he touched her calculator, though, she might not be able to control herself.

"So, you're Uncle Frank's niece." Bean shook his head. "I thought you'd be . . . different."

Little John felt Uncle Frank's name in her ears like she'd dunked her head into a bucket of cold water.

"My dad is A.C.," Bean continued. "Andrew Clark. You've heard of him?"

Little John arched her eyebrows in assent. Of course, she'd heard of A.C.—he ran the Boston Butchers, so called because they liked to stab their victims rather than shoot them. Uncle Frank's greatest rival.

"A.C. was pretty happy when he heard you took out Uncle Frank," said Bean. "That guy had been a stone in his shoe for as long as I've been alive." Bean tapped thoughtfully on her calculator keys but didn't press down; Little John's fingers twitched. "Only problem was, Frank owed us money—a lot of it." Bean's lips pursed. "That's where you come in."

The bucket had become a dunking tank, and Little John was swimming in it. She and Daisy Chain had come to Maryland precisely to get away from any ties with Uncle Frank, and yet the tie was here, in her office, now swiping a pen from the cup of identical blue ballpoints and tucking it behind his ear.

"How much?" Little John asked, because with the Butchers, there was no arguing. Not if you wanted to keep your guts intact. Still, she thought about the pens—about whether she could get the cap off and the point into his neck faster than he could withdraw the blade hidden in his shoe, or his shirt, or tucked into his belt. Probably not, and besides, what would happen to Daisy if she found Little John bleeding out on the office floor?

"Five million."

Little John raised her eyebrows again, this time to the point where she felt the muscles in her forehead strain. She didn't have five million dollars—not anymore.

"Not now," Bean clarified, his voice benevolent. "After you've gotten a million dollars from each of the girls."

"The other girls? How would I even know—"

"Oh please." Bean crossed his arms. "Skillet's been out of jail this month, and where she drives, White Rabbit's in the passenger's seat. Daisy Chain is downstairs, and as for Robin . . ." He smirked. "What kind of best friend would you be if you couldn't track her down?"

"So, we have a week?" Little John asked. She wouldn't acknowledge his comment about Robin. That girl was like a sand crab, and Little John wasn't ready to wave away her cover.

"I'll give you two." Bean put out his hand. Little John noted the curved nails, the slight shine of their surface. Crabs under beaches, all of them. "But if you don't deliver—"

"Save the threats." Little John put her small hand in his smooth one. "Your daddy will have his money."

He left his embossed card, which made Little John think of the old-fashioned gangsters who proudly displayed their symbols and lists of enemies. Bean had no such marks of a killer; just his name, Bernard Clark, and a phone number that probably went to a burner phone or a voicemail linked to an anonymous email address. Or maybe the number went to nothing at all; when Little John had the money, she would know where to find him. Under the number was a familiar saying—Massachusetts's state motto, *Ense petit placidam sub libertate quietem.*

By the sword we seek peace, but peace only under liberty.

"Every criminal thinks he's a hero," muttered Little John, and she shoved the card into her desk's top drawer and slammed it.

CHAPTER THIRTEEN

FINE FIXERS HADN'T CHANGED MUCH IN three years, but for the yellow plastic bag tied onto one of the pumps to indicate it was broken and the loss of the letter O in the open sign. In many ways, "pen" was a more appropriate name for the plot of dust and the garage door propped open with a shovel. The radio blasted Madonna in her ears.

"Mikey?" Little John yelled.

Mikey's head appeared from the right side of the door. He'd shaved the mustache, leaving a black shadow like a cartoon thug and the red bowling ball head propped on top of his stained collar.

"Little John?" His face went a shade redder, or maybe that was just the effect of the Florida sun on his sensitive skin. "What are you doing here?"

"Looking for Robin." Little John's eyes darted behind him, under a Toyota Yaris, in the store. No sign of Robin amidst the bags and bottles; no sign of anyone. Little John wondered how Mikey kept his cover with such an unconvincingly successful establishment.

"You should have called first." Mikey dabbed at the sweat on his neck with a towel. "I haven't seen that girl in years."

"Oh really?" Little John's eyes drifted to the outline of the second garage. "So, you wouldn't mind if I take a look, then?"

Mikey's sweat had gone from beads to little rivulets following the contours of his veins. "Be my guest." He threw her the keys and then went back in the shop.

Little John's hopes vanished. She had been so sure . . . but Mikey wouldn't just let her into the garage alone if Robin was there, would he? Still, she had come all this way, and she followed the footprints of one pair of boots in the sandy dirt all the way back to the door even as she knew the effort was wasted.

Sure enough, the lights were off, and the lines of motorcycles preserved in perfect aisles. No Robin, though Little John walked through the whole room just to be sure—just to postpone to inevitable panic already rising in her like a tide. She was no leader; she had never wanted to be, not even when Robin made a mistake like agreeing to a job for Uncle Frank, and then another job, and then another. Little John needed her school of fish, to feel the bodies on both sides, to follow the straight line of someone in front who would guide her down a safe path—or be eaten in the process.

Little John went back to her car, a rented SUV that Skillet would have called a gas guzzler as though she didn't drive her own heavily loaded truck, blast the air conditioning, and speed at least twenty miles over the speed limit.

Did she still drive that way?

Could she even drive at all?

Little John saw Skillet's body on the cold cement surrounded by her blood, like a heavy bag of sand during hurricane season. If she closed her eyes, she could still smell the metallic tang, the sweat from nights of training, the mold, the boxes of open baking soda Blake used to soak up the scent. *This isn't a cake,* Robin had always teased. *Buy an air filter like a normal person.*

Little John got in the car and pressed the on button. She hated driving—hadn't even learned to do it until they got to Maryland, where there had been no Skillet to serve as chauffeur or Robin to serve as substitute—and she still gripped the wheel at ten and two so hard her hands turned white at the knuckles. As she pulled out onto the highway, she overshot and ended up a foot over the line.

The only music that she didn't find distracting was classical, but all she found on the panhandle stations was praise music and talk radio. Frustrated, Little John slammed her hand against the radio dial and drove on in silence. She thought about what she would say to Daisy Chain, who had believed, as she always did, that everything was going to work out.

Suddenly, a motor revved somewhere close to her on the left.

Little John flinched, and the SUV lilted over the middle line and then steadied. In her left side mirror, she saw the driver wave her over, as though saying *Get out of the way.* Little John honked her horn—yellow line didn't allow passing, and besides, motorcycles made her nervous—but the person behind her kept waving.

Wait.

Little John looked back again. To the road in front of her. Back again. That red hair, flying from out from the sides of the helmet like licking flames. The small frame of her body. The enormous black boots.

As though she had the same realization, the girl on the bike suddenly turned into the opposite lane and went back.

"Oh no you don't," muttered Little John, and after checking to make sure no cars were incoming, she awkwardly U-turned. The SUV was like a hulking bull rotating to charge. After a brief drive over the grass on the other side of the road, Little John righted the vehicle in the center of the opposite lane. She slammed her hand on the radio and left the station on gospel tunes—after all, she was probably about to die—as she pressed down on the pedal.

The SUV revved, jolted, sped.

The motorcycle was a mouse in front of Little John's reaching claws. Every time she increased her speed, the motorcycle went faster. *If that isn't Robin . . .* Little John thought, imagining the awkward police interrogation as a stranger with red hair accused her of stalking—but no, she was sure. How many times had she followed her best friend down this same road, at this same speed, holding her breath as she waited for a crash?

Robin turned off suddenly, and Little John followed her. The SUV bumped over a mound of sandy dirt, bumped again, again, and Little John's head snapped on her neck. Greenery on either side of the road stayed an indistinct wall.

The motorcycle turned again, this time onto a path just wide enough for the bike and a pair of narrow shoulders. "No!" yelled Little John as her SUV slid past the entrance to the path, but even if she could get turned around, she knew she would never be able to follow.

"Fine," she mumbled as she put the SUV in reverse. Under her wheels, plants were mowed down like pins under a bowling ball. "But you can't hide forever, Robin."

* * *

LITTLE JOHN DROVE BACK TO FINE FIXERS and parked behind the second garage, where she wouldn't be spotted. "Keys," she yelled to Mikey, who was bent over an engine, and he threw her the ring without removing his left hand from the part. "And if you tell her I'm here, I swear to God—"

"Not a word," Mikey said. He put his right hand up again, as if to swear. "I want her out of here just as bad as you do. That girl thinks she's the boss of the world."

Little John went back to the second garage and unlocked the door. Then she locked it behind her again. With the lights on, she made a mental map of the room, then turned the switch off again and made her way to the right row on her hands and knees so that she could feel for the furthest tire. Then she counted the motorcycles as she felt the next tire with her cautious fingertips. When she got to ten, she veered left and hid behind the frame.

The room was dark and warm, and Little John wondered what Florida creatures lurked in the walls or under the dark spaces between tires and floor. Roaches, she was sure, and spiders. Some fleas. Even worse, invisible bugs like biting midges, called no-see-ums, the pesky bloodsuckers that Little John had only seen at the beach, but still . . .

A key clicked in the lock.

The door squeaked open.

The lights flickered and then stayed on.

Little John held her breath, though Robin couldn't possibly hear her light inhales and exhales from fifty feet away. Little John had planned out what she would say on the plane, rehearsed it in the car, and yet now, she couldn't remember a word.

"You can come out now," Robin said.

Little John stood up. Her back ached, and she stretched a few times on either side to get feeling back in her muscles and to delay speaking. Robin was still by the door, helmet under her arm. Her hair was longer, the way Daisy Chain's used to be before Little John asked her to cut it because she couldn't stand the snakelike hairs she found stuck in the drain—and because her hair had always been the part of Daisy Chain that Little John loved the most.

Second cousins can make things work, but first cousins have to get over it and move on, she had told herself that day. *It's over, Little John. In fact, it never even began.*

"You look good," Little John told Robin. And she did— not just her hair, but the black tank top, the tight leather pants, the muscular arms all reminded Little John of why she'd developed a crush on her best friend when she'd first met her—a femme biker chick who looked like she could just as easily pose as a model in a magazine ad as beat someone senseless.

"You too," said Robin.

Little John wondered what Robin really thought of her new look—designer blazer, salon-cut bangs, black eyeliner, and a silver watch with diamonds around the face—and whether she knew what Little John had been up to since she'd inherited her millions. She knew what Robin had been up to without asking: hanging out at Mikey's, riding around in the marshlands, and generally fighting with the demons of her past.

People never change.

Robin slung a rag over her shoulder and picked up a grayish blue tool chest that looked older than her. Then she went to a bike in the second row, banged the toolbox open, and pulled out a wrench.

"What are you doing?"

Robin didn't look up as she used the wrench to crank off some kind of cover. "What does it look like?"

Little John decided not to answer.

"I'm changing the oil filter," Robin finally said.

"So, you're a mechanic now?"

Robin shrugged without stopping her work. She seemed to now be trying to get the bike vertical, and then she bent down to check something through the porthole on the side of the crank case.

"Cool. Well, while you've been playing Mikey Junior, we've been getting into some deep trouble. It's a long story, but one of Uncle Frank's competitors wants his money back and—"

Robin held up the wrench as if she was a conductor cueing her orchestra to cut off a note. "My money's still in the account. Take the slip of paper in the pencil case on the desk and transfer it."

"But Robin, I'm trying to explain—"

"I'm out," Robin said. She had gone back to her work. "I don't do that kind of thing anymore."

"But just listen—"

There was a radio attached to the bike, and Robin pressed the power button to drown Little John out. Country, surprisingly, and classic country at that. Little John wondered whether Robin even knew Skillet was alive. Was that all this petulant behavior was about?

Either way, Little John was starting to get angry. She hated that emotion—logic was the better strategy, both for her and for whomever she felt frustrated by—and the fact that Robin had managed to get under her skin made her even angrier. To calm herself, she closed her eyes and put herself in Uncle Frank's basement, where Blake had trained her and the other kids to calm their minds by finding their mental safe space. He thought himself some kind of guru and had even made them sit cross-legged as he guided them with his smooth voice. *What do you see?* he asked. *An island? A special treehouse? Your kitchen table?*

Little John had tried to visualize a beach, or a park, but all she had seen was a calculator. Numbers appeared, and she added, subtracted, multiplied. Instantly, her whole body relaxed.

This is where you'll go if you're ever caught and tortured, Blake had explained, *but also to stay calm in lower-stakes situations like a robbery or knifing.*

Robin had whispered that her safe place was in Blake's bed, and when Little John opened her eyes a slit, she saw Blake frowning in their direction. Quickly, she closed her eyes again.

Now, Little John could go to that safe place with her eyes open—as long as she focused on her counting. In desperate situations, she even tapped her fingers against her leg until she could breathe normally. She looked around the room and found a license plate, which she added and then multiplied times itself, and then she tried to talk again.

"Give me one minute to just—" Little John said, raising her voice.

Robin raised the volume.

Little John took a deep breath. *Count down from ten.* Ten, nine, eight—

Robin raised the volume again, preemptively.

Little John felt the rage boiling up again. She tried to focus her eyes on a number, any number, but she could barely see straight.

Then she lifted the radio off the handlebars and smashed it on the ground.

She hadn't meant to . . . and yet, as the device meteored into the cement and divided, she couldn't help but feel a small thrill of victory. Robin had slept with Daisy Chain, even after she found out that Little John loved her. Robin had lied to them about stealing from Uncle Frank. Robin had gotten Skillet shot.

Worst of all, Robin had abandoned them.

"Feel better?" Robin asked.

Little John deflated like a blown tire. She knew, just as Robin knew, that no matter how many strikes Robin had against her, Little John would still follow her into any mission, anywhere, at any time.

"That's why I can't come back," Robin said, as if she had read Little John's mind.

"You have to." Little John took another deep breath. She suddenly remembered the words she'd written on the plane. "Do you know what happens to monogynous ant colonies when their queen dies?"

Robin's eyebrows arched. "No . . ."

"They die. It might happen slowly, and they might lay a lot of worker ant eggs first, but eventually . . ." She lost her train of thought, worked to pick it up again. "And the truth is, yeah, you made some questionable decisions in Nottingham. But before we met you, we were just individual ants waiting to get squished. At least together, we were a colony."

Robin sat back and rested her hands, still holding the wrench and rag, on her knees. She looked like the girl Little John had met back at Uncle Frank's, before she'd dyed her hair red and started training with Blake, when she'd cry out at night from the nightmares about *before*.

"Skillet's alive," Little John said softly, "and she's out."

Robin nodded. "I know. I might seem disconnected, but I keep tabs on all of you." She put down the wrench and wrung the rag with both hands. "So, what's the plan? Track them down and then give those gangsters their money back?"

"Their money?" Little John shook her head. "No. It's *our* money."

Robin stopped wringing the rag. "So, what, then?"

This was the hardest part. Little John was a student at a desk taking a math test, and Robin was the final question.

"We take them all down."

CHAPTER FOURTEEN

THE CROWD WAS SHOULDER TO SHOULDER; in the darkness, their cell phone lights were like those glowing sea creatures that Robin would have been able to name, had Little John voiced her thought. She couldn't talk, though—or rather, couldn't be heard—over the excited mob. The smell of beer mingled with fried dough, sizzling chicken, and car fumes. Outside the glow, the black and blue bruise of the fields and sky seemed detached from their revelry.

"You're sure she'll be here?" Little John asked loudly through her visor. They had kept their helmets on so that they wouldn't be recognized, and her hair itched from the weight and heat. Her desperate fingers tried to run up the back of her head, got stuck, and retreated.

"I'm sure," said Robin. She had changed clothes before the trip, and Little John wondered how she could wear a motorcycle jacket in the Georgia heat. "Are you ready?"

Little John nodded, the helmet rocking a little on her too-small head. She felt nervous. To try to relax, she counted the cars lined up behind the starting line. *One, two. Three, four.* There would be several matches, each one an opportunity for fans to bet big, lose, bet again. Little John wondered how her assistant manager was getting along back at The Nott, but then the revving of engines brought her back to the present.

A flag girl waved the first pair off, and they peeled away, their competing engines like bees buzzing around the same flower. In their place, two new vehicles moved forward, like soldiers soon to be sent into battle.

"That's her," said Robin.

Little John squinted at the purple truck with red flames. "How do you know?"

Robin didn't answer. Little John tried to see the driver, but the cowboy hat obscured their face. In Nottingham the hat would have been a giveaway, but here, hats seemed as essential as underwear. Then Little John's eyes shifted past the truck to the assistant, a familiar woman with a black t-shirt with zeroes and ones printed in the shape of a middle finger. From her mouth, a sour straw dangled like a frog tongue.

Robin got back on her bike, which she had explained was something called an "Aprilia," and Little John did the same, struggling to reach the right height to get her leg over the back seat. Then she gripped Robin's waist tightly.

White Rabbit climbed into the passenger's side of the truck.

I hate motorcycles, Little John thought.

The flag girl moved her hands up and then back, like a bird about to take flight, and the motorcycle hummed to life. Robin threaded through the crowd as the trucks shot forward; as soon as they were clear of human life, she accelerated to match the trucks' speed. The two vehicles were on both lanes of a bumpy backroad, which meant that to drive parallel to their progress, Robin's motorcycle swerved into the grass. *Please don't have potholes*, Little John prayed to the ground.

Please don't have any creepy creatures that decide to get in our way. One mistake and . . . Wind slapped at her cheeks, flew under her shirt, battered her sides like water batters the hull of a boat. *Please, please, please.*

As if incensed by their presence, Skillet's truck shot forward and then veered left onto a different side street. The other truck didn't follow. "She's leaving!" yelled Little John. Robin made a hard left, crossed behind the other truck, and zoomed after her.

The road narrowed and became a trail, just two tire lines in the grass, and Robin guided the bike into the right line. The truck bounced like a bull trying to throw its rider, but it didn't slow. Behind them, lights came on in windows, but Little John couldn't keep her eyes off the road long enough to see what curious faces had been awoken by their activity.

If she was about to die, she wanted to see the log or stray dog or fallen signpost that killed her.

"Hold on!" Robin yelled, as if Little John wasn't already holding on for dear life, and then she swerved farther to the right to pass the truck. Skillet increased her speed again, but the truck seemed to be maxed out. Robin's Aprilia, on the other hand, was like an animal that had been straining against her leash and then released. In a few seconds she had passed the truck and shot forward.

She's going to do a burnout, thought Little John. Her eyes closed, as if she could imagine herself out of the situation, then squinted open to watch. *Please, please, please, I don't want to die before I see Daisy again, and what about—*

Robin used the throttle and clutch to slip the back tire as she hit the front brakes. Little John whipped around like a kid on a teacup ride and came to a stop. She took a deep breath to calm herself and then remembered that there was still a truck coming directly toward her.

The truck was like a big fist already aimed, and it plowed toward them even as Skillet slammed on the brakes. Little John spotted White Rabbit in the passenger seat, hands over her eyes.

Violent ends, Little John thought.

The truck brakes screeched even louder.

Dust clouded around them.

Little John waited to die.

Then silence took back control of the path. No one moved for a full minute. Eventually, the opening truck door on White Rabbit's side indicated human life.

"Steal from the rich?" a voice asked tentatively.

"Give to ourselves!" Robin and Little John put their fists in the air.

White Rabbit came through the dust like a real rabbit emerging from a thicket. She was smiling, which was a good sign, and when Little John hopped down from the bike, she grabbed her around the middle and swung her around.

"How have you been?" White Rabbit asked.

Little John thought about The Nott, which she still hadn't managed to bring up with Robin. "Same old," she said with a shrug. There would be time. "And you two?"

White Rabbit looked back at the truck. "Better," she said.

Now Little John heard a door flip up and then a new sound. The dust had settled enough for the hydraulic lift to come in sight as it brought Skillet's chair down to ground level, and to make the pushes of her arms visible.

"Is she . . . ?" asked Little John.

White Rabbit nodded. "But nothing stops my girl."

"You bet." Skillet approached them. "And if you'd been driving a truck, I still would have beaten you."

"I know," Robin said. "That's exactly why I didn't."

The two girls stared at each other for a while, and Little John looked between them. Judging by her lack of surprise, Robin had already known about Skillet's wheelchair use— had probably sequestered herself at Mikey's because of it—and Little John wondered why she hadn't told her. Maybe she felt guilty; maybe she knew Little John would tell her it wasn't her fault.

"What are you doing here?" White Rabbit asked.

Robin looked at Little John as if to say, *You tell them.*

"We have a job," said Little John.

"A job?" Skillet took off her hat and put it on her lap. Her hair was sweaty at the roots. "What kind of job?"

Little John was about to say *The dangerous kind,* but she found herself unable to speak. Skillet was more than familiar with the dangerous kind of job. How could Little John ask her to put her life on the line again? Why had Robin let her get into this situation?

"I see," said Skillet. Even after three years, they could all still read each other's minds. Skillet put her hat back on. "Then we're in."

"But—"

"I'm still the same gal, Little John. Clear?"

Little John nodded yes.

"Good. Then let's go inside and talk about it over dinner."

Only now did Little John realize that they were standing directly in front of a small yard sign that said Nottingham Grove. Past several live oaks, a small house with a ramp built up to the door was indistinct but for the line of trucks parked in the driveway. Even with millions of dollars, they had tried to recreate Nottingham—as had Little John, in her own way.

The four of them went inside, where Skillet hung her keys on a spare nail in the wall next to five other keys. The lights were already on, as if they had been waiting for their arrival, and illuminated a cozy den decorated in Skillet's southern style on the left and a dark office with glowing computers on the right. Down the hallway and through an installed barn door, the kitchen had the same southern flair, from the *Home is where the heart is* cross-stitched picture to the wrought iron chandelier made to look like deer horns.

"Nice," said Robin of the bench-style kitchen table before taking a seat. She picked up a plastic pear from the wicker basket in the middle, returned it.

Little John stood awkwardly behind her, waiting to be invited. She always felt like that—the outsider—and she counted the rings on the table to relax. At fifteen, Skillet drawled, "Sit down, Little John," and Little John took a seat on the bench next to Robin.

Skillet pulled out a cutting board from a drawer, balanced the cutting board on the open drawer, and began chopping onions from the pile of vegetables. As she worked, White Rabbit put a skillet on the stove and heated the oil. Then she took the prepared onions, and Skillet started again with the peppers. Little John loved watching them cook together, like a partnered dance, and she wondered if she would ever feel so comfortable around someone else. Even though she and Daisy lived together, they had opposite hours; besides, even when they were home at the same time, Daisy Chain went around the apartment making a mess while Little John followed her cleaning it up. No synchronized action. No affection.

And still, Little John loved her.

"Want a drink?" Skillet asked. Somehow, a beer had found its way onto the cutting board.

Second cousins can make things work, but first cousins have to get over it and move on.

"No thanks," said Little John. She imagined the last time she'd watched one of her patrons stumble down a step and then puke into a planter.

It's not my fault I fell in love with Daisy Chain before I knew we were related.

Little John could still remember the day she realized how she felt—not the first day Daisy Chain arrived, or even the first month, but a year later, when the two of them were sitting outside in Robin's Adirondack chairs with Robin on the ground below them letting a caterpillar inch down her sheathed knife. Little John was making a list of that month's expenses when Daisy Chain asked her for her birth date and time through elaborate Shakespeare quotes Little John had needed Robin to translate. Then Daisy Chain began scribbling wildly on a piece of notebook paper. *What's that?*, Little John had asked Robin. *Your aspects and houses*, said Robin, *so she can read your horoscope.* Little John had laughed. *So, it's a bunch of hocus pocus?* Robin had cocked her head to the side and replied, *It's math.*

And that was it. There was something in the way Daisy Chain wildly poured the geometric angles of the locations of the planets for Little John's natal chart onto the page with her rainbow-leaded pencil that captivated Little John's number hungry heart. She hadn't felt that way since seventh grade Algebra, when Mrs. Austin had written out the quadratic formula.

"Are you thinking about her?" Robin asked.

Little John shook her head. "Mrs. Austin?"

"No." Robin furrowed her brow. "Who's Mrs. Austin?"

"Long story." Little John looked at Skillet and White Rabbit, but they were in the middle of a heated debate about butter versus vegetable oil. "And yeah, I guess I was thinking about her, but I wish I wasn't." Little John counted the rings again. She wished she could go back in time and keep her mouth shut about Daisy. Then she could have suffered alone.

"It takes time," Robin said. "What is that Shakespeare line she's always quoting? *Oh teach me how I should forget to think?*"

Little John shrugged. Would the conversation ever end? Fifteen rings. *Skillet and White Rabbit should get some drink coasters.* Now she moved to the baskets on the shelves behind the table. Fifteen again. The number of pencils in the smallest basket. Five.

"I found out, you know." Robin took a long sip. "About Daisy and Uncle Frank."

"You did?" Little John stopped counting. "What happened?" She and Daisy Chain had never talked about that day. She wondered how Robin knew, but apparently even in her isolation, she kept tabs on all of them. Little John wondered if she already knew about The Nott, too.

Robin shook her head. "It's horrible. Apparently, he found out his wife had gone to the cops and . . . well, you know Uncle Frank."

Little John felt sick. She'd known Uncle Frank was a cold-blooded killer, but to take out his own wife? Sure, he hadn't exactly been a role model for Little John, but after what happened to her dad, he had at least taken her in and given her a way to support herself so that she wouldn't have to go live with her mom. Now she hated the idea of even sharing a last name with him.

"I know," said Robin. "It's horrible. And to think Daisy Chain stood five feet from him in Nottingham so many times without saying a word. Then, when the opportunity presented itself . . ." She made a gun with her right hand.

Skillet and White Rabbit brought over the skillet and tortillas. "What about a gun?" White Rabbit asked.

Little John shook her head slightly. White Rabbit and Skillet knew Uncle Frank was dead, but outside of Little John and Robin, no one else had any idea that he and Daisy Chain were related.

"Nothing," Robin said quickly, "just something I saw on the news."

"Got it." White Rabbit took a big bite of her fajita and then said, through a full mouth, "Well, how about telling us what you've been up to the last three years?"

Robin looked at Little John. Little John looked down. There were fourteen red pepper pieces and ten green pepper pieces. She liked that they were both even numbers.

"Robin's been working on motorcycles. And . . . I've been working at The Nott," she finally mumbled.

"The Nott?" asked Skillet.

Robin burst out laughing. "Little John is our very own Meyer Lansky!"

Skillet and White Rabbit didn't get the reference, but Little John did. Curse Uncle Frank and his training.

"It's a casino!" Robin explained. "Little John has been running a casino!"

Now they were all laughing. Little John frowned. What was wrong with a casino? It was better than hiding in a garage tinkering with motors all day long, or sitting in jail, or hacking into innocent people's computers.

"Can't you just imagine her in her blazer ordering her employees around?" asked White Rabbit, and Skillet replied, "I sure can, bless her little entrepreneurial heart."

"I'll have you know—" Little John tried to say, but she couldn't make her voice heard over the racket of the other three girls. She crossed her arms and waited until they finally stopped laughing. "—that casinos are actually very impressive establishments."

White Rabbit laughed so hard that she spilled her drink. Skillet choked on a pepper, and Robin had to pound her back. Little John went back to the baskets.

One, two, three . . .

Her mind drifted back to Uncle Frank. When she first arrived at the school, the kid at the door had taken her up to the fourth floor, much like she and the Misfits had been brought up three years before, only that time, Uncle Frank had peered at her over his desk and said, "Are you a girl, a boy, neither, or both?"

"I'm a mathematician," she'd answered.

Uncle Frank's bushy silver eyebrows had risen at that. "Oh really?"

"Yeah." She crossed her arms. "And I'm here to work."

Uncle Frank crossed his arms too and sat back in his chair. "Your father would be furious if he knew you were here. I promised him I would never let you get wrapped up in all of this."

"My father's dead," Little John said. "You were at his funeral last week. Ten white lily arrangements. Three bible passages. Fourteen attendees, twelve of which were fellow fisherman and none of which were Delia. Seventy-two shovels full of dirt over the casket and twenty taps to pack the ground flat—"

"I get it." Uncle Frank smiled slightly. "You like math. But won't your mother come looking for you?"

Little John thought of the events of the last seven days: fight in Macy's when her mom made her try on bras, fight in the grocery store when she said chocolate would make her skin break out, fight with her two horrible stepsisters about whether cheerleading was a sport, fight with her lawyer stepfather about everything else. Little John was like a crazed boxer swinging at air, ready to take down anyone who got too close.

"I doubt it. She only wanted me because she wanted to win, and now my dad's dead, so there's no one to beat anymore. Plus, I don't fit into her perfect new life." She was not exaggerating; her mother had literally used those exact words the day before.

"Persuasive argument." Uncle Frank smiled again. He seemed amused by her, like humans are amused by their small dogs when they bring them sticks, and she knew if she could keep his attention, he would let her stay. She could not go back to Delia—not ever. "What kind of math can you do?"

She thought about what would be most useful to a mobster. "I can balance a checkbook," she said, "and do quick, accurate mental math on demand. I can count cards. I can guess the weight of a fish—uh, I mean, a bag of money—just by holding it in my hands. I can remember long numbers up to twelve digits. I can—"

Uncle Frank raised his hand. "Alright. You can stay. But if your mother tries to sue me, I'll hand you over faster than a stolen car when the sirens start coming, understand?"

Little John put her hand out and shook on it.

* * *

"Little John?" Robin waved her hand in front of Little John's face.

"What?" Little John blinked a few times. "Sorry, I got distracted."

"Skillet was just telling us about how your mom and stepdad got her out of jail." Robin looked upset. "Why didn't you tell me?"

Skillet went back to her story, but Little John didn't want to hear it, so she walked out of the room without excusing herself. She could still hear her mom's voice on the phone, distracted by some conversation she was having with her assistant, and Little John had needed to yell to make herself heard. "I'm your daughter!" Little John had finally exclaimed, and the background had ceased immediately

"What do you want?" Delia had asked quietly.

"What do I want? That's how you greet your long-lost kid after all this time?"

"Lost?" Delia snorted. "You think I didn't know you were at Uncle Frank's this whole time? Who do you think has been sending him all those checks for your upkeep, then?"

"Money doesn't solve everything!" Little John yelled, but she was shaken. She hadn't known about the checks.

"You're right. But neither does running away." Delia took a deep breath. "I'm about to go into a very important client meeting, so why don't you tell me what you want."

Right. Because designing the perfect living room for some rich lady in Beacon Hill is more important than talking to your own daughter. Of course. Little John fumed, but she kept her thoughts to herself. She needed Delia—or rather, Skillet did.

"I want your husband to represent my friend Skillet," Little John said as calmly as she could. "She got injured protecting me and couldn't get away from the cops. I want to get her out."

"Of jail?" Delia laughed unkindly, and Little John almost let the words slip out again. To calm herself, she counted the thumbtacks on her office wall. Skillet needed her help.

"Please, Mom?" Little John asked softly.

Her mother did not say anything at first, but then she let out a long sigh. She sounded older, more beaten down, and Little John wondered what she looked like now. Did she still wear power dresses with belted waists and cupped sleeves? Did her pointy-toed shoes still warn of her arrival? Was her hair still pinned back in a tight bun and as black as Little John's, or had she gone a distinguished gray?

"Thank you," Little John said.

"Don't call here again," her mother said quietly. Then she hung up.

CHAPTER FIFTEEN

FOR ALL THEIR LAUGHING ABOUT THE NOTT, the girls demanded that they use the casino as their headquarters. Early the next morning, they packed into one of Skillet's trucks and drove toward home. The car was quickly too hot, and the collar of Little John's blazer itched against the back of her neck almost immediately. By South Carolina, she had removed the blazer and aimed the fan directly at her face. Sweat dropped from her forehead. She couldn't escape. Didn't the other girls notice the way the car seemed to get smaller the longer they drove? Her legs itched. How could they sing along to the radio like a bunch of kids on the bus ride to camp? She opened the window, but the humidity made everything worse. She unscrewed the cap of her water bottle. Drank a sip, counted to three, drank a gulp, counted to nine, drank another gulp, counted to twenty-seven.

81. 243. 729.

"I need to pee," she practically yelled.

"Pee?" White Rabbit checked her smart watch. "We've only been driving for an hour."

"I know." Little John shook her empty water bottle. "I guess I drank too much water."

They weren't anywhere near a bathroom, so Skillet found a gas station with dirty windows and cigarette ads pasted up, where Little John had to ask the woman behind the counter for the key and suffer the humiliation of her silent but obvious annoyance that they weren't buying anything. Little John was tempted to voice her own opinion about the number of empty candy wrappers on the counter near the register, but she didn't feel like dealing with the repercussions. She needed a quiet, lonely space to gather her thoughts.

That lonely space turned out to be worse than the station, just a toilet with no seat and a small sink with rust and no soap. The smell was almost unbearable. Little John looked at herself in the mirror and tried to take a deep breath. Her wide eyes looked like two zeros. What was wrong with her? The anxiety was an old foe, but why had it decided to appear now, as she drove with her friends? She couldn't figure it out. Was it Daisy Chain? The close quarters of the truck? The realization that she had likely asked everyone to risk their lives—again—and that this time, it would be her fault if something went wrong?

Or was this the same old voice that had always been there, as old as Little John herself?

She thought of her father out on the sea, wrestling against a strong wave like David against Goliath. She thought of him in their bathroom, talking to himself in the mirror once he thought she was asleep. *Get it together. You must get it together.* That was the night before he went on the bender that eventually took him out to sea, drifting like a piece of wood until the waves finally tugged him under. She had wished she could do something to make him feel better, the way his medication was supposed to.

"Little John?"

Robin again. Little John ran the water for a minute and then unlocked the door. "Yeah?" she said, making her voice sound impenetrable.

"Here." Robin held out a plastic pill box. "I snuck back to Nottingham a year ago and found these in your medicine cabinet. Figured they might come in handy."

Little John could have hugged her—if she was the hugging type. Instead, she nodded, took the pill box, and closed the bathroom door. Her mouth was moist enough from all the water drinking that she could take the Xanax using a dry gulp and a few more swallows of spit. She would need Zoloft, but there was a bottle at home that she was already supposed to be taking.

Once she could breathe again, Little John went back outside. Robin was there, sitting on the curb to the parking lot.

"I told the girls you have a UTI," said Robin. "You know, so you could pee whenever you need to."

"Great." Little John rolled her eyes, but then she started laughing. "That's actually really smart."

"I thought so." Robin stood up and brushed dust and gravel from her pants. "Are you okay?"

What a word. *Okay.* Not great, not even good, but *okay.* Was she okay? Little John took stock. Hands no longer shaking. Eyes more focused. Breathing normal.

"I'm on my way to okay," she said. "Thanks."

"Any time." Robin put her arm up but didn't touch Little John. This was the way they hugged—always a choice, and one that Little John often didn't make, depending on whether she felt *okay* or not.

This time, she settled under the weight of Robin's arm, and they walked that way, like one monstrous person, all the way to the truck.

* * *

LITTLE JOHN DOZED AGAINST THE WINDOW. They passed through North Carolina nothingness, Virginia nothingness. The girls stopped for fries, pizza slices, sodas, beer, anything to get them out of the truck and into a nondescript restaurant where a local asked them where they had been, and where they were going. Skillet drove the whole time, but she didn't seem to mind—her trucks always seemed like an extension of her, like a snail and its shell. Plus, driving meant she could work both the hand controls for speed and the radio for music, and lucky for her, country stations were abundant.

They talked sometimes too—or, rather, the three other Misfits talked, and Little John listened between real naps and the times she kept her eyes closed so that no one would think to ask her questions. She found out that White Rabbit had been teaching computer science classes under a fake name, and that, in addition to stealing supplies, she had recruited some of her best students to work on a side project she called Infiltribe. Like the program she had used to steal Uncle Frank's money, Infiltribe functioned as a heist system, only this malware worked on banks by creating fake transactions.

Skillet had made friends with some of the most dangerous inmates due to the legend of Uncle Frank's murder, and that when they asked if she'd been the one to pull the trigger, she winked. From that day on, she'd had an easy time getting assistance when she needed it, as well as contraband like a cell phone on which she and White Rabbit could plan her release.

Even Robin had drifted into the occasional bike heist, she admitted, and there was that one time when she couldn't resist breaking into a vacation home to take a joy ride on the owner's M16.

"What's that?" Little John asked, then remembered she was supposed to be asleep.

"A three hundred and nineteen pound body of mostly carbon fiber, including the fuel tank and fender. Let me tell you, I was tempted to keep the thing, but the owner had taken such good care of it that I couldn't bring myself to take it home. Now, if they'd left it muddy . . ." Her eyes went dreamy.

"And what about you, Little John?" asked Skillet. "What kind of messes have you and Daisy Chain been up to at The Nott?"

Little John shook her head. "No messes."

"Really?" White Rabbit turned down the radio to hear better. "You're the only casino in America that's on the up-and-up?"

"Guess so."

Little John didn't explain—couldn't explain—that being around Daisy made her want to be a better person. Not just because of her work at Tiny Notts, but in the careful consideration of every action, from buying a cup of coffee (What about the disposable cup? Was it fair trade? How much did they pay their workers?) to the patio installation of a vertical garden made of holes in rows of PVC pipe. She often stood with her watering can raining down on them and muttered, *"And this our life, exempt from public haunt, Finds tongues in trees, books in the running brooks, Sermons in stones, and good in everything,"* and Little John would whisper the lines later, remembering the way her voice mingled with the sounds of the city.

They arrived at The Nott at 2:50 A.M. "You can park in my spot," said Little John. She didn't actually own a car, but she still liked the plate that said "Reserved for Owner" hung on the wall in front of the best spot on the first floor. Skillet glided the SUV into the narrow spot, and then they all got out and stretched their legs.

"No need to get your suitcases," Little John told them. "We'll send someone."

"*We'll send someone*," mocked Robin. Then she took her suitcase out of the truck bed. "I can get my own luggage, thank you very much."

"Suit yourself."

They exited the lot and walked to The Nott's tinted black door. Music oozed through the crack between the two doors, soft piano notes that invited passersby to come on in, just for a minute. The bouncer, Luis, nodded at Little John without a word and opened the right door. The music volume increased, mingled with voices, stopped. Little John checked her watch. At 3:00 A.M., the nighttime pianist swapped with the early morning pianist. Right on schedule.

The Nott was a 24-hour establishment, but the patrons still present past 1:00 A.M. were the people Little John called zombies. Now they lilted from one table to another; now they gulped, gulped, gulped. Now they followed the scent of a pulse, someone they wouldn't remember the next morning.

"No messes, eh?" said White Rabbit.

Little John stopped a waitress, adjusted a glass too close to the edge of her tray, and nodded her away. "They choose to come here and spend their money," she said, her eyes on the room. "I just take it."

And the money did flow. Chips clinked like pennies loose in a purse. Bills rustled as they were exchanged. Bartenders swiped cards. In a few years, Little John would have been able to pay off the Boston Butchers herself—but she didn't have a few years.

"Come on," she said, ushering them ahead. "Daisy Chain is waiting."

Little John had called ahead, and by the time they got to her office, there was a spread of late-night favorites: pizza, artichoke dip, and fried green beans. Typically, the chef left at 1:00 A.M., and Little John wondered how much the meal had cost them in overtime; then she pushed the thought out of her mind. Her friends were here—were alive—and they needed to celebrate.

Daisy Chain had been making chains of small slips of paper when they came in, her now-chin-length hair a wall in front of her face, but when she spotted Robin, she dropped her work. Little John noted that Daisy Chain had dressed up for the occasion in a purple tie-dye summer dress and her favorite amethyst gem, though she wasn't wearing shoes. Daisy Chain leapt from her chair, circled the desk like a bird turning wildly in the wind, and flew into Robin's arms. Little John knew she was scowling, but she couldn't make herself stop.

"*If we do meet again, why, we shall smile,*" said Robin as she twirled Daisy Chain around.

"Not more of that silly Shakespeare," said Daisy Chain with a laugh.

Robin stopped twirling. "You're talking!"

"I've always been talking," said Daisy Chain. "But for a long time, you were the only one listening."

Yuck. Little John tasted the sweetness of soda on the back of her throat. *How can they do this in front of me?* Then she remembered that she and Daisy Chain were related, and that she couldn't tell anyone how she felt. Better for them to think she had moved on; better for them to be happy.

"Food, anyone?" she said. Then she impolitely took a piece of pizza first and shoved the end into her mouth to give it something else to do but frown.

They finished all three plates and rubbed their greasy fingers onto the black cloth napkins. White Rabbit and Skillet filled Daisy Chain in on their activities, as well as adding some new details, such as the fact that Skillet's nickname in prison had been Uncle Killer. "Subtle," mumbled Little John. Then they asked Daisy Chain about Tiny Notts, and Daisy Chain showed them the slips of paper, which turned out to be wishes the kids had written down with her help. Apparently, she planned on hanging them up as the tracks of a train that said *Goals* to help them visualize that they were the train conductors of their own destiny.

"Are they going to understand all that?" asked Little John.

"What a great idea!" said Robin at the same time.

They looked at each other.

Little John made herself smile.

Night became early morning. "We should sleep," suggested Little John, and as if a spell had fallen over them, they all yawned. "Robin, you can stay—"

"With me," said Daisy Chain. Then she looked down shyly. "If you want to?"

"—with Daisy Chain, if you want to," finished Little John, though she had been going to say, *On the futon here in my office.* Her stomach clenched again. She regretted eating so much pizza. "Skillet and White Rabbit, you'll take the foldout couch."

"Ay-ay, conductor of our destiny," said Skillet with a salute.

Little John led them back through the casino, where the zombies, chased away by the light through the windows, had left empty glasses and crumbs in their wake. The cleaners fought back the mess with vacuums and rags, and Little John shook each of their hands on her way across the room, being sure to make eye contact and say, *Great work.* She knew the other girls would make fun of her sincerity, but she didn't care. *Loyal employees are a vital asset.* Little John used quotes from business blogs the way Daisy Chain used her Shakespeare, though she never voiced her mantras.

Their apartment building was a modern black building, and inside the front doors, the lobby screamed new money. In their three years at The Addison, the room had been renovated twice, the most recent shift from the previously trendy minimalist to the currently trendy maximalist of yellow and blue accents amidst gold-framed mirrors, marble fireplaces, five types of wall lamps, and something called a settee. The elevator had matching marble floors and gold mirrors, along with its own small chandelier. Up on the fifth floor, they followed the blue carpet and silver fixtures to 504, recognizable among the other matching doors for the dream catcher hanging from the silver handle.

"Let me guess which one is yours," said White Rabbit. She tapped her chin thoughtfully.

"Yeah, yeah." Little John hated that dream catcher, and when she unlocked the door, her anxiety spiked even more from the assault of colorful tapestries, vintage bookshelves, incense burners, half-used candles, and bean bags Daisy Chain claimed were chairs. When they had first moved in to 504, Little John had set a firm rule—shared space is clean space—and yet now she basically lived in a thrift store. She knew she should just tell Daisy Chain that the mess bothered her—not to mention the piled dishes from Daisy's recent attempt at quinoa burgers, or the fallen ash smudged into the carpet like old eyeshadow, or the smell of homegrown cheese—but every time she tried, she just ended up so anxious about how Daisy Chain would react that she ended up buying her roommate another gem or salt lamp just to assuage her guilt.

"Oh, Daisy Chain." Robin shook her head. "Someone's been giving you the run of the house, haven't they?"

"What do you mean?" Daisy Chain asked, while at the same time Skillet crushed an incense stick under her wheel and then bumped into an essential oils diffuser that was on the floor.

"I mean: Little John hates mess." Robin waved her hand across the room. "You're basically torturing her."

"I am?" Daisy Chain looked genuinely shocked. She turned to Little John. "Am I torturing you?"

"I . . . Well . . ." Little John looked down at her feet. There was a broken flowerpot that Daisy had sworn she would fix two years ago, and Little John counted the shards. *One. Two. Three. Four.* "It's not that bad . . ."

"It's terrible." Robin went into the kitchen and rummaged around for a minute; then she returned with a plastic trash bag. "Alright girls, everyone pick up five broken or useless items and throw them in the bag."

In less than five minutes, Robin did more to clean the apartment than Little John had managed to do in three years. Yet Little John felt more upset than ever. With every clang of a finger cymbal or painted glass jar, Little John realized that Daisy Chain would never do anything to stop Robin from throwing out what she had claimed, over the years, were her "prized possessions."

Because she loved her.

Little John should have seen it coming. The two girls had been in a long-term fling since Daisy Chain's arrival, and yet they had always seemed so casual, so temporary. Breaking them up had been as easy as voicing her feelings to Robin that day at her grandmother's house. Yet Little John had never considered that every equation has two sides; she couldn't solve for the variable of x without considering both of them.

When would this terrible night end?

At last, Robin carried the malformed trash bag out the door by hoisting it over her shoulder like Santa's sack. When she returned, Little John had to admit that she could breathe easier now that she could actually see the black leather cushions of the couch, and the remote for the DVD player they'd been unable to use for a year, and the coffee table where her tax documents had been buried under a display of beading tools and plastic beading organizers. She could breathe easier—but she wasn't happier.

"Good work, team." Robin gave the other girls high fives. "Now we'd better get some sleep. We have a lot of planning to do tomorrow."

Like the good soldiers they were, the Merry Misfits went their separate ways. Skillet and White Rabbit to prepare their bed; Robin to join Daisy Chain in hers. Little John skipped brushing her teeth and went right into her bedroom, the only space in the apartment untouched by Daisy Chain's "artistic" hand.

She closed the door and leaned her back against it. *Breathe in. Breathe out.*

The room was as she'd left it: White comforter tucked on all four sides. Black pillows. White desk organized with a black file cabinet, pencil case, and paper clip holder. Not a single decoration on the walls. Even her books were boxed and slid under her bed, where she could refer to the alphabetized list on top for the contents.

She wished she knew how to cry.

A knock came at the door. Little John stepped away from it and then turned the knob. "Yeah?" she asked a waiting Robin, who had already changed into a pair of Daisy Chain's rainbow pajamas.

"I just wanted to check that you were okay," she said. She squinted at Little John. "Are you?"

"Of course."

"Great. I thought so. I just . . . Well, I wanted to make sure you weren't still harboring secret feelings for," she cocked her head to the right, toward Daisy's room, "you know who."

"No. I would tell you."

"Cool." Robin hesitated. "But if you decide that you're not okay with it—"

"I'm fine." Little John's voice was angrier than she meant it to be. She took another breath. "I'm fine," she repeated, "just tired. But thanks for checking. And thanks for the whole gas station thing earlier, and the living room thing just now . . . You're a good friend."

And she meant it. Even after three years apart, Robin still understood her better than anyone else—better than she sometimes knew herself.

"I've really missed you." Robin put out her arm, and Little John accepted her embrace. "Life isn't nearly as fun without you."

"Same." Little John pulled away. "Now go get some sleep."

This time, after she closed the door, she slid between the mattress and the tight covers and pulled them over her head. Things were too complicated, and Little John preferred things simple. Clean. Right and wrong. Straight like a number, like the counting of the little white dots she saw when she concentrated on her closed eyelids.

But she was both jealous of Robin and happy that she was back.

Both angry that Daisy Chain loved her and completely aware that they were perfect for each other.

And worst of all, both content in the realization that she would always be alone and utterly destroyed by it.

* * *

LITTLE JOHN COULD NOT SLEEP, EVEN though she knew that sleep was one of the most important elements of her sanity. *Why not be useful?*, she thought, and decided to go back to The Nott for an hour and help set the kitchen up for the breakfast shift. There were several hotels with bad restaurants on their street, and they often got an influx of visitors from 8:00 A.M. to 10:00 A.M.; plus, they sold bottomless mimosas seven days of the week.

Maurice, the dining room manager, was in his office closing out the previous night. He did not seem surprised to see her, a harmless ghost who wandered in and out at odd hours, and after saying good morning, he went back to his stack of receipts. Little John continued down the hallway to the kitchen, where Jillian, the sous chef and daytime head honcho, was giving her staff orders. Jillian had once asked Little John out for a drink, perhaps as friends but more likely as something more, but Little John had said she was too busy.

"Want to add anything?" Jillian asked Little John suddenly.

Five expectant faces turned toward her.

"Front of the house staff mentioned a few complaints about the popovers?" Little John shrugged, acknowledging that she didn't even make her own meals, let alone know a single thing about baking high quantities of bread. "Maybe they're in the oven too long?"

"Okay," Jillian said, noting this on the clipboard in front of her. "Check into popovers. Thanks, Boss."

Little John made herself useful retrieving the crates of clean plates from where the dishwasher had stacked them a few hours before and setting them at different stations along the line. She liked the way the columns of dishes looked, and she always set them down in twenty-plate increments. Then she put pats of butter into the ceramic dishes—three pats per bowl—and covered them with plastic wrap to wait until a server needed one. Finally, she filled the salt and pepper shakers to the brim, tucked some sets of silverware into their napkin beds, and removed some stubborn crumbs off the dessert display table with a scraper.

None of these tasks were hers—nor were they appropriate for the owner of a casino to complete, if she was honest with herself—and yet everyone at The Nott had come to expect such strange behavior from her. In fact, they seemed to like it—she was one of them. She wanted to tell them that her father had been a fisherman who cleaned the guts from his catches with a knife and his bare hands, and that the blood had sometimes turned black under his fingertips, but she couldn't bring herself to say the words out loud.

Now, she looked up at a painting of a similar man waiting for a bite as the day drew onto the canvas of a calm sea and imagined that man was her father. There were twenty-nine similar pieces of art throughout the Nott: two in the waiting area at the front of the building, fourteen around the main casino floor, seven in the dining room, two in each bathroom, one in her office, and one in Maurice's office. *I'm more of an expressionist kind of guy,* he had told her when she tried to hang a Rembrandt print, but she could not have twenty-eight matching seafarer paintings and one blurry field, so she had tracked down a Renoir print called "La Grenouillère," which was technically of a restaurant on a frog pond but at least had a boat in it. According to Maurice, it was the nicest thing a boss had ever done for him, which said much more about the industry than it did about her selfish desire for matching décor.

Out of kitchen chores, Little John went back to Maurice and asked him if he needed anything else done.

"You can take the trash out," he said without looking away from the computer screen.

"Okay, and after that?"

Maurice turned toward her with a look Little John knew well, the one that indicated she had missed something obvious. "I was joking."

"Right. Of course." Little John buttoned and unbuttoned her blazer. "So, nothing, then?"

"Just get some sleep, okay Boss?"

If only it was that simple. Little John eyed "La Grenouillère" nervously, unsettled by the middle-class revelers on the restaurant's barge and the empty boat that floated by the gang plank. The decorator had explained that the name "La Grenouillère" meant frog pond, but it also meant loose women—not prostitutes, exactly, but unattached women who followed their youthful whims wherever they took them. *Like the Misfits*, Little John had thought as the decorator's assistant threaded the wire over the hanging hooks.

But actually, Little John had never followed her own whims as a Misfit—she had followed Robin's. The Nott was the first choice she had made on her own in years; maybe that was why the casino meant so much to her.

On the way out the back door, she took the plastic trash bags by their knots and hauled them to the dumpster.

CHAPTER SIXTEEN

LITTLE JOHN AWOKE TO THE SOUND of girls' voices outside her door. Something about a *bull in a China shop*. She checked her phone. 11:00 A.M., just six hours after she'd fallen asleep. Her body ached. Her eyes threatened to close again. Blink. Blink. She forced them open. Turned her body and got out of bed. Tucked in the covers.

In the kitchen, Skillet and White Rabbit were putting away clean dishes. On the table, the remains of a feast of pancakes, eggs, baked beans, and sausage spread across four plates. Little John wondered where they had gotten the meat, considering Daisy Chain was mostly vegan and Little John ate all her meals across the street, but couldn't find the energy to ask.

"You've been busy." Little John ignored the food and went, instead, to the coffeemaker to pour herself a generous cup. She drank until her brain worked and then asked, "Where's Daisy Chain?"

"Over at Tiny Notts. She wanted to stay and help us plan, but apparently it's something called Career Day?"

"Oh no!" Little John dropped her half-full mug in the sink. "I was supposed to speak to her class today. Oh god. It's so late, and they were so excited, and—"

"Hold your horses." Skillet put up a hand like a crosswalk officer telling a car to stop. "Robin's filling in for you."

In more ways than one, Little John thought. She scowled, and then consciously worked her mouth into a straight line. "Perfect."

Since she had the time, she poured herself a second cup of coffee and went out onto the patio, where she could grumble to herself in peace. She sat in one of the wrought iron chairs, put her feet up on the low table, and glared across the street at the door that said Tiny Notts. Somewhere behind that door, Robin was telling a room of awestruck kids that she fixed motorcycles for a living. Somewhere behind that door, Daisy Chain was falling even more in love with her.

The sliding glass door opened behind her. "When you're done with your coffee," Skillet said, "holler at us. We have a few ideas we want to run by you."

Little John gripped her mug handle tightly as the door closed. Wasn't the whole reason that she'd made Robin leave Fine Fixers that she needed her to lead the Merry Misfits? Yet there she was, gallivanting across the street to Tiny Notts to captivate small children like the bloody pied piper, while in the meantime Little John would still need to clean up their mess.

She counted the bars of the patio railing. Fifteen. She counted the intertwined circles of the coffee table's pattern. Thirty-six. Her breathing slowed, became more regular.

"Alright," she said, finally. "Pull yourself together."

Little John went inside and joined Skillet and White Rabbit at the dining room table, which had been cleared and then covered in pieces of crumpled paper. Apparently, their system was to come up with a moneymaking scheme, decide the scheme was a bad idea, crumple the sheet, and then later retrieve it after a string of even worse ideas.

"What do we have so far?" Little John sifted through the clutter, picked out a few pages. "Bank robbery. Counterfeit money. Hostages." She held up the last sheet. "Really? You thought 'hostages' was an idea worth reconsidering?"

"Skillet came up with it," said White Rabbit. She feigned moving her chair away from her girlfriend. "Apparently, prison has really changed her."

Skillet rummaged through some of the pages and then waved one in the air. "If I'm so bad, then why did you write 'counterfeit drugs'? That crud could kill people!"

"Crud?" White Rabbit leaned in and kissed Skillet. "Your southern substitutes are adorable."

"Don't change the subject." Skillet smiled. "Or do."

Little John rolled her eyes. She had forgotten how lovey-dovey these two could get, and apparently, absence had made the heart even fonder. Didn't anyone care that a gang leader had them on his hit list?

"Wait." Little John thought back to the truck ride. "Didn't you say something about Infiltrate? Infantile?"

"Infiltribe?"

"Right, that's the one. What if you sent up the program to steal just a small amount—say three dollars—from every account over a certain amount?"

White Rabbit seemed to be thinking. Then she smiled. "So, steal from the rich . . ."

"Give to ourselves," finished Little John.

* * *

By the time Robin and Daisy Chain got back from Tiny Notts, the apartment had again been subsumed by materials—only this time, instead of gems and hemp bracelets, it was plans scribbled out on pieces of paper and every computer and screen Little John could dig up. White Rabbit was on a group call on a burner phone with people who had equally ridiculous nicknames: Black Cat, Spider, Mushroom Head. Mushroom Head sounded about twelve years old, and to make matters worse, had a cold that made him sniffle into the phone. The one time Little John asked White Rabbit what she was doing as she typed rapidly on her computer, she fired back without stopping, *There's no way I can explain it to you, so let's not waste time trying.*

"What's going on?" asked Robin as soon as she closed the front door behind her. She had borrowed some of Daisy Chain's clothes, and she looked completely different in a hippie dress and red hair loose down her back.

"Business." Little John noted that Robin and Daisy Chain were holding hands and then averted her eyes. "I solved our financial crisis."

"How?" Robin scanned the papers, and then peered over White Rabbit's shoulder. "Are those bank accounts?"

"You'd know if you hadn't . . ." Little John trailed off.

Robin raised her eyebrows.

"Are you stealing?" asked Daisy Chain. Luckily, she seemed to have missed Little John's jab. "I thought we didn't do that anymore."

She was right. They didn't. Little John felt instantly guilty. What had she been thinking? Was she so jealous of Robin that she'd lashed out at a bunch of rich strangers? Hadn't she worked so hard these past three years to do things honestly, even if that made them harder? What about all that mush about Daisy Chain making her a better person, blah blah blah? Had she just been lying to herself?

"What choice do we have?" Robin asked Daisy Chain.

"What choice?" Daisy Chain dropped her hand. "The only one that matters: to be criminals—or not to."

Robin rolled her eyes. "Nothing is that simple, Daisy. If we don't give Andrew Clark his money, then we die."

"At least we would die nobly," said Daisy Chain. Her chin thrust in the air. She might have been a character on the stage delivering her final lines before a losing battle, sword in the air and valiant resolve on her face. Her lower lip shook.

"This isn't a play," said Robin. She might look like a flower child, but her voice was steel. "It's real life. If we die here, we die for real. I, for one, am not going to let that happen to my friends."

"Do what you want," whispered Daisy Chain. "I'm out."

She disappeared into her room and closed the door softly behind her. Everyone left exhaled, along with the group chatters, who had apparently been listening to the fight, and then Little John whispered to Robin, "Thanks for having our backs."

"It was the right thing to do. Daisy Chain means well, but she's very naïve." Robin bent over White Rabbit, all business. "What other supplies do you need?"

White Rabbit told her a list, which Little John heard as a bunch of foreign words strung together. She was still stuck on Daisy Chain, and on the way that Robin had so quickly taken their side. Did that mean Robin didn't love her? No. Little John knew her best friend better than that. Misfits first, lovers second, no matter which man or woman had her attention at the time. That was what made her such a great leader—and such a terrible girlfriend.

Little John felt guilty—the whole Infiltribe thing had been her idea—and yet strangely satisfied knowing that though she had lost Daisy Chain, she hadn't lost her best friend.

"Did you get all that?" asked Robin, breaking Little John's concentration.

"Uh." Little John blushed. "Sorry, I wasn't exactly listening . . ."

Robin smiled, and Little John realized she was teasing her. "Don't worry, I made a list. Want to go pick this stuff up with me?"

"Uh." Little John looked back down the hallway, thought about knocking on Daisy Chain's door, and then turned away. "Sure."

They took the casino's company van, usually used for picking up last minute produce the kitchen needed or rented audio equipment. Little John had assumed they would go to Best Buy, or maybe even Walmart, but Robin drove them out of the city in silence and then further, to the suburbs where the distance between houses was enough to build whole duplexes, and where people planted gardens lush with green leaves. White Rabbit had given her an address, and when Robin repeated it, Little John said she'd never even heard of it.

"Good," said Robin. "Small towns mean less cops."

And it was small. A gas station much like the one at Fine Fixers, just two pumps and a stall. A post office. A Walmart. Lots and lots of empty space. No officers for miles, and even if they had seen the telltale sheriff title in all capitals, they were way more likely to get pulled over for speeding than their private business.

The house where they ended up looked somewhere between artistic and abandoned. Dirt driveway, dirty windows, broken front step; but also, dog statue made of old tools, wind spinner butterflies, and a fairy garden half-hidden under a bush. "Keep out," said one sign, and then a second, "Smile, you're on camera."

The girls parked behind a rusted truck missing a wheel. Little John wondered how they got anywhere without a ride; then again, in their line of work, maybe everyone came to them. Robin led them to the front door, with Little John trailing behind. She counted the bushes. Five on one side, four on the other. She hated when things weren't symmetrical. Robin knocked three times, waited a few seconds, and then knocked five times. Eight. Little John wondered what was the significance of the numbers.

"Yes?" asked a voice from a speaker under the peephole.

"Code word: dynamite," said Robin.

The door lock clicked open. No one was on the other side. The only light was from the windows on the far ends of the house. "Come downstairs," the voice commanded through the speaker. "Straight to the kitchen and then right."

The house gave Little John the creeps. It was full of thrift store furniture, but every cushion had a fine layer of dust. The pictures in the frames looked like models, and every family was different.

"It's a front," explained Robin. "She doesn't actually live here."

Little John didn't care. She kept waiting for a serial killer to grab her shoulder, or a ghost to pop out from the old-style box television. *Count the sconces,* she tasked herself. *One, two three . . .*

The kitchen showed no signs of use. No dishes in the sink, no fruit in the bowl in the middle of the kitchen table. They turned right, found the door, and descended. The room below was a blue glow, like the ramp to an alien ship in a movie where they would surely be dinner. Robin took her hand. Her palm was dry and cool, like the basement air. At the bottom of the steps, they suddenly came face-to-face with a hundred versions of themselves. Or rather, a hundred screens projecting a feed from the many security cameras around the house, looping and doubling back to the moment when they had passed them.

"Hello?" asked Robin.

"Took you long enough." A chair turned amidst the screens, centered like the pistil between the petals of a flower. In the middle was a girl—or a woman, rather, at least a few years older than Little John—with tightly curled black hair and large black glasses through which she examined them. Even as she stared, she continued to type without looking down at the keyboard attached to her swivel chair. She wore a white button-up shirt closed to the neck, as if she was a secretary in an old movie. Her socks were rolled to the place where they met her leather loafers. "Thirty-two minutes and fourteen seconds, to be exact, which is long considering your average speed of sixty-five miles an hour."

"That's a *mean* thing to say," said Little John.

The woman blinked at her.

Little John blinked back.

They both started laughing.

"I don't get it," said Robin. "Why is stating our average speed mean?"

Neither of them explained the pun. Little John felt instantly at home with the woman, whose name was Wanda, though she went by WandWizard online. Apparently, Wanda had hacked into not only the garage and traffic cameras on their way, but The Nott's old footage as well. "I was impressed by your counting," she admitted to Little John.

"How did you know I was counting?" she asked. If she had a tell, she needed to know what it was to avoid it.

"Your eyes bounce back and forth on the floor as you figure out the index number. See?"

Wanda pulled up footage from her last night at The Nott—the night that she'd met Bean Clark. Sure enough, her eyes bounced four times before she looked up at Eliza.

"Thanks," said Little John, and she meant it. She especially appreciated Wanda's use of evidence to support her claim. "That's excellent constructive feedback."

"I'm glad you are open to criticism. Oh, and maybe try tapping your fingers together instead," advised Wanda. "Other counters will never think to look at your hands. Plus, you wear those ill-fitting blazers, so your fingers are often covered anyway."

Little John raised her arms and looked at her partially covered hands. "Good point. I'll incorporate your suggestions during my next shift."

Robin had been looking back and forth between them, and now she snapped her fingers in the air where their eye contact met. "Hey nerds. If you're done flirting, we have some equipment to pick up."

Wanda had not been flirting with her—had she? Little John thought it over while Wanda showed Robin the box full of supplies she had prepared for them—something about proxy servers and a list of personal data saved on a USB. Had she really been flirting? Had Little John wanted her to? Robin told Little John to pay Wanda while she called White Rabbit, and Little John went to take out her old-school Velcro wallet only to find her hands shaking.

"Nice wallet," said Wanda.

"Thanks. It's the most effective way to carry money."

"I agree." Wanda removed her own wallet from her pocket, also Velcro but purple instead of black. "All of the benefits of a traditional man's wallet, but more durable, and with the added protection of the closure abilities."

"Are you really flirting with me?" Little John asked. She had not meant to say it, but she hated ambiguity.

"Let me evaluate." Wanda looked up, as though to think through their short list of interactions. "I find you very attractive, and I appreciate our shared interest in math. However, I worry about the age difference between us and whether you'll enjoy my favorite activity, playing D&D on Friday and Saturday nights with my two primary friend groups. If you're anything like me, using creative thinking is hard enough without adding a bunch of curious strangers into the mix."

"You're right, that sounds terrible." Little John envisioned herself surrounded by druids and dwarfs. "But Friday and Saturday nights don't work for me anyway because of The Nott's peak hours. What do you do on Sundays?"

"Rock climbing. I find the combination of physical activity and problem solving to be an effective stress reliever."

Rock climbing explained her arms, which were quite muscular for a computer nerd, as well as the dexterity of her hands, which Little John had noted earlier as she typed on the computer. The sport was outside of her comfort zone, but she did enjoy physical problem solving in other settings, like a pick-up soccer game with the Merry Misfits.

"I'll join you next Sunday, then—if I'm still alive," said Little John. "Would you please send me the address?"

"Better, I'll add you to my Google calendar and send you a reminder." Wanda retrieved her cell phone and entered Little John's number. A few seconds later, she got a text— *Hello. This is Wanda. Please send me your email address at your earliest convenience.*

Robin hung up and came back to them. "What did I miss?" she asked.

"A lot," said Wanda. "But nothing pertaining to this trans-action. Can I assume that White Rabbit found my products to be acceptable for her current venture?"

"Uh, yeah." Robin gave Wanda another weird look—the same one she usually gave Little John when Little John tried to explain how her budget infographics worked. "We're all good."

They emerged back into the light of midday blinking and blind, like two moles dragged from their holes. The retrieved information went into the glove compartment, and the box of supplies sat between them.

"Wanda reminds me a lot of you," said Robin as she reversed out of Wanda's driveway. "You liked her, didn't you?"

"I guess." Little John shifted her gaze out the window. "I just figured it might be time to date someone a little bit more . . ." *Logical. Compatible. Not related to me.* ". . . you know."

"Yeah, I do."

They drove for a while in silence. The landscape shifted back to suburban. Little John guessed that Robin was upset about what had happened with Daisy Chain, and that the problem was not just a single fight but a fundamental difference between them: Robin, as leader of the Merry Misfits, put crew above everything, whether it be law or love. Daisy Chain followed her emotional compass like how a dandelion seed floats in the wind. Both thought their values were morally superior, and thus could not respect the choices of the other.

This is why I need someone logical in my life.

And yet Little John felt guilty about liking Wanda, as though she were cheating on Daisy Chain—and that feeling was not logical either. Asking Wanda out had happened too quickly, so naturally, spurred on by the fact that they all might die in a week, that only now did she realize that she probably would not be able to disentangle herself from her crush in time to make a meaningful relationship with someone else.

But she had to.

Enough is enough.

Her mind went to Daisy. The smell of incense, soy candles, and flower petals. The whisper of Shakespeare in her ear. She felt these things so intensely that she shivered. *Enough is enough. Enough is enough. Enough is enough.* Drum rhythms through a closed door. Beads clicking against each other. Bangles tapping.

"Little John?"

"What?"

Robin put her hand out, and Little John held it. Back at Uncle Frank's, they would fall asleep this way, just two tough kids looking for any kind of comfort. Little John thought of her father, and the way his hands had been calloused too, more so even from all the gripping of fishing poles and slicing up fish with knives. The smell of Daisy slowly gave way to her father, salty and metallic from the blood on his apron.

"Do you think having a mom made you better at loving people?" Robin asked suddenly.

Little John raised her eyebrows. "You think *I'm* a good model for relationships?"

They had never talked about their families, not even in the middle of the night back at Uncle Frank's as they contemplated escape. Robin's policeman father had been a complete shock, though looking back, academy training explained so much about Robin's loyal demeanor and drive for success.

"It's just . . ." Robin's eyes were on the road, but they also seemed to look farther—all the way back to the past. ". . . Sometimes I wonder if I would be better at relationships if my mom hadn't died. I know most of that gender essentialism is bullshit, but I just can't help wondering . . ."

Little John expected her stomach to clench and her palms to sweat. Delia usually manifested this way first, like a flu. Instead, she felt surprisingly calm.

"Trust me," said Little John, "not all mothers are good. Sometimes they're the ones that mess you up the most."

Whenever she thought of her mother, the only memory that came to mind besides the most recent call was Little John's view from across a wide wooden table with Delia facing her, future husband by her side, pen tapping impatiently on a pad of notebook paper. Delia had used her inheritance to sue for full custody several times, even though she had looked at Little John's gelled hair and tomboy clothes and hissed, *My god, Anthony, she's not your son. Don't you have any pride?*

"My mother thought she was too good for my father," Little John explained, "and she expected me to leave him the way that she did. We were both a source of constant disappointment to her."

Had that table scene finally become the past, no longer to repeat endlessly in Little John's mind like the decimal version of a recurring fraction?

"What makes me so mad now," Little John thought out loud, "is the fact that she should have been proud of him. Born and raised by a bunch of mobsters, he made his own living honestly, and he never asked Uncle Frank for help, even when he needed the money most." *Like for custody battles*, she thought, *or therapy bills.*

"And yet here we are," said Robin, pulling her hand away in order to turn into the parking garage, "just a bunch of thieves."

CHAPTER SEVENTEEN

THE IMPLEMENTATION OF INFILTRIBE'S PROGRAM WAS as easy as accessing the bank accounts from the list, inputting their stolen passwords, and watching the dollars roll into their own shell corporation. From this account, they could transfer the money to a second account owned by Andrew Clark. Skillet served tall glasses of iced tea and chips with salsa while they waited, as though they were at a backyard barbecue and not committing another federal crime. No one touched any of it. White Rabbit shifted between screens with shortcuts, since she never used a mouse. Her fingers pressed, held, added, released. They were like two dancing spiders.

"Make the call," she said, still typing.

Little John took out her burner phone. Her hands shook. She removed Bean's card from her wallet and dialed. On the first ring, his voice greeted her with a confident "Hey there!"

"We're ready to make the transfer," she said. She felt sick. They were about to hand over a lot of money to a criminal organization like Uncle Frank's—worse, even—and there was nothing she could do about it. Maybe Daisy Chain had been right. Maybe they were making a big mistake.

"What's the number?" she asked. Then she put the phone on speaker.

"Hi, you beautiful bandits." Bean knew he had an audience. "I'm a huge fan of your work. The redhead especially, though the computer geek also gets me—"

"Just give us the number," Robin said.

"Fine. Just trying to make a little small talk." He read out a string of digits for the account and routing numbers, which White Rabbit recorded. Little John added them up: 87.

"Done," White Rabbit said as she hit enter.

"Great. It was a pleasure doing—"

Little John hung up and smashed the phone against the table, breaking it into two unusable pieces.

No one moved.

Little John thought of her father. Of his callouses. Of the way that, when his own father had died, they had driven in a line of family cars to the cemetery, five sports cars and a beat-up truck with a missing fender. The bed of their truck smelled like fish, even after her father had scrubbed it clean that morning. Everyone had laughed at them.

"We did the wrong thing," she said softly.

"I know." Robin sat down at the table and put her head in her hands. "We've gone soft. We're just a bunch of regular girls who want to go back to our regular lives, even if that means funding a drug cartel or weapons for a gang or whatever those Boston Butchers decide to do next."

"Yeah." White Rabbit closed her laptop. "This is the first time I've felt bad about a job."

"Slow your roll. You mean to tell me," Skillet raised her eyebrows, "that you didn't feel bad that time when we realized there was a kid in the back of that tow truck we stole? That was a hot mess."

"Okay," White Rabbit assented, "That was bad. But we gave her a thousand dollars and a bus ticket, remember? Who knows what would have happened to her if she had stuck with him instead? Or worse, us."

"I reckon you're right." Skillet put her arm around her girlfriend. "But what can we do about it now? We gave Bean the money. It's over."

Little John looked down the hallway at Daisy Chain's closed door. Was she standing right behind it, listening? Or had she opened her window to look across the street at Tiny Notts, where they had done so much good over the past three years?

Not we, Little John corrected. *Daisy. I just fund the place.*

Funds.

Places.

"That's it." Little John was so excited that she waved her arms, sending the half of the phone still in her hand across the room. "We can steal the money back. And not just our money—all of it."

"Are you talking about another job?" Skillet asked.

"It's the same job," corrected Little John. "The second half. We take down the Boston Butchers, and then we use all the money for . . . something good." The word sounded strange in her mouth.

"Good?" White Rabbit asked. She seemed just as uncomfortable. "Like what?"

"I don't know." Little John thought about what it had felt like to help that girl in the truck—even if it was just handing her a stack of cash. "We could fund programs for teens. Girls like us who need a new start."

"Well butter my butt and call me a biscuit," Skillet said. She was grinning.

"Helping girls like us." White Rabbit smiled. "I like the sound of that. I could have used some help five years ago, that's for sure."

"Me too." Little John wondered what her life would have been like if she had been able to ask someone for help— someone besides her uncle.

Everyone looked at Robin. When she lifted her head off her arms, she was crying. She put her fist in the air. "Steal from the rich," she chanted, "and this time, we give it to the poor."

"Steal from the rich and give to the poor!" they all echoed.

The door at the end of the hallway swung open.

PART FOUR
DAISY
CHAIN

CHAPTER EIGHTEEN

FRANK'S BLOOD ON THE FLOOR WAS like a blossom, wet and red and swaying in and out of her vision as the waves of her memories pulled Daisy Chain backward, forward, backward again. A tug-of-war with herself.

* * *

HER MOTHER'S BLOOD WAS ON HER hands, like gloves. Her mother's blood was on her boots, her linen dress, everywhere she pressed her body like a stamp. *Mom, Mom, Mom.* Dab, dab, dab.

* * *

HER MOTHER TOLD HER TO HIDE in the closet, behind the shoe boxes. Her mother told her that she should be in school, and that meant that no one would think to look for her there. *Let's play the quiet game, Rosalind,* her mother said, finger to her lips. Her nails were blood red. *Silence is a true friend who never betrays.* Rosalind knew this was Shakespeare talking, not her mother, because she used her teacher voice. In the closet she thought about silence, about true friends, and the way that Jinny told everyone at school about her crush on Cara the week before. She touched the boxes, felt through the holes for the leather toes and pointy heels. The bedroom door crashed into the wall.

* * *

THEY NAMED HER DAISY CHAIN. SHE liked the metaphor of intertwined stems in a circle, the way the Merry Misfits had threaded together in Nottingham. She liked the allusion to her real name, another flower—though she wasn't that girl anymore. She thought of Ophelia in Shakespeare's *Hamlet*, and the way that her madness manifested in the giving of flowers. Yet Ophelia had been conflicted, and Daisy Chain was not.

She would kill her father.

* * *

THE FIRST MAN TO STOP FOR Rosalind wore a black suit and purple tie. He was on his way to a meeting. *In Providence*, he said, as if she should know where that was. She nodded and slid into the passenger seat. *Are you old enough to ride up front?* he asked. She said she was, even though she wouldn't be twelve for another three months. His car showed signs of younger children—snack wrappers, kid cups, a doll. Her mother had told her never to talk to strangers, and so she buttoned her mouth, even when he put his hand on her knee. *Where are your parents?* he asked a while later over the voices of a talk radio station, and she said Providence, because it was the only place she could think of. *Changed your mind about running away, huh?* She said yes. She asked if he had more snacks. She had not eaten since breakfast; her mother had promised to take her to get vegan burgers after she got back from her errand. *I'll do you one better,* he said, and pulled off at the next exit, where he ordered her a burger and fries. The burger was not vegan. Her mother was dead. Rosalind ate the burger while he watched her, and then they kept driving.

* * *

"THEIR SYSTEM IS IMPENETRABLE," SAID WHITE Rabbit. Her fingers made rain on the keyboard. "We're going to need to get in. And then get out before they can—" She slapped her hand on the table. Daisy Chain jumped.

"Shaina has our back," said Robin.

Daisy Chain did not trust the police. When she saw a woman or man in blue with a shiny silver badge, she felt like there were bugs all over her body, like back in Nottingham the time she had fallen asleep with a drink in her hand. She had itched for weeks.

"But she's one cop," argued White Rabbit, "or best case a few, if she manages to convince her team. Do you actually think that's any match—"

"Alright, don't get your knickers in a knot," said Skillet. Her hand went to White Rabbit's shoulder. A long time ago, Robin had touched Daisy Chain the same way, and just the press of her palm against a tight muscle had calmed her. Now, they never touched. Robin was on one side of an enormous chasm, and Daisy Chain was on the other—or, maybe, the chasm was inside her.

"Let's just say, for argument's sake," said Little John, who had gone on another date last night, who wore the secret smile of new love, who had once loved Daisy Chain in the way that Daisy Chain loved Robin, "that we do have an army of cops behind us. That still doesn't solve the true problem: How do we get in? The Butchers know what we pulled on Uncle Frank—they're not going to let us near them."

"I could go," volunteered Wanda.

"No way," said Little John.

"Yeah, no way," agreed Robin. "You're a terrible liar. This morning Skillet asked you if her new hat looked good, and you said, 'I don't know the beauty standards of your geographical area.'"

"What?" Wanda looked around. She was pretty. Daisy Chain felt jealous of her. Not because Little John loved her, but because anyone did. "That's an accurate statement."

"My point exactly." Robin tapped her fingers on the table, four horse hooves trampling across a wooden tundra. "We need a Caligo."

"A what?" Wanda asked. She did not yet know that every metaphor Robin made was natural.

"An owl butterfly. You know . . . the ones with the huge eyespots? Native to rainforests?"

Wanda blinked at her.

"*We'll so bestow ourselves that, seeing unseen, We may of their encounter frankly judge, And gather by him, as he is behaved,*" quoted Daisy Chain.

"Right. A spy." Robin looked at her gratefully, but Daisy Chain's mind drifted away before she could smile.

* * *

THE SECOND MAN TO STOP FOR Rosalind took her home to his wife. She was one big hug. Her white hair had clots of corn bread batter in it. She wanted Rosalind to stay for dinner, and then for dessert, a fresh apple pie cooling on the windowsill like in an old movie. Rosalind ate three slices. She watched the man, who at the end of dessert got up and walked into the living room, and listened for the murmur of his voice under the banging of his wife's. "May I use your restroom?" Rosalind asked politely.

The woman clasped her hands to her heart and said, "What a darling little thing you are."

On the way to the bathroom, Rosalind stole two hundred dollars out of the woman's worn leather purse and a photo of two babies in matching Christmas sweaters. The bathroom window brushed up against a hedge, which she used as a ladder down to the ground.

Maybe the cops came soon after that, or maybe the couple had to wait alone in their living room for half an hour, wondering whether they'd done the right thing.

By then, Rosalind was in another car, with another man, moving down a square on the game board of highway between her and the end of the line.

* * *

BACK IN NOTTINGHAM, IN THOSE EARLY days of uninter-rupted quiet, the butterfly flitted through the early morning light and alighted on a blossom. Its wings flicked in the wind like a paper airplane held in the pinched fingers of a nervous child. Daisy Chain reached up her hand to touch the creature, but Robin threaded her fingers through Daisy Chain's out-stretched hand and pulled it downward, to where they lay in the grass. The earth was warm, the grass in thin patches over the sandy panhandle dirt. A cloud hand muted the mouth of the sun. Daisy Chain thought of "Sonnet 116." *Love alters not with his brief hours and weeks, But bears it out even to the edge of doom. If this*

be error and upon me proved, I never writ, nor no man ever loved.
And she did love; and the edge of doom barreled toward her.
They would go to the house of her father. He would die.

* * *

ROSALIND NEEDED TO TRANSFORM. SHE COULD not be
recognized, not even by herself in the mirror—not if she
hoped to make it all the way to her father's side. When the
nurses removed the tape and plastic splints, the girl who was
once Rosalind looked at her reflection and saw someone who
was not her mother's daughter. That nose, that face, were
those of a stranger. After the surgery, she dyed her hair so
often that the texture became frizzy and brittle. She covered
her body in layers, in bangles, in braids.

Viola, she called herself.

And that was her name.

* * *

ROBIN, SKILLET, AND WHITE RABBIT WENT to their
apartment across the hall. Little John and Wanda went to a
movie. The apartment was quiet. Daisy Chain drifted into
her room, the only place still surging with energy, and
inhaled the sweet scent of incense and essential oils. She
existed there, in that chaos, the pieces of herself scattered
like seed pods dropped from a tree. She was the quartz on
the shelf. She was the wooden jewelry box lined with shells.

When Robin had ordered them to scrub the apartment
clean of her like wiping away a set of fingerprints, she had
told herself she didn't mind. Her love for Robin had a way of
doing that. But now, when she ventured out into the sterile
rooms, she wanted to cry.

If the evidence of Daisy Chain disappeared, then who was she? *All the world's a stage, and all the men and women merely players. They have their exits and their entrances; And one man in his time plays many parts.* Daisy Chain knew that her time as this version of herself was almost over. For weeks, she had felt the change like a coming storm. She had a new mission: she would call herself Portia, she had decided, like from *The Merchant of Venice.* She would transform, like a caterpillar awakening its sleeping cells, into a gruesome beauty. This new woman would trick Bean, A.C.'s son, into loving her.

These were the facts of her existence—and yet, now that the heaviness sat on her chest and the thunder rumbled closer, she suddenly wanted to grip onto her life like a child gripped the banister of a set of steps she was not quite big enough to climb. *Many parts.* Rosalind, the child. Viola, the miscreant. Daisy Chain, the Misfit.

Exits. Entrances.

Escapes.

She had a set of boxes saved at the bottom of her closet, which she dragged from beneath her dreamcatcher comforter and unpacked. One for Robin. One for Skillet. One for White Rabbit. One for Little John.

And one for Daisy Chain.

In the small Daisy Chain box, she put only four items: a leather-bound journal, a copy of *Shakespeare's Sonnets,* her amethyst necklace, and the only letter that Robin had ever written her. She tore a piece of paper from the journal and retrieved a pen from her desk.

Dear Robin.

CHAPTER NINETEEN

ROSALIND WAS HIDING. HER MOTHER STEPPED somewhere on the other side of the curtain, her feet padding against the carpet like a careful predator. Rosalind held her breath. She knew this was just a game, yet a thrill of anticipation and dread moved through her body in a chill. *Where are you, Rosalind?* her mother whispered. Rosalind closed her eyes. The curtain against her arm was rough and heavy. She told herself to become the curtain, the way the class chameleon blended into the green poster board behind her tank, and imagined herself growing heavy, thick, unmoving even in strong wind. She hung, lifeless. She shielded.

"Got you!"

Rosalind was lifted and swung. Her mother found her soft belly and tickled. Rosalind hung, limbs weak from her laughter. No longer a curtain, she flooded with new life, overflowing out of her in a manic giggle-scream.

* * *

ALL THAT LIVES MUST DIE, DAISY Chain warned as the rode the elevator up to the fourth floor.

Nobody paid attention to her, and that was better, for she felt a howling hurricane start up around her, like one of Prospero's storms. She could barely see the hallway as she passed through it, using the bodies in front of her as light-house beacons.

"Stay alert," Little John whispered,

"Always," Robin said.

Daisy Chain was not alert. She wasn't even sure she *was*. Rosalind had surged up inside of her, a scared and angry child, and tried to cast Daisy Chain off like a costume. The boy knocked on Frank's door, and Daisy Chain felt the reverberations of the sound through her whole body.

"Come in."

His voice was older, more of a low growl, but she would have recognized it among a million similar echoes. How many times has she heard him in her dreams? And there he was, at his desk, his left hand flat as if he was calming his animalistic desk and right hand slowly scribbling on a piece of graph paper. Daisy Chain looked at Robin and then the fish tank that held her gaze.

"I thought you vowed never to set foot in Boston again?" Uncle Frank said to Robin, but Daisy Chain felt like he was speaking directly to her. She held her breath, but Frank noticed Little John and ambled over with the use of a cane and inspected both girls like an incoming shipment. Not once did his eyes drift to his daughter's face. The hurricane around her roared, battered her face and chest like the bullets that had once assailed her mother, and yet she suffered in silence. *Not yet. Not yet. Not yet.* Even when Robin introduced her, a supposedly new recruit, neither she nor her father even made eye contact. Her eyes were on the gun in the guard's holster. She knew how to use it, and how close she had to be in order to not miss.

"Deception by those you love the most," Frank was saying to Robin. "I know all about that."

The hurricane circled faster and faster. She thought of the last storm, when the winds had blown trees from their posts and brought the waters up so high they had almost had to leave Nottingham behind, and how the noise had been like a woman screaming one long, endless scream. *You know nothing*, she wanted to add to the noise. Or, in the words of the mariners weathering Prospero's fury, *All lost! to prayers, to prayers! all lost!* Frank had stolen everything from her, and now he spoke of deception like he knew the meaning of the word.

Robin got hold of a gun and aimed. *Not yet*, Daisy Chain wanted to say, *I have to be the one to kill him.* She had to get a gun, but how? Her eyes roamed the room, the guard, Frank's desk. The other girls were distracted by the USB, as though money or information or whatever Robin planned to extract had any relevance to the here, the now.

Out of nowhere, Little John handed her a gun.

Daisy Chain stared down at it, that *deus ex machina*, in awe. She had held guns before, but they had felt heavy, pulled down by their literal metal and their abstract power. This gun was light as air. Something happened out of her line of vision, something to do with Robin, but Daisy Chain focused her attention on aiming the gun at Frank's chest.

The sins of the father are to be laid upon the children.

The hurricane went silent.

* * *

Viola was always on the move.

The many cars became a continuous journey; the many drivers at their wheels became one. Ride, sleep, ride, sleep, with meals and hotel stops and cash in her pocket and neon lights after midnight and blankness. The only people she remembered were the ones who broke the cycle, who took her home to their families, who wanted nothing from her but to feel that they had helped.

Many of these people called the police.

* * *

Portia applied blood-red lipstick to her pouting lips using the visible part of a mirror behind the bar and then put up a hand to flag the bartender. "Vodka cranberry," she said. Her eyes moved to the door, where a young man in a suit and goofy yellow tie entered with two friends who, judging by their muscular arms and black t-shirts, were bodyguards. The young man looked like a boy who had dressed up in his father's clothes. His hair was too long, too messy. He had spent too much time shining his shoes.

"Thank you," Portia said to the bartender, and traded him a twenty-dollar bill for the drink. "Keep the change."

She watched the young man in the mirror. He was at the far end of the bar. She adjusted her black bangs and ran her fingers through her bob.

A few feet from her left shoulder.

Behind her.

Portia turned abruptly and spilled her drink onto his shirt. The cold liquid splashed onto her hands, and she hid her shiver by throwing her shoulders back.

"Hey, watch where you're going," the young man yelled.

"It's not my fault you're invisible," Portia snapped back.

The bodyguards arched their eyebrows.

"Invisible?" the young man huffed. He turned to the guards. "Did she just call me . . . ? Did you hear what she . . . ?"

"Oh, get over yourself." Portia rolled her eyes and turned away. "And maybe buy a better-fitting suit."

She made it to the other end of the bar before she heard, "Hey! Hey, girl in the red dress!"

Portia turned slowly. This had to seem like a great inconvenience. Her stiletto heels ground into the bar floor. "Yes, boy in the dad suit?"

He smiled sheepishly, and she saw the child in him. "Let me buy you another drink."

* * *

Robin sat in the chair by Daisy Chain's window. The rain torrented against the window, a million missiles falling to the ground of Nottingham keeping her in Daisy Chain's trailer rather than her own. Daisy Chain lay in bed pretending to sleep. Usually when the Florida rains came, she put on her yellow raincoat and danced barefoot down the path, but all she wanted to do now was look at Robin looking at the rain.

When shall we three meet again? In thunder, lightning, or in rain?

Shakespeare's words, but true. There were three people in the room: Robin, Daisy Chain, and Rosalind. Only around Robin did Daisy Chain feel that part of herself, that soft core, exposed. Daisy Chain protected it with Shakespeare, with casual nights and lonely mornings, with a vacant expression whenever anyone asked her to do anything. She had only one goal here in Nottingham, and until she achieved it, no highway robbery could distract her.

And yet . . .

Robin turned and caught her eye. The side of her face that should have been lit by the window was molted from the raindrops interrupting the daylight glow, but she still looked beautiful—even more so. Dark like the darkness of her soul. Daisy Chain knew nothing about Robin before her intersection with Frank—What was her real name? Where did she come from?—but she did know that the real girl inside of Robin wanted to remain as anonymous as Rosalind did.

"I might go get some food at Skillet's," Robin said. Her eyes went back to the rain. "Want to come?"

Parting is such sweet sorrow, Daisy Chain thought, but she could not even speak this quote out loud for fear of sounding how she felt. Instead, she shook her head no, and the beads in her hair tapped out her answer.

"Suit yourself."

Robin left in the same clothes she had worn the night before. When the door clicked closed, Daisy Chain climbed out of bed and found her raincoat in the small closet hidden in a wall panel of the kitchen. The pockets were heavy, and she removed three smooth stones, a crushed dandelion, five bottle caps, and a silver lightning bolt necklace she wore whenever she ventured into the rain in honor of Zeus, God of bad weather. *It's what Daisy Chain would do,* she thought, and then reminded herself that she was Daisy Chain. Usually, she had no problem staying in character, but when she spent too much time with Robin, the edges of her blurred, broke apart, overlapped. She was two waves crashing and separating and crashing again.

Outside, the rain tapped her on the head. Instantly, her skirt was soaked. Her feet crashed into one puddle, the next, the next. She stamped out the water . . . Rosalind . . . love. Before she disappeared into the forest, she couldn't help glancing back at Skillet's window, where bright light illuminated four Misfits huddled around the stove like primitive women around a fire.

She was a part of the Misfits too, she reminded herself, and at any point she could join their circle.

Then she turned into the rain and ran.

* * *

"I'M IN," PORTIA SAID INTO THE pay phone receiver. A girl that she used to know breathed a sigh of relief. *Robin*, she thought, but then she wiped the name away like the condensation from her breath on the pay phone glass. "Tell me what to do."

* * *

"WAIT." BEAN CAUGHT HER HAND AND held her back from the restaurant door. He looked handsome in his tailored suit, the one she had picked out for him. She was about to meet his father. She should have been nervous, but she felt completely calm. Portia was not fazed by any man.

"I got you this." He handed her a velvet box. Inside was an amethyst the size of a loquat, surrounded by diamonds and dangled on a silver chain.

"How did you—?"

"I saw you looking at them last week," Bean said shyly. "Do you like it?"

Portia felt like something was stuck in her throat. She coughed a little, but the sensation remained. The necklace

had made her think of her mother—Rosalind's mother—
and the way she had moved Rosalind's hair in order to clasp
a similar stone around her neck. She could almost feel the
soft hands on her back. Rosalind's back. The waves returned,
crashing, and drifting, and crashing again.

"Well?" Bean asked. He clasped and unclasped his hands.
Portia had this effect on the men around her.

"*My crown is in my heart, not in my head, Nor decked with diamonds and Indian stones, Nor to be seen; my crown is called
contentment; A crown it is, that seldom kings enjoy.*"

The words just slipped out. As soon as Portia's red lips
uttered Daisy Chain's thought, the waves subsided, drifting
her back into her present. Bean cocked his head.

"I mean that I'm happy," Portia said. She touched the
amethyst, but the feeling did not return. "Thank you."

* * *

"I HAVE AN IDEA FOR A new meeting location," Portia whispered into Bean's ear. He was almost asleep, and he turned
toward her without opening his eyes. She recited the words
Robin had told her to say, and he agreed to them without
question, as she'd known he would.

After Bean fell asleep, Portia slipped out of bed. Her
silk nightgown breezed against her legs as she stepped
over the places she knew the wood creaked, learned over
many sleepless nights. She did not feel tired at all; in fact,
she wished she was back in Nottingham so that she could
run through the forest until the stones and broken sticks
made her bare feet bleed. Something was pushing inside
of her, like a caterpillar struggling against its cocoon. She
thought of *King Lear: Come, let's away to prison. We two alone*

will sing like birds i' th' cage. But who were the two? Portia and Daisy Chain?

Was the pain she felt the splitting of her center?

Portia pulled out a bag of chamomile tea from the box in the kitchen and dropped it in a white mug. Then she filled it with water and stuck it in the microwave. The mug went around and around, closer, and then farther away. Before the timer went off, she turned away and went out onto the balcony.

Their street was quiet. The lights were on, as they always were after nightfall, but no soul interrupted their bright beams. Occasionally, a car sped past and then disappeared into the darkness, but even those stopped coming after a time.

"I want to go home," Portia whispered. But the thought unsettled her even further, for she wasn't sure, anymore, whether home was Nottingham or Boston. The microwave reminded her of her tea, but she did not pass back through the open door to retrieve it. Chamomile tea was Daisy Chain's drink anyway; Portia preferred nightcaps.

"Portia?" Bean stood in the doorway in his sweatpants and no shirt. His hair was a messy garland around his head. After a few seconds in the cool spring air, he shivered. "Are you okay?"

Now she remembered why she needed to take the tea out of the microwave—the beeping always woke him up.

"Fine," she said. She felt like she was a million miles away, or very high up, looking down on him.

"You sure?" Bean pointed to the open door. "You're letting all of the warm air out."

Beeping microwave. Open door. These earthly matters couldn't reach her.

"Sorry," she said, for that was what she was supposed to say in this kind of situation. She suddenly remembered how in spring Robin would always sleep with the windows open, no matter how hot her trailer got, just to listen to the loud crickets serenade her to sleep.

Robin.

She was the person Portia should be sleeping next to.

"Hey." Bean bent down so that he could look into her eyes. "Are you here?"

Here. She almost laughed that he thought the problem was a question of where and not whom.

"I love you," he said.

"I love you too."

She did not mean the words as she said them—but she almost did. The line between the two was surprisingly thin. She knew that if she stayed any longer, she would cross over, and she might never be able to cross back.

"Good." He pulled something out of his pocket. He was already on one knee, so all he had to do was open the box. "Will you marry me?"

CHAPTER TWENTY

THE PARTY WAS A COLLAGE OF faces, some familiar and many new. Beers sweated down ringed hands; martinis tilted like ships in a harbor, almost spilled, and then straightened. The women had fake breasts and collagen lips. Portia touched her own smiling mouth and realized she could not remember what that part of her body had felt like *before*.

The music was loud, but the high-pitched laughter of the women sitting on the deck was louder. They wore mini-skirts and high heels. The diamonds on their neck were collars tethering them to the small group of men in the cabin talking about things no one outside the room knew.

"Portia?" Bean was at the door of the cabin.

He ushered her inside but didn't follow. Compared to the revelry of the deck, this room was somber. The men smoked cigars and drank Bean's whiskey. His father, Andrew Clark, sat at the head of the table facing her. He always wore a gray suit and tie. His gray hair, thin at the temples, was slicked back against his head. She had met A.C. before, but every time they came face to face, she was struck again by the thickness of him, like a human wall.

"Bean made a lot of money for us last month," A.C. said. He spoke at a low volume, but everyone heard him. "When I thanked him just now, he told me you had something to do with it."

Portia dropped her chin down to her chest in gratitude.

"Come now," said A.C. "You can't fool us with that act."

Portia looked up quickly. She scanned the faces, which seemed more curious than angry. Did they know?

"That's more like it." A.C. swirled his drink. "You single-handedly created a program that steals money from people's bank accounts without alerting them. You procured the necessary equipment. You transferred the money to our offshore account without a trace. So, tell me, Portia Moretti . . ."

Portia took a deep breath.

". . . What's a girl with your brains doing with my son?"

Portia exhaled slowly, so the men didn't notice. Once she regained her composure, she said, "I love him, of course."

A.C. snorted. "Oh, really? Are you sure we're talking about the same guy?"

"He's sweet to me," she insisted, "and he's easy to read. He wears his heart on his sleeve."

A.C. rubbed his chin. He seemed to be trying to decide.

"Isn't that what you love about the girls on deck?" Portia asked. She forced her mouth into a wry smile. "Or is it really just about how they look in bikinis?"

A.C. stared at her blankly for a second. Had she taken this too far? It was one thing for a man to insult his son, but it was another thing entirely for a strange woman to compare Bean Clark to a bunch of his gang members' wives.

Then A.C. burst into a laugh that sounded like a lawn mower starting up, and the other men at the table joined in.

* * *

HER FATHER WAS IN A MEETING with his friends in their dining room. Rosalind put her ear to the sliding wooden door and listened. Their voices were deep murmurs, glass hitting glass, a fist pounding a table. She liked when his friends came over; they brought her little treats, like a *pignoli* from the bakery or a small wooden keychain Pinocchio from a recent trip to their homeland. They put their big hands on her head and weighed her to the ground.

"Rosalind?" her mother called from the kitchen.

She dutifully followed the voice. In the kitchen, her mother stirred something in a big pot on the stove. "Meatball soup?" she asked, but her mother said it was white bean. Rosalind made a face.

"It's your father's favorite," her mother said, as if this fact would change her taste buds. "Were you listening at the door again, *amore mio*?"

"No."

"Oh, really?" Her mother seemed to be trying not to smile, which means she knew Rosalind was lying. "Then what were you doing?"

"I was . . ." Rosalind thought, ". . . playing dolls. Yup, I was playing dolls, Barbie and Ken go to adopt a baby. The baby was Mr. Monkey, and when they saw him, they had to try to figure out how to fit him in their house. The box is too small, so they tried cutting a hole in the roof. When that didn't work, they added a second box—"

Her mother turned abruptly and sank to one knee so that she could look in Rosalind's eyes.

"*Whose tongue soe'er speaks false, Not truly speaks; who speaks not truly, lies.* Do you understand?"

"Yes, Mama."

But she didn't—not really. The lines of Shakespeare fell around her like rain, sometimes landing on her head but mostly just close enough to keep her standing under the protective umbrella of her mother's orders. *No listening at the door. No riffling through your father's drawers. No searching for games on your father's cell phone.* Her mother seemed to want to keep her from her father, but Rosalind didn't understand why. She'd married him, hadn't she? She loved him, didn't she?

Yes, her mother always said with a sigh whenever Rosalind asked her, *and yes. But some things are more important than love. One day, you'll understand that.*

* * *

"This is it," Bean whispered. He took Portia's hand. They would walk into the warehouse together and lead the Butchers in the greatest heist in history. "And it's all happening because of you."

* * *

On Tuesday and Thursday nights, Rosalind and her mother went to rehearsals for the Boston Women's Shakespeare Company. This season they were doing *Much Ado about Nothing,* and her mother was Hero, one of her least favorite roles. "It's impossible to give her a spine," her mother said as she honked her horn at the stalled traffic in front of her. "She's in love with an idiot who wants her dead because she supposedly cheated on him, and even her own father can't stand the sight of her. Then, when the incident gets resolved, she just goes back to normal. Can you imagine?"

Rosalind had no idea what her mother was talking about. She had been thinking about Bianca—the daughter of the woman playing Beatrice—who had also been named after a Shakespearian character and who looked like one too with her wavy blond hair, bright green eyes, flouncy dresses, and headbands of interwoven plastic flowers. During the last rehearsal, Bianca had whispered to Rosalind and Marco, son of the play's Benedick, that they should learn the lines and put on their own version of the play by filling in for their parents. Marco had promised to bring a friend today to play Claudio, and Rosalind wondered who it might be. She thought Marco was cute, and she hoped that his friend would look like him and not every other awkward sixth grader at school.

They arrived twenty minutes late, and the rehearsal for Act V, scenes iii–iv, was already in motion, with a chair standing in for the missing Hero. Marco was sitting in the back row of the auditorium, with an unknown person with short black hair on one side of him and Bianca on the other. Rosalind felt the thrill that always came with arriving at rehearsals, as well as a sense of apprehension. What if the boy didn't like her?

But she needn't have worried, for the black-haired stranger was a girl. "My neighbor," Marco explained. "Sorry, Rosalind, but I just couldn't convince any of my friends to listen to Shakespeare outside of school."

"That's okay," she lied. She noticed that Marco and Bianca were holding hands on Bianca's side of the armrest and frowned. "We can just skip practice."

"No," said the black-haired girl, "let's do it anyway. I want to be an actress, and Marco promised me this would help."

Rosalind shrugged. She didn't care about anything except the couple holding hands, and the way that Bianca didn't so much as look at her as they slipped out of the auditorium and into a classroom across the hallway. Of course, Bianca and Marco wanted to run lines for the same part of the play that the adults were practicing: the final scene, when everyone marries and kisses and lives happily ever after.

"Fine." Rosalind rolled her eyes. "Whatever you guys want."

Everyone knew their lines but the new girl, so they gave her their copy and recited their own lines by heart. The new girl, now Claudio, got the surprise of his assumed-dead fiancé coming back to life, and then Benedick and Beatrice claimed not to love each other but then admitted their true feelings.

"Peace! I will stop your mouth," said Benedick. He kissed his bride, and then kept on kissing her, until it was obvious that the play was over and Benedick was Marco again and everything that had ever existed between Rosalind and Bianca was gone. And what had existed between them? Rosalind wasn't quite sure; or rather, she knew, but couldn't name it.

"Come on." The new girl, who said her name was Tina, put her arm out like a gentleman, and Rosalind threaded her hand through the triangle and then rested it on Tina's forearm. "Let's get out of here before I throw up."

* * *

FOR FATHER'S DAY, THE TINY NOTTS made clay families stuck onto cardboard box lids. *You can make your parents,* Daisy Chain explained as she wove through the two-seater tables, *or anyone else in your life you feel has served as a mentor or friend*. She did not want those without fathers to feel left out, or for those with bad fathers to feel that they must craft clay idols of false gods. The clay people were melon-headed and blue-faced. They had bloated arms and legs, as if they wore snowsuits, and startled O's for mouths and eyes. One child had to prop a top-heavy father up with three toothpicks, turning him into a spider mutant. Another accidentally decapitated her father with her backpack when she riffled for her pencil. Little John was there too, helping, and she winked at Daisy Chain over the bent heads.

"Beautiful," Daisy Chain told Katie, who was working hard on her mother's long, blond hair. She had taken her time on the outfit, a long dress with flowers etched into the waist.

"It's you!" Katie said proudly.

Daisy Chain looked down at her likeness, but for some reason, she felt panicked. Who did she think she was fooling with this Mother Theresa act? None of her work could ever make up for what she had done. *That was Viola*, she told herself, but for some reason this time, the disassociation didn't work. She had the urge to squish herself pancake flat against the desk. If only she could get away from all those fathers. If only she could—

"Miss Daisy?" Katie's brows furrowed. "Do you like it?"

Daisy Chain needed to tune out that voice. She thought of Shakespeare quotes, not relevant but anything, *Shall I compare thee to a summer's day—Something wicked this way comes—Get thee to a nunnery—*

"I love it," she said over the noise. "What an honor."

She told Little John she needed to use the "potty." The bathroom was for children, with a short toilet and low sink, bright pink soap, and a step stool. It smelled like coconut sunscreen. In the mirror, her body stopped at her shoulders; above the neck, she could have been someone else.

I am someone else.

* * *

ROSALIND'S FATHER ANNOUNCED THAT HE WAS taking her for ice cream.

"Why?" she asked.

"Can't a man take his daughter out on a beautiful Saturday afternoon without arousing suspicion?"

He drove her to Cone-O-Copia, which was across town, rather than her usual soft serve from the McDonald's down the block. In the car he was quiet but happy, humming along with the radio and tapping his thick fingers against the steering wheel to the beat. She barely ever spent time alone with her father; she felt both elated and unsettled. Her legs itched. She wondered what her mother could possibly be doing with an afternoon to herself. She looked out the window, and then at her father again. He looked weird in jeans and a polo shirt—normal dad clothes.

The ice cream shop was packed. Little kids stood in puddles of bubble gum and mint and rocky road, and bigger kids stared into space, bored, while their parents yapped at them about something unimportant. Everywhere was loud. Rosalind ordered chocolate-covered cherry, and her father ordered raspberry sorbet. *The closest to gelato,* he explained. He got a small cup; she asked for the cone on the right, with the pointy end—not the one that looked like an upside-down sandcastle. There were no empty seats at any of the tables.

"We'll eat in the car," her father announced, refusing to let his plan go awry.

Outside was hot, and the car was even hotter. Rosalind and her ice cream cone dripped in unison. Frank rolled down the windows, and a slight breeze made the air bearable—for a while.

"So, I want you to do me a favor," Frank said. His eyes stayed on Cone-O-Copia in front of them. "It's something only you can do, and it would mean a lot to me."

Rosalind perked up. A favor? From her?

"I want you to keep an eye on your mother," he said. His bowl was empty, but he kept scraping at the Styrofoam. "She might seem fine to you, but the doctor says she's been having delusions—mostly about me."

Rosalind's heartbeat raced. Her mother was sick? Why hadn't she told her? Had there been signs? She thought back. Her mother did always warn her not to get too close to her father's friends, or to listen at the door, or—

"I don't want you to spy or anything." He waved his spoon. "Just keep an eye out, you know? For anything fishy. That way I can take care of her."

Rosalind nodded very seriously. She felt like a superhero tasked with saving the world. She would watch her mother's every move; she would listen to her every phone call; she would help her get better.

"Good talk." Her father smiled at her. "Now we'd better be getting home."

CHAPTER TWENTY-ONE

A.C. PUT THEM IN CHARGE OF a job. "You'll run point together," he said, intertwining his fingers. "Think of this as training wheels." The instructions were simple: kidnap, ransom, return. The target was Adelaide Meeks, the daughter of a city councilmember, someone A.C. needed to cooperate on a zoning bill—and who he hoped to extort a million dollars from in the process.

They had three days.

On Monday morning, Bean and Portia rented a car to stake out the house in Melrose without leaving a trail. Though they planned on parking by 5:00 A.M., Bean insisted on making a pit stop first. He emerged from the gas station with lukewarm coffees and glazed donuts, which they ate while they waited. The house was hidden by a protective gate, the kind that all the wealthiest people in Melrose used to shield themselves from the distasteful events of the common people, so they could not see much but for a stern gray roof and the tops of three well-pruned trees. Without taking their eyes off the gate, Bean and Portia talked about their favorite time-killing topic: puppies. Bean wanted a Treeing Walker Coonhound; Portia wanted a Golden Retriever.

"But a Coonhound could help us track down our enemies," reasoned Bean.

"I don't want our dog wrapped up in all of this." Portia checked the time, and then brought her eyes right back to the gate. "I want him wagging his tail when we come home from a long day."

"That does sound nice," Bean admitted. He felt for her hand and held it. "You know, working with your fiancé really has its perks."

At 7:30 a.m. on the dot, the gate swung open, revealing a two-story house with expansive yellow gables and a set of white lounge chairs on the porch. A basset hound lay at the door, probably waiting to be let back inside. At first, no one appeared, but then a teen in a blue plaid uniform and black loafers slipped through the gate in a hurry and veered left. She had long red hair that swished against her back. Bean started the car and inched forward, following her.

"Isn't school . . . ?" he asked.

"Yup. The other way." Portia squinted at Adelaide's retreating back as she turned again and disappeared into the hedges around her yard. The prickly green branches shook a little and then went still. "But I have a feeling she isn't going to school."

A minute later, a different girl left the protection of the bushes and dusted off her ratty jeans. Her loafers had become black boots. Her shirt sported the name of a band Portia had never heard of. She wore an empty backpack that sunk against her body. Portia's throat felt tight, like she was choking on air. Adelaide was the spitting image of—

Stop. Don't even say her name.

Adelaide looked left and right, then crossed the street and got into a bright blue van. The lights came on, and the van moved forward, driven by someone else who must have been waiting for her. "Follow them," Portia said, and Bean slipped into the road again.

The van's driver was sloppy with indicating and terrible at lane merges. Portia wondered whether the person up front was seventeen too, and whether their parents had an idea that their vehicle was on I-93 south. They passed Middlesex Fells Reservation and Wright's Park, and then ended up at Tufts University fifteen minutes later. Students flooded the sidewalks, crosswalks, and green spaces of the school grounds. Adelaide and three other students wearing similar outfits climbed out of the van and joined the flock, and then the driver disappeared. Portia thought of Skillet.

"What are they doing?" Bean asked.

Bean and Portia left the car parked without paying the meter and followed the small pack of high schoolers through the college grounds. There were so many graduate students and teachers jammed onto the busy sidewalks with the undergrads that no one noticed two people in their twenties, even when they had to run to catch up with Adelaide's gang. They passed a group of hippies playing drums, followed by a stand giving out free condoms, a sorority selling cookies, and a group of friends all checking their cell phones. Suddenly, Adelaide and her friends turned into a place called Tisch Library and disappeared through the doors.

Portia put her hand out to stop Bean from following. "They must have swipe access. We'll need to wait for them here."

Students poured into and out of the library, but none of them were Adelaide or her friends. The morning turned hot.

Bean insisted on getting another cup of coffee from the café on the bottom floor of the library, and when she threatened to leave him if Adelaide came back, he gave her the keys. He returned with two iced coffees and a blueberry muffin to split.

"You're terrible at this," she said as she broke off half of the muffin.

"And you're excellent at it." He leaned over and kissed her, and she kissed him back with her eyes open and trained on the door. "Is it my fault my fiancé is so distracting?"

Portia understood, as Bean did not, that the *training wheels* comment had been meant for her. Bean was the extra accessory, to be removed from her jobs once she proved herself capable. Sure, A.C. would still send his son on errands, but they would be simple ones, like a dog sent after a stick. Portia was the one he trusted.

Whatever Adelaide and her friends did in the library took an hour and twenty-three minutes. In the meantime, Portia daydreamed about what it would have been like to go to college, though she didn't even know what subjects they taught or what her major could have been. The last time Portia had been in school, they'd been learning about *Romeo and Juliet*, algebra, and introductory biology. How much had she missed? She probably would have been an English major like her mother, though Frank would have tried to convince her to do business so that she could run his line of delis—and the secret work that they covered up—after she graduated. Little John would have picked statistics, and Robin would have picked conservational biology, and—

Adelaide and her friends reappeared. Their backpacks looked much heavier than when they had entered, and even the smaller front pockets were now full. They hurried back the opposite way as fast as they could, weighed down like snails by their shells. Probably stolen books, Portia thought, since that was what the Merry Misfits would have done in a library.

Adelaide paused and tightened her bag, leaving her five, ten, twenty feet behind the others.

"It's now or never," Portia whispered.

She grabbed one of Adelaide's arms, and Bean grabbed the other. The teen opened her mouth to scream, but Portia said they had weapons, which was true—they both had guns in leg holsters. Up close, Adelaide looked much younger than before, just a kid under a layer of eyeliner and hair dye.

"If you want to save all of these people's lives, then you'll come with us quietly," Portia ordered. Portia knew this would work because it would have worked on Robin. One life easily traded for the life of others. Adelaide set her mouth into a grim line and let her arms go limp. They fell away from the rest of the group and disappeared into the crowd, taking the long way back to their car so that no one would see them. When they got back to the rental, they stuck Adelaide in the back of the car, and Portia took the seat next to her. She removed her gun and aimed it so that Adelaide knew they were serious.

"How much is the ransom?" Adelaide asked once they were moving.

"A million," Portia said. She felt unnerved. Looking at Adelaide was like looking directly into the past—someone else's past.

"You'll get it." Adelaide leaned back into her seat and closed her eyes, as though she was at a spa and not her own kidnapping. "You can use my cell phone. He's listed under A-hole with the Credit Card." Portia could not help smiling a little at that. A-hole with the Credit Card. It was exactly the kind of thing Robin would have done, and then she would have been sure to let the person see it the next time they called.

They took Adelaide to a motel where the owner owed A.C. a favor. Even the motel sign looked shabby, coated in pollen and dirt and surrounded by dying Dwarf crape myrtle, and the rest of the U-shaped building was worse. The staircases hadn't been cared for in years, and flecks of black paint came off in Portia's hands as she ascended. The key card didn't work the first three times. Upon opening the door, Portia smelled chlorine, mold, and old gym socks.

"I'll make the call," Portia said.

Bean took Adelaide inside to wait, and Portia stayed outside with Adelaide's cell phone. As she waited for someone to answer, she watched a woman in a shimmery silver dress come out of an alcove at the end of their side of the building with an ice bucket and then disappear into the room three doors down.

"Adelaide? Is everything okay?"

Portia straightened up. For some reason, she had not expected Congressman Meeks to answer himself.

"We have your daughter," Portia said in a voice much lower than her normal one. "If you want to see her again, then you need to listen very carefully."

Congressman Meeks did not sound terrible at all—he sounded like a worried father who would do anything to get his daughter back. *Just don't hurt her,* he said repeatedly. *She's everything to me.* Portia wondered what her own father would have said in his shoes.

Inside their room, Bean and Adelaide were in the middle of a poker game at the table.

"He said yes?" Adelaide asked nonchalantly, and Portia nodded. She watched them play, both laughing when they got terrible hands and smugly slapping down their cards when they got good ones. Then she had a thought that shocked her.

Someday, I might want to have children with this man . . . and I don't want them wrapped up in all of this.

* * *

DURING THE DAY, WHILE THE OTHER girls go out on jobs, Daisy Chain wandered around Nottingham and the surrounding woods. She picked dandelions and spun so fast that the spores waltzed off into the air. She spied on a fox asleep in a tree hole. Shakespeare quotes flowed from her lips and fell flat on the ears of the other Misfits.

Little John thought she was insane and mentioned it several times a week.

Skillet and White Rabbit ignored her.

Robin was the only one who wanted to spend time with her, and the only one who tried to read between the lines she recited. She never asked Daisy Chain to tell her about *before*. She never asked Daisy Chain anything at all. When she found Daisy Chain lying in a field watching leaves fall, she lay down beside her without saying a word and let them fall onto her face and hair. Ants crawled on their arms, and birds came to rest on branches close to their still forms.

"I need to tell you something," Robin said quietly. Her voice was melodic, and the birds were not startled from their roost. "But I don't know if you'll want to hear it."

Daisy Chain's heart beat quickly in her chest. She felt jarred from her earthly rhythm.

"Ever since you came here, I've felt . . ." Robin turned her head, but Daisy Chain didn't look at her. "I've felt that . . . Well, what I'm trying to say is . . . Uh, I think that I lo—"

"*Don't waste your love on somebody, who doesn't value it,*" interrupted Daisy Chain. She kept her gaze at the sky. Her blood gonged in her ears.

"Right. Okay. That's . . . Right." Robin turned away again. "Just pretend I never said anything, okay?"

When the clouds turned into afternoon haze, Robin got up and left Daisy Chain to her silence. Two squirrels chased each other from tree to tree and then disappeared into a hole. A butterfly undulated in the calm air like a conductor waving her hand. Daisy Chain tried to puzzle out how she felt, but everything was muddled—the butterfly, Robin, her mother. She drifted from play to play, looking for the right words. She did love Robin. Her mother was dead. The butterfly was looking for nectar. Her father must die. Shakespeare did not have the words for this feeling, this bloodlust that turned even a pure emotion like love into something dark and ominous. She thought of Prospero's storm, and the words that Ferdinand yelled as he dove overboard: *Hell is empty and all the devils are here.*

And Daisy Chain was the worst devil of all.

* * *

"Hi, Dad. This is Rosalind. Well, I guess you know that." She took a deep breath and exhaled into the receiver. She wondered where he was, and whether anyone else would hear her message. "Anyway, I just wanted to call and tell you that Mom went out for the afternoon again and wouldn't tell me where she was going. She kept calling this guy 'officer' on the phone before she left. Okay, call me back! It's Rosalind. Your daughter. Okay, bye!"

After she hung up, she went upstairs to investigate her parents' bedroom for clues. Her mother's side showed the signs of her afternoon preparations: lipsticks scattered across the top of her vanity, two discarded shirts cast onto the chair back, and a pair of fuzzy black slippers. Maybe her mother was having an affair, she thought. That would have explained why she had to dress up to get milk, which was what she had told Rosalind before she left, though Rosalind knew that her mother would never have left her at home to go to the store, where they had free cookies and balloons that Rosalind should have been too old for but wasn't.

Rosalind slid her feet over the fake fur and put on a shirt with small pearl buttons down the front. She pinned her hair back with her mother's black bobby pins and modeled left, right, left in the mirror. Something was missing. She opened the jewelry case, filled with gifts from her father, and added a pair of diamond earrings to her ensemble. More, she thought, and added gold bangles. Underneath the stack of bracelets, she found a small piece of folded paper that contained a phone number, a list of dates, and a location: laundromat on Westland Ave.

She thought about calling her dad again, but something made her fold the paper back up and return it to the bottom of the box. Guilt sat in her stomach like a full meal. What if her mother wasn't crazy at all? What if she had been right about Rosalind's father and the other men who whispered in the dining room and smoked cigars inside and always called her Bella, though they knew her name?

What if Rosalind had made a mistake?

Rosalind watched her father throughout dinner, but he did not acknowledge her voicemail or even look at her. His eyes stayed on the television, a football game between two teams that were not the Patriots. When her mother asked him to pass the pepper, he kept his eyes on the screen as he slid the grinder across the table as far as he could reach without getting up. "I'm tired," he said as soon as the game was done, "I think I'm going to go to bed."

That night, Rosalind stared at the wooden coat rack on the wall with her name written in big pink letters across the top and wondered what, if anything, would happen next. She felt sick to her stomach. She pulled the sheets up to her nose and even pulled her old teddy, Mr. Brown, into bed with her, but nothing worked. When the morning sun chased away the shadows of her reading chair, she was still wide awake. Her eyes ached, and her muscles felt like she had been through the hardest gym class of her life.

"Are you sick, *amore mio*?" Her mother turned away from the omelet on the stove and pressed the thin skin of her wrist against Rosalind's forehead.

"No. I don't know." Rosalind checked the hallway closet; her father's black jacket was gone. Hopefully he was at work at the deli. "Can I stay home with you today?"

"*Ovviamente.*" Her mother hugged her, and Rosalind inhaled the oniony scent of her clothes. "Now why don't you try to eat something, *sì*?"

The eggs were tough and tasteless; the translucent pieces of onion and wet threads of spinach made her gag. When her mother wasn't looking, she slid the contents of her plate into the trash and covered them with an unfolded napkin.

"Mama?" she asked.

"Yes, *amore mio?*" Her mother turned on the faucet and began to wash their plates, though they had a dishwasher right next to where she was standing. It's how my mother did things, she always said, of the handwashing but also the laundry line in their backyard and the homemade soap and the washcloths she knit at night while she relaxed in bed.

"I need to tell you something. I told Dad about the officer you've been—"

Her mother dropped the plate in the sink, and the sound seemed as loud as the contents of a recycling bin dumped into the back of the truck.

"Rosalind." Her mother was using her I'm-trying-to-stay-calm voice. She took a deep breath and turned around. "What, exactly, did you say to him?"

"Nothing much, I swear. Just that you've been going out in the afternoons sometimes, and that you called that officer guy a few times. That's all. No big deal, right?"

Her mother looked pale. Her hands shook as she wipes them on a towel. "Listen to me," she whispered, "we need to pack our things right no—"

A knock came at the door.

Her mother didn't move.

"Mama?" Rosalind looked toward the front of the house. "Aren't you going to answer the door?"

* * *

PORTIA WAS SO TIRED THAT SIFTING through her purse for her apartment key felt like an impossible effort. She had been up for three nights straight staking out the home of one of A.C.'s guards, who he suspected of leaking information to the feds, with a gun by her side in case she did see him leaving in the dead of night to make any suspicious calls. During the first day, she had also tapped his house phone and installed cameras in his daughter's stuffed animals. When she tried to close her eyes to get a few hours of sleep between shifts, all she could think about was the fuzzy fur against the palms of her hands and the worn neck of a bear long strangled by a loving arm.

"Tell Bean you're working an undercover gig as a burlesque dancer or something," A.C. had told her without looking up from the open folder on his desk. "Whatever you need to say so that he doesn't ask questions. Bernie's been in the family for over ten years, and Bean would take his death hard, should things come to that."

But they hadn't, to Portia's relief, and now she was finally home again. The key jangled against her wallet, and she scooped it from the crumb-covered bottom of her purse and unlocked her front door.

Wait. What was that sound? She paused, with the door open only a few inches, and pressed her ear against the surface. *Tap-tap-tap-tap.* Pause. *Tap-tap-tap-tap.* Pause. Slowly, she inched the door all the way open and looked down.

Pale yellow face.

Black nose.

Floppy ears.

Portia sank to her knees in exhaustion and surprise. The puppy bounded onto her knees and then thighs, and then, balancing his little back paws, jumped up and put his front paws against her chest. His little pink tongue licked at her chin and cheeks.

"Portia?" Bean appeared in the hallway in pajama pants and no shirt and rubbed sleep from his eyes. The puppy, upon hearing his voice, hopped off her legs and scurried back to its original owner. "I missed seeing your face. Were you surprised?"

"Beyond. But I thought you wanted a coonhound?"

The puppy, feeling its allegiances divided, ran back and forth between them.

"I did," Bean said. He came over and hugged her, and she put her hands on his warm, bare back. "But I wanted you to get what you wanted more."

Portia looked down at the puppy, whose tail wagged just as enthusiastically as she'd imagined. "What should we name it?"

"Well, first of all, you should know he's a boy." Bean said as he got down on his knees and rubbed the puppy's head. "What about Shakespeare?"

"What?" Portia felt all her joy sapped. "Why would you say that?"

"I don't know." Bean looked up at her. "I just assumed he was your favorite author—you know, because you're always quoting him and stuff."

Portia felt unsettled, but she tried to hide the feeling. Besides that one time with the crown of contentment, when had she quoted Shakespeare? Were the other voices in her head slipping out, unnoticed, like spirit possessions?

"Not Shakespeare." She forced herself to smile even though she didn't feel happy anymore. "How about . . ." All the names that came to mind were from Shakespeare's castes. Romeo. Claudius. Mercutio. Ariel. ". . . Marlowe?"

"Marlowe." Bean tried the name out a few times as he petted the puppy. "I like it."

He went to make her a cup of chamomile tea, and Marlowe followed him. Portia wondered if Bean even knew who

Christopher Marlowe was, but she was too tired to follow the train of thought much further than that. She didn't love Bean for his brains, and besides, who else would surprise her with a puppy at exactly the right time without even knowing it?

Wait.

Love?

She examined the thought and found it to be true. Somehow, at some point in the last few months, she had fallen in love with Bean Clark. How could she have let this happen? And now the Shakespeare quotes came rolling in again, starting with Cassius: *Men at some time are masters of their fates: The fault, dear Brutus, is not in our stars, But in ourselves, that we are underlings.* She had thought herself in control this whole time, and here she was, too far down the rabbit hole of Portia's personality, in love with her enemy, about to crawl into bed with not only him but also their sweet new Marlowe. Even worse, she was smiling about it!

Lord, what fools these mortals be!

* * *

WHAT FOOLS THESE MORTALS BE, ROSALIND thought as Marco and Bianca snuck out of the auditorium. One of these days, the two of them would get caught. In the meantime, Rosalind watched the rehearsals until the lines ran through her head when she closed her eyes and greeted her each morning, starting with *I learn in this letter that Don Peter of Arragon comes this night to Messina.* The only good nights were the ones when Tina tagged along with Marco, since at least Rosalind had someone to sit with and discuss the progress of the players.

"Your mom is the bomb," Tina said. She sighed and sat back against the rough red fabric of the auditorium chair.

"Ew."

"No, I didn't mean—"

"Sure." Rosalind sat back so that their faces were closer, and they could whisper. "Just keep your fangirling to yourself." She listened in to identify the actors' place in the play and then whispered, "While we're on the subject of bombs, though, Marco's mom is going to bomb on opening night."

"Yeah." Tina did not turn away from Rosalind's mother, though Marco's mom was on the opposite end of the stage. "She's terrible."

She was more than terrible—she was a mess. According to Rosalind's mother, Marco's parents were in the middle of something called a trial separation, which sounded like a nicer name for a divorce. Whatever it was, it meant Marco's mother cried at every line about love until her mascara ran and the director had to call for a fifteen-minute break. Even when she wasn't crying, her version of Beatrice was less solitary tiger tamed into cohabitation and more timid kitten; Benedick suffered just as much, for the two characters were written as a mirror in which one person's sarcasm and bravado reflected the other. Without a solid performance of Beatrice or Benedick to enchant the audience—and only the obedient Hero and easily duped Claudio to entertain them in the meantime—the play fell flat like a body into a grave.

The next Tuesday, Marco and his mom skipped practice. Then they missed the Thursday after that. Even Bianca stayed home the following week, though her mother, who played Benedick, still came, and practiced her lines with Mr. Hamby, the director.

Tina was the one to finally break the news: the separation had indeed turned into divorce, accompanied by the reveal of a secret girlfriend and her recently purchased beach house. Marco's mother was inconsolable. The women on the block, including Tina's mom, had brought over casseroles and sat with her for hours like they were attending the funeral of her old life, but no one could inspire her to move.

"So, we're screwed." Mr. Hamby threw his clipboard in the air and collapsed dramatically into his seat. He was a volunteer, but everyone knew he had taken on the project to show the school board he would make a great drama teacher when the current one retired.

"Not exactly." Tina pointed at Rosalind. "She already knows all of the lines by heart."

Mr. Hamby and the rest of the cast looked at Rosalind. She waited to feel nervous, but instead, she felt only anticipation.

"Throw something at her," Mr. Hamby ordered Bianca's mother, who played Benedick.

"Uh . . . *I pray you, what is he?*"

Rosalind closed her eyes. Not because she needed to remember the lines—she had instantly recalled the passage—but because she wanted to *become* Beatrice before she spoke. She imagined herself a cold, confident woman who neither needed nor wanted any man except as the object of her laughing scorn.

"*Why, he is the prince's jester,*" she mocked, "*a very dull fool; only his gift—*"

"Another!" Mr. Hamby ordered Benedick.

"*Fair Beatrice, I thank you for your pains.*"

Rosalind laughed, as Beatrice might have. She imagined a corset cinching her waist, making every deep breath an intense effort, and tight shoes that pinched her toes. "*I took no more pains for those thanks than you take pains to thank—*"

"A final cue!" Mr. Hamby cried, his voice almost gleeful. "*Tarry, good Beatrice. By this hand, I love thee.*"

Rosalind paused. Again, she knew the line; again, she took the time to adjust her character. By this point in the play, Beatrice lamented the wrongdoing against her cousin, who had been as faithful to Claudio as any woman could be and yet accused of cheating. "*Use it for my love some other way than swearing by it,*" she said in a cool, calculated tone. She wanted Benedick to take Claudio's life; she wanted revenge.

The whole cast cheered. Rosalind's mother alternated between hugging her tightly and pulling away so that she could smile at her in amazement.

"One thing," Rosalind said as the clapping died down. She felt Beatrice's confidence in her veins.

"Anything," said Mr. Hamby.

"It's about the role of Hero." Rosalind winked at her mother. "I know we can't add lines, but what if we add a silent scene where Hero learns that Claudio regrets her death? That way she won't take him back without at least some gesture of true love? Girls these days don't need more examples of spineless devotion, right Mr. Hamby."

Mr. Hamby stroked his brown mustache thoughtfully. "A silent scene," he mused. Then his eyes drifted somewhere above her, as though he was playing out the changes in his head and imagining the critical attention. "Yes, I think that would *ado*—" he chuckled at his own joke, "—quite nicely."

All the women cheered again, none louder than Rosalind's mother. They set to work discussing the new scene and set—after all, they were three weeks from their first performance—but Rosalind slipped away and found Tina in the back of the auditorium, where she was now the only viewer left. Tina put her hand up, and Rosalind gave her a high five.

"You're a natural liar."

"Guess so." Rosalind tilted her head. "But how'd you know?"

"These two." Tina pointed at the empty seats where Marco and Bianca usually sat. "You're in love with both of them, but you never let it show. I figured if you could hide that huge secret, playing an overly honest Beatrice would be a piece of cake."

Rosalind opened her mouth, but she could not think of a comeback. She really had loved Marco and Bianca—at least for a while. Instead, she decided to use Shakespeare's words:

"Life's but a walking shadow, a poor player that struts and frets his hour upon the stage and then is heard no more. It is a tale told by an idiot, full of sound and fury, signifying nothing."

"Dark," Tina said. "But you're more of a Beatrice than you think. You're not going to let an idiot tell your story—or Mr. Hamby."

"Seems like you think you know me pretty well."

Tina's face went sober. Unlike Rosalind, she was not very good at hiding her feelings. "I guess we've all got our own Biancas. High five for being two lonely losers?"

Tina put out her hand again. This time, instead of giving her a high five, Rosalind held it.

"I guess you don't know everything about me after all," Rosalind said.

* * *

"MORE COFFEE, HUN?"

Viola picked her head up off her arm and blinked against the attack of sun, bright lights, and red paint that had turned the dim diner radiant while she slept. She slid her cup to the end of her table. "Thanks."

The waitress filled her mug and then continued her rounds. When Viola had arrived late the night before, she had been the only patron; now, almost every booth was full of parents and their offspring, who colored on paper mats with stubs of old crayons or played football with folded napkins and their fingers as goals. How tired all of the parents looked; how oblivious to their parents' exhaustion the children were. She wondered if her own parents had found her as draining and decided that the answer was likely yes.

Viola now turned her attention to finding her next ride. The last one had been a family too, or rather a father and his twin girls, and he'd kept his eye on her the whole time, even when one twin hit the other twin with a stuffed bear. Still, he'd given her fruit snacks and a package of tiny bears that tasted like honey graham crackers, and even let her sip some of his Slurpee. Viola had liked him; she had felt he was a good father to his children.

What about these people sitting around her?

Not the mom scolding her toddler; she seemed too uptight, and after all, he'd only dropped his pacifier a few too many times. Not the man reading the paper while his wife poured syrup over the pancakes of their two kids. Maybe the couple sitting alone, completely absorbed in their phones but at least hipster-wannabees in sandals, ripped jeans, and fedoras, or maybe the older woman who spread cream cheese diligently over every surface of her bagel before closing her eyes and taking her first bite.

"You need a ride?"

It was the waitress talking again, only she had changed from her black pants and white apron into normal mom-wear—horizontal striped shirt, loose jeans, and comfortable sneakers like the ones they wore in retirement homes.

"I'm off for the next three days," the waitress said. She slung her coat over her arm. "Else I wouldn't offer."

"Which way are you headed?" Viola asked. She had forgotten about her coffee, so she sipped it now, lukewarm, and too creamy from the milk she had probably put in twice.

"South to my mom's in South Carolina."

Viola had only asked to be polite—she didn't care where the woman was headed. Unless she got a ride soon, she'd be stuck in middle America forever.

"Great. Thanks." Viola got up, and the room spun briefly before settling back into place. She was tired; she hadn't slept more than an hour on the table. "Hey, mind if I use the bathroom first?"

Viola passed by all of the families, now full from their enormous helpings of pancakes, eggs, and bacon, and quieter in their stupor, and followed the bathroom sign. Right as she was about to turn and go through the door, she happened to look behind her. The manager's door had been left open, and though the light was off, she could see the white phone sitting on his desk.

Should she?

Viola went into the office and closed the door behind her. Only then did she turn on the light, though she need not have worried, since the diner was so bright that no one would notice the extra shine. She knew the number by heart, and she dialed it now and held her breath. *Don't answer. Don't answer.*

The phone rung five times and then went to voicemail.

"'*Tis ever common that men are merriest when they are from home.' That means we're out, but leave us—*" Someone picked up, cutting off her mother's voice. "Hello?"

Viola hung up on her father's voice. Her hands shook against the keys as she dialed again, this time a different number.

"Rosalind?"

She took a deep breath. "How did you know it was me?"

"Because you're the only one that calls me from out of state, and the only one who calls me besides my mom. I'm a kid, remember?" Tina paused and then added, "And so are you."

"So you keep telling me." Viola tried to twirl the phone cord around her finger, but the whole thing shook. "How are you?"

"Good, I guess. I'm Puck in *Midsummer Night's Dream* with the Boston Women's Shakespeare Company. They tell me I'm a good actress, but I know that if you were here, they'd give you the part."

"No, they wouldn't. You're a natural." Viola looked around the desk to a picture of the manager and realized that he was the man reading the paper. Who went to their place of work on their day off to eat brunch?

"See. You sound so convincing, but then I remember you haven't even seen me act." Tina's voice became more serious. "When are you coming home?"

Viola looked at the picture again. In a few seconds, she would need to hang up in case Frank was tracking her. "'*Tis ever common that men are merriest when they are from home.*'"

* * *

THE MISFITS WERE GONE AGAIN. DAISY Chain lay in the dusty dirt, her arms by her sides with her fingers pointed down into the ground like roots. Her legs moved apart and then together, apart, and then together, as though she was making a snow angel. Frank had come and gone again, but he would be back. The time was almost right. She envisioned his death like a tomato plant, turning now from green to juicy red. He had not even glanced in her direction when he'd said to Blake, *That's an odd one.* And now Blake was dead. Robin thought that no one had noticed, but Daisy Chain knew the smell of fresh blood.

Her fingers burrowed further into the ground. She felt grass, stones, sand. Her mind drifted away from her body and up into the clouds, like a kite only barely grounded to the earth by its string. She might drift off. She might never come down.

From above, she watched her body stand up and brush itself off. What a strange body it was too, all loose limbs and skipping legs and hair like seaweed in a steady flow of water. The body moved away from Nottingham toward the north end of their grounds, where Robin and Little John had buried Blake in the middle of the night and Daisy Chain had watched them do it from her hiding spot in the woods. The dirt was still freshly pressed, and therefore easy to grab by the fistful and move out of the way. The excavating hands found Blake's face, his shoulders, his torso.

I wonder why my body is doing that, Daisy Chain thought.

The body unearthed Blake's whole form and dragged it from its grave. Blake was heavy, and the body struggled to lift him completely, so he ended up half in the grave and half out of it.

What a strange effort.

When her body had most of Blake on the higher ground, it took out the knife she kept in her boot and set to work adding holes to his chest. The holes seemed very intentionally placed, and in fact, familiar—the pattern of bullet holes that she saw when she closed her eyes. When its work was complete, the body rolled Blake back into his grave and returned the layer of dirt with a few shoves and pats, as if it was tucking him in to sleep.

A useless activity, Daisy Chain decided. *Absolutely pointless.*

Her body went back to its spot in the clearing, and Daisy Chain felt her mind reeled back into it. Any moment now, she would feel the breeze again, feel the sand, feel the wet blood on her palms. She decided that she didn't want to go back, so like a desperate fish, she flailed away from the body that was coming closer, closer, closer. *Help. Help. Help!*

Breeze.

Sand.

Blood.

CHAPTER TWENTY-TWO

DAISY CHAIN SLID INTO THE AUDITORIUM seat in the first row and smiled at her neighbor, an overzealous mom-type with her cell phone out to record her daughter's lines. Daisy Chain could not even remember the last time she had left Nottingham, let alone watched a production of a Shakespeare play. "You're just in time," the mom whispered as the lights dimmed and the curtains pulled back. The scene was Verona, Italy, imagined by this director as a balcony, two sets of stairs, two archways, and a lot of fake ivy.

"*Two households, both alike in dignity, in fair Verona, where we lay our scene, from ancient grudge break to new mutiny, where civil blood makes civil hands unclean.*"

Daisy Chain mouthed the words. Sampson and Gregory appeared with their swords, then Benvolio and Tybalt, and the play was off with the biting of a thumb and a drawing of swords.

"Daisy Chain? Come in, Daisy Chain?" Robin asked in her ear.

Right. She was there for a reason. Without drawing her eyes from the stage, Daisy Chain ran her hand over the back of her seat, across the armrest, and into the mom-type's purse. Keys, cough drop, and voila, a wallet. Her hand withdrew like a warrior in retreat, but the wallet came with her and went into her own bag.

"*I was seeking for a fool when I found you,*" she said softly as she got up.

"Okay," said Robin. "I'll take that line as 'Copy that.'"

This time the woman was elderly, at least eighty, and staring somewhere off-stage with an intent but confused expression. *Is the day so young?*, Romeo, or rather the middle schooler with acne and a high voice playing him, asked. Daisy Chain found the woman's purse, unclasped it, and rummaged around. There was more in there, at least a few tissues and a lot more hard candy, but Daisy Chain found a coin purse and pulled. Into her bag it went, a newfound treasure into her chest.

"A few more," Robin ordered in her ear, "and then get out of there, okay?"

There was fear and uncertainty in her voice. The Misfits had been reluctant to send Daisy Chain on a job, even when that job had been her own idea in the first place, and they'd only agreed to let her spend fifteen minutes in the auditorium. The crew only needed a few hundred dollars, just enough to buy a new truck now that Skillet's had blown its transmission, and Daisy Chain figured that a private school in Tallahassee would do the trick.

Besides, she had been in Nottingham six months. She needed to prove that she was part of the crew.

"*How now! Who calls?*"

"*Your mother.*"

Daisy Chain's palms began to sweat. To distract herself, she moved to the fifth row, this time next to a bald man, and then the seventh row, where another mom had been so trusting as to leave her purse open on the seat between them. The purse was black imitation snakeskin, or maybe the real thing—Robin would have known.

"I'll look to like, if looking liking move: But no more deep will I endart mine eye than your consent gives strength to make it fly."

Daisy Chain froze. The woman's matching snakeskin wallet in her hands fell back into the purse. Daisy Chain was suddenly ten years old listening at the door to her parents' bedroom the night after her father had held one of his secret dinners. She held a glass to the door the way she'd seen on TV, hoping to amplify the sounds of their voices.

"I don't like him," her mother was saying.

"You don't like anyone," said his father.

"Not true. I like lots of people." Daisy Chain heard the clink of her mother's earrings into the dish on her nightstand. "I just don't like men who look like serial killers, that's all."

"Markie is not a serial killer." Her father laughed, and then something happened on the other side of the door involving a lot of rustling of fabric. Maybe they were getting into bed. "He's a good guy. Just look at him with a little less judgment next time, okay? You might be surprised."

"I'll look to like, if looking liking move," her mother said.

"Daisy Chain?" This voice was Robin in her ear. "I think they're onto you."

Daisy Chain blinked. She couldn't orient herself. *Romeo and Juliet* had been the one play her mother refused to act in—*I don't do creepy child stalkers*, she'd always said—and yet there was that line, echoing through time.

"That girl stole my purse," the woman in the first row cried out.

"*O, then, I see Queen Mab hath been with you,*" Mercutio began on the stage, unaware that he had lost his audience.

Daisy Chain felt like the darkness of the theater was consuming her, an enormous mouth swallowing her whole. Her mother's voice came in and out, like a tide, and in between there were the strange lines from the stage and Daisy Chain's own racing thoughts. Queen Mab, the fairies' midwife—*through lover's brains*—why hadn't Rosalind just realized that her mother hadn't trusted her father's friends because she didn't trust Frank himself?—oh, God—*when maids lie on their backs.*

"I think she's ill," the snakeskin woman said, her eyes two reflected beads of light, and then someone had her in their arms and was pulling her back, back, back.

"She's my sister," Robin was saying. Robin—who had come from the van outside, who was a convincing actress, who she loved—had rescued her again. The bag fell from her arm, or was taken. "She's a bit of a klepto, but it's all there, I promise. Make way! Make way, she needs some air!"

The lights attacked her, the bright lights, the lights of *now.* Robin was there, and Little John, and they each took her by an arm and carried her down the hallway filled with trophy cases and awards and student artwork of self-portraits that looked like no one. Then the lights were gone, and they were in the rental car, and Daisy felt the cool breeze come through Skillet's open windows.

"*We know what we are, but not what we may be,*" Daisy Chain whispered.

"Shhh." Robin hushed her as she petted her damp hair. "I know."

* * *

AFTER VIOLA HUNG UP WITH TINA, she walked back into the main area of the diner to find the room completely changed. The first thing she noticed were the empty booths; then the silence. A child whimpered, alerting her to the fact that the families who had once been lounging post-gorge were huddled under their tables, and that's when she saw the gunman wearing a ski mask. Behind him, Viola's waitress had taken cover next to the jukebox.

"Oh," Viola said. Then, because she had no fear of death, she walked right up to the man in the mask and whispered, *"Do all men kill the things they do not love?"*

"What did you just say to me?"

Viola was now close enough to see his plain brown eyes, framed ornately with long lashes, and to smell the maple syrup on his breath. So, he had been one of the breakfasters, now intent on stealing the very money he had just paid— with a lot of interest.

"Step back," the man warned. His voice was young but hard. He had been dealt a bad hand; she could tell. Pain recognizes pain. Still, he seemed well-off now; his gun was the same one Frank owned, which he had let her hold once he'd taken the bullets out. He wore a gold watch. His shoes were real leather and unscuffed.

"I need a ride," Viola said.

The man looked around him without lowering the gun and then asked, "Are you talking to me?"

"You're the one with the H&K USP Compact 9mm. I figure if you've got an expensive gun like that, you probably have an even better . . ." she raised her eyebrows ". . . car."

"What are you even talking about right now?"

Viola smiled her most winning smile, the one she'd used on her mother whenever she wanted something at the mall. "I'm talking about combining forces. You're Marc Antony, and I'm Cleopatra." He still didn't say anything, so she added in her most frustrated yet flirtatious voice, "Do I need to spell it out for you? I need a ride, and you need a female sidekick."

The man hesitated. His gun wavered and aimed again. "I still need the money out of the cash register."

"I don't care if you rob this diner or the World Bank," Viola said, and she found that really didn't. None of these people mattered, only Frank. "I'll meet you outside."

She passed by the robber, and he let her. Outside, the sun shone off the shiny hood of an otherwise nondescript black sedan, a little bent up but unquestionably the nicest car in the lot, and Viola tried the passenger door. Sure enough, it was unlocked. The car still smelled new, and she wondered if he'd purchased it or stolen it.

She found didn't care about that either.

The keys were in the ignition as a DIY getaway plan, so Viola turned them and reclined her seat a little. She needed to sleep, though she would still need to convince the masked man to let her tag along first. There would be time, later, to sway his intentions toward her father. The robber had anger in him, great anger, and that was enough.

Bored, Viola watched a large ant walk across the windshield and thought of one of Hamlet's lines: *What a piece of work is man, How noble in reason, how infinite in faculty, In form and moving how express and admirable, In action how like an Angel, In apprehension how like a god, The beauty of the world, The paragon of animals. And yet to me, what is this quintessence of dust? Man delights not me; no, nor Woman neither.* Nor myself, she thought as the ant made it to the end of the windshield and began the descent down her window. I would put myself in front of a million barrels to win one chance at revenge. *Man delights me—*

The gun went off in the diner. *Bang, bang, bang.* The sound was smooth and quick, though the screams that followed seemed to last for all of eternity.

* * *

RIGHT BEFORE SHE PULLED THE TRIGGER and killed her father, Daisy Chain saw her mother. Not there, in Frank's office, but at home, in their living room, with her stocking feet propped up on a stool and a thick script on her lap. She mouthed her lines quietly. Daisy Chain, now Rosalind, tried to hear what she was saying, but even when she bent her face down so close that she could feel her mother's breath, no sound came out.

The result of forgetting.

"Mama?" Rosalind asked.

Her mother turned toward her. There was a white glow on her face, and now Rosalind remembered that it was Christmas. She turned around to face the tree, tall and austere in all-white lights and crystal ornaments and found the one Popsicle stick angel made by her own hands that morning. A few presents waited on the white velvet skirt: a gold chain for her mother, a doll and stroller for her, and a watch for her father. Or maybe the watch hadn't been wrapped yet, since she was sure there had been more gifts than those three that had disappeared from her recollection.

"Would you like to play a part?" her mother asked.

Rosalind nodded. Her mother pulled her up by the armpits and sat her on the center of her lap, from which vantage point she could see the squiggly lines.

"But I can't read," Rosalind reminded her, almost embarrassed.

"That's okay. Just close your eyes and pretend you *are* the character, and then repeat after me."

And so, Rosalind "read" her first lines of Shakespeare: *If music be the food of love, play on; Give me excess of it, that, surfeiting, the appetite may sicken and so die.* Her mother had to explain the quote by Duke Orsino, and how the first half of the sentence was often misquoted as a call for more music, when in reality, the rest of the quote meant that the music would actually kill his love.

"Why would he—"

"I'm home," Frank called from the front hallway. "And I have presents!"

Rosalind scooted off her mother's lap and made for the hall. At the last second, she looked back to see if her mother was following, but she had already disappeared back into the script. Her mouth moved, but the volume muted again.

Rosalind turned away.

* * *

"WHO ARE YOU?" THE MASKED ROBBER asked Viola, who was now unmasked and revealed as a young man in his early twenties with a scar across his right cheek and a faded tattoo on his neck, asked as he sped away from the diner.

Viola opened her mouth to tell him her name, but she found that no matter how hard she tried, she couldn't speak.

"*That is the question,*" she finally got out. "*Whether 'tis nobler in the mind to suffer the slings and arrows of outrageous fortune, or to take arms against a sea of troubles, and, by opposing, end them?*"

"You're weird," the man said. Then he looked at her again, and she could tell that he was going to let her stay. "My name's Aiden. What's yours?"

* * *

"DO WE HAVE TO GIVE HER back?" Bean asked. He and Portia were in a new rental car, this one nicer with leather interiors and satellite radio, watching Adelaide on a bench across the street. They had not thought about a change of clothes for her, so she was back in her school uniform again. The plaid and high socks made her look so much younger, so much more innocent, than she was.

"I know." Portia linked her fingers with his, but not too tightly, since at any moment she might need to reach into the glove compartment and pull out her gun. "I liked playing house too."

A man in a muscle t-shirt, fitted black pants, and dark sunglasses appeared. He looked around quickly, spoke into an earpiece, and then grabbed Adelaide by the arm and told her something that made her hurry away, as if she was late for a class. Right before they rounded the corner, she looked back over her shoulder, her eyes searching for two now-familiar faces. Then she was gone.

"What if we did this for good?" Bean asked. His voice sounded as sad as she felt.

"What? Kidnapped children for ransom money?" she teased.

"No, Portia." He frowned. Apparently, he wasn't in the mood for jokes. "Played house."

Even though she felt the same way, she knew she could not admit it. They had parts to play, and until the curtain closed on the final act, they could not step off the stage.

"What, and give up all this?" She reached her hand back and patted the duffel bag full of money they had picked up from the allotted dumpster. "I have a million reasons to wait on that step."

She had expected him to frown again, but Bean grinned instead. "You just said *wait*," he pointed out as he started the car. "That means you're thinking about it."

"Just focus on the road for now," she instructed, and he pulled out of the spot and onto the road that would take them home.

"Alright, I'm focused." Then, after a pause, he added "*and* waiting."

Portia let the conversation drop, but she could not help imagining what that white picket fence life would look like. A nice neighborhood, where the children played together after school and on the weekends and they switched off with other parents to have date nights. A house like the one where she grew up, clean and warm and *home*. Her bedroom would look like her mother's, with a king-sized bed and a recliner where she knitted hats for the new babies at church, a walk-in closet filled with dresses she never wore and a second for her shoes and Frank's suits, and a vanity with a mirror that reflected every well-earned wrinkle.

Not that her mother had many wrinkles when she'd died.

And that, right there, was the problem.

No matter how many times Portia insisted on a separation of business and pleasure, any house that she and Bean owned would end up having visits from A.C. and the

Butchers—just like her childhood home had been overrun by Frank's crew. Her kids would find stolen watches in the sock drawer. They would play spy on their parents just to overhear plans for upcoming jobs like the one she and Bean had just finished.

She would always be waiting for that knock at the door.

"Dad's here," Bean said, and Portia shook her head, trying to orient herself. They were at A.C.'s Victorian row home in South End, where he spent only a few weeks of the year. Usually, they met him on one of his boats, or at his vacation home in Martha's Vineyard, and Portia was surprised he'd asked them to bring ransom money there.

Bean's mother opened the door. "Darling!" she exclaimed, thrusting out her enhanced chest. Judging by the over-zealous greeting, she had already visited her pill bottles that morning.

"Hi, Mom." Bean went up the front steps and kissed her on the recently Botoxed forehead. Portia took her time getting the duffel bag, and by the time she got to the door, Bean and his mother had gone off somewhere—probably to have some celebratory champagne, even though it was 11 A.M. Poor, innocent Bean, who was so sheltered and privileged that he did not even notice his own mother's addiction, did not even read between the lines during her most recent trip to a "creativity retreat"—especially considering his mother did not have any artistic talents.

Portia was about to follow their voices when she heard her name called. She dropped the duffel by the gilded loveseat in the hallway and then followed A.C.'s voice to the office, where he sat, as her father often had, among stacks of manila folders and handwritten papers. He closed the window open on his computer with a quick click and then shut the monitor off for good measure. "Close the door."

She did as she was told.

"You did it," he said. He folded his hands over his stomach. "Not that I ever doubted you."

"Bean was a huge help, sir." Her gaze went to a miniature Porsche poured in yellow gold sitting on the desk nearby. "I couldn't have done it without him."

A.C. chuckled. "Sure, sure. Let me guess: he took at least two breakfast breaks during your stakeout and then got himself emotionally attached to the kid?"

She was a good liar, but A.C. was an even better lie detector. She kept her mouth shut.

"I thought so. Portia, you might not be my daughter yet, but you're already more like me than my own son."

She shook her head as though brushing off his compliments, but she could not help the little thrill of pleasure she got from his words. A.C., head of the Boston Butchers, thought *she* was a good criminal.

"Fight it all you want, but you've earned my admiration— and my trust." He paused and picked up the Porsche. In his hands, the small car looked miniature, a Hot Wheel. "Bean tells me you have an idea for a new warehouse space for the Butchers?"

She raised her eyes to his and held her breath. Had she done it? Had she fulfilled her mission?

"You officially have my approval to move forward. In fact, you can take the duffel bag with you on your way out."

"Thank you, sir." She exhaled slowly. "You won't be disappointed."

"I know." A.C. clicked his monitor on and then his mouse.

Dismissed, Portia left the office and closed the door behind her. Then she leaned against the wall between two silver sconces and closed her eyes. She could barely believe she had gotten this far, and that she only had a month to go as Portia. Thirty days from now, she could cast off her heels and her tight-fitting tops and turn back into Daisy Chain, reciter of Shakespeare, flower child of the forest, member of the Merry Misfits.

But what if she couldn't go back?

* * *

VIOLA BEGAN TO FORGET WHAT HER old room looked like. She stopped looking over her shoulder for her father's men. She got a nose job, her hair dyed, a boyfriend who drove her wherever she wanted and knew the black market.

Yet Rosalind was like a layer of covered paint. With the right scrape, she showed through.

This happened at inconvenient times, such as in the grocery store, as she stared at a box of English Breakfast tea and remembered how her mother used to dunk the bag repeatedly as she read; or as Aiden, her boyfriend, punched the face of a man who owed her money and became her father beating at the bag hanging in their basement. He used to hit until he bled at the knuckles, or until her mother yelled *Enough* because it was 3:00 A.M. and he was angry, but she was angrier.

"This is all for you," Aiden told her. Then he kicked the man who now lay down on the driveway, who in a minute would reveal the address of her father's new "school." The man looked like a father in an old t-shirt and gardening gloves. He probably carried a picture of his children in his wallet.

It's all for me, she had thought when she heard about this new venture—Frank's School for Misunderstood Youth. He was baiting her, like a fish to a worm. *But Frank, I'm not misunderstood.*

Oh really? a different voice asked. *Not even by yourself?*

Shut up, Rosalind.

Fine. But you might want to take a good look around, "Viola." Look where you are.

She was nowhere. She was in Miami, at a stranger's house, in the middle of the afternoon. There was a fern bed leading up the driveway. Rake and shovel in the grass. Glass of lemonade, or maybe beer. She looked down.

The stranger was dead.

His children would never see him again, even in a casket.

I'm home.

* * *

WHEN THE GIRL WITH BLOOD-COLORED HAIR found her at the rest stop, Viola was not actually alone. She does not remember, anymore, who she was with, but they were rich, very rich, and they had stopped their car so that she could pick daisies while they used the restroom. *Parting is such sweet sorrow.* She had known that the girl would derail her plans—or, as it turned out, just delay them for a while—but, yet, she had collected her flowers and left with the girl called Robin anyway because, for once, she could not make herself do otherwise.

* * *

DAISY CHAIN WAS STILL INSIDE OF the Christmas memory when she pulled the trigger. She knew her father at the end of the hallway with his arms outstretched was not real, that this version of Frank had only come now to stop Daisy Chain from what she was about to do, and so she aimed at the wrapped gift held in front of his chest anyway. *You still love him*, her mind told her, *and he's still your father. What would your mother think? Would she really want you to—*

Rosalind leapt the last few feet of the hallway toward young Frank's arms, like a bird into the safety of a tree's branches.

Daisy Chain pulled the trigger.

The shot was like the caps her neighbor had once smashed with rocks, only louder, like all of them going off at once. The memory disappeared. The room where she stood was dark and smelled like blood and urine. Uncle Frank, as the other girls called him, had a widening red circle on his white shirt.

"Daisy Chain?" Robin asked, but Daisy Chain barely heard her. She didn't feel better; in fact, she was angrier than she had ever been. She had finally killed her father, and yet the black hole at her center was still there. She swung her gun wildly and found Frank's bodyguard. *Give me excess of it, that, surfeiting, the appetite may sicken and so die.* Maybe if she shot him too, if she shot every last one of them, she might feel like herself again.

Robin was calling her name, her voice like an anchor holding her still against a vicious tide. Robin was forming her from the clay of her confusion. If only she focused on those words, she might be able to pull herself out of this fugue state.

Daisy Chain.

Daisy Chain.

Daisy Chain.

And that was who she was.

* * *

IN THE PARKING LOT OUTSIDE THE Butchers' new warehouse, Portia stopped walking. Bean tugged at her arm like
an insistent dog against its leash, and then stopped too.

"What's wrong?" he asked.

Portia checked her Gucci watch, a one-year anniversary
gift, and saw they had one minute left. She looked past him,
to the warehouse, a nondescript building with rusty red
siding and a large black door where the Butchers had been
meeting for months. The windows were pollen-dusted. The
roof was covered in wet leaves. Inside, the Butchers sat
around a long table, with A.C. at one end and an empty seat
for Bean, the heir apparent, at the other. Whiskey glasses
around the table reflected sunlight like the dazzling bulbs
around a Hollywood mirror. Piles of fruit and tiny muffins
baked by Bean's mother covered silver trays.

The chair next to Bean's was reserved for her.

"I just have a bad feeling." She kept hold of his hand,
squeezed it. The underside of her engagement ring dug into
her finger.

"What kind of feeling?" Bean asked.

No other man in that warehouse would have stopped fifty
feet from the door and had this conversation. No other man
was Bean. She looked into his eyes and saw trust there, the
kind of trust that she hadn't had for another human being
since her mother's murder.

"A feeling that we need to go."

"Go?" Bean looked back at the warehouse, at her, at the
warehouse again. "But . . . What about . . . ?"

"Bean." She took his other hand, so that he could not
easily look away. "When I first met you, all you cared about

was the Butchers. But over the past year and a half, you've become a completely different person. You take vacations. You speak your mind in meetings. You are *more than just your father's son.*"

"And that's all because of you." Bean stopped trying to turn around and just smiled at her. "You've changed my life."

"And now I'm going to change it again." Portia dropped her voice to a whisper. "Do you see those bushes to the right." Bean started to turn again. "No, don't look, just move your eyes."

Bean shifted his glance to his right. At first his face was blank; then recognition set in. His lips pursed.

"They aren't alone," she said. "There are more behind those parked cars. I can see their shoes."

"What?" His eyes darted right, left, right. His breathing quickened. "We need to tell—"

"Bean." Her voice was firm. She sounded like her mother. "There's no time. You can either go to prison with them, or you can drive off with me."

Bean looked back at the warehouse. Then he glanced back at their Ferrari twenty feet behind her. She remembered what it felt like to split down the middle, and she knew that if he followed her, it would be a long time before he was whole again.

"On three," she said without moving her mouth, and then she counted them down. On three, she turned and ran, her heels like stilts adjusting her gait forward, toward escape. A second set of footsteps followed her. Bean unlocked the door, threw himself into his seat, and started the car. No one fired a shot, but Portia felt eyes on her, judging her, mourning her. As they reversed out of the lot, the warehouse closed in on itself—the doors locked, the windows barred, the vents in the walls released a gas that would put every Butcher leader to sleep. These same walls had been recording them for a month, gathering enough evidence to bring down every man involved in their operation for life. *A smart warehouse*, Robin had described it on the phone, *and all you need to do is get them there.*

A wolf in sheep's clothing, Portia had thought as she hung up the phone, but the fable did not feel right, for she had begun to forget who was the sheep and who the wolf. She was losing herself. In the words of Shakespeare, *There is nothing either good or bad, but thinking makes it so.* If she had stayed Portia any longer, she would think herself out of the plan—and out of herself.

Now, Robin was somewhere in the bushes, or behind the parked cars, wondering what had happened to her friend Daisy Chain . . .

. . . and Portia was gone.

PART FIVE
EPILOGUE

DURING THE NEXT SESSION OF NOTTINGHAM, Robin again stands behind the curtains. She has given up trying to give the opening remarks—instead, she will stand beside Skillet and wave, vaguely, at the crowd of excited teens.

For now, she hides here, in the dark—alone.

"Robin?"

Robin turns around. The lights are like a truck's high beams, and she can barely see anything for a few seconds. Then a stranger with a long dishwater-blond braid wearing leggings and ballet flats comes into view. Robin tries to place her. Something about her secretive smile, and the way she shyly looks down from Robin's gaze, seems so familiar.

"*All the world's a stage,*" the woman says.

Robin only knows one person who would have the audacity to sneak backstage to utter a Shakespeare quote. "Daisy Chain?"

The woman smiles fully now, and her happiness turns her into a stranger again. Did Daisy Chain ever smile that way around her? Skillet calls Robin's name, but she can't move. She feels rooted to the ground; or rather, completely uprooted, like a tree whipped around in a tornado.

"I actually go by Imogen now," Daisy Chain says. She points to her nametag, which says Imogen Cress. "But you can call me whatever you want."

Rosalind. Viola. Portia. Robin thinks through the Shakespeare plays she has read since Daisy Chain left and places the name Imogen: the virtuous wife of Posthumus in *Cymbeline*. She wonders if Daisy Chain picked that name for the meaning it conveys, or because she had already used up the rest of Shakespeare's cast on other personas.

"What are you doing here?" Robin asks, because she can't think of anything else to say.

"My daughter." Daisy Chain points past her, to the crowd. "She brought home your brochure from school, and I . . . Well, I just thought . . ."

They both stare at each other.

"So, you're married?" Robin asks. She should be elated just to know Daisy Chain is alive, but she feels sick to her stomach. Has she just been living a normal life for all these years, unaware of how much pain she caused them all?

"Widowed," Daisy Chain says. "As of a few years ago."

"I'm sorry." Robin isn't sorry. She feels angry. She wants to rip the nametag off Daisy Chain's shirt and shred it to pieces. Twenty years, gone like sand through open fingers—or the dust from a long drive washed away. Twenty years of wondering.

"I should have contacted you," Daisy Chain says. She steps closer. "But I didn't know how, not after I just left you all like that. I was a different person then, and . . . After years of therapy and medication, I . . . There were all these memories that I couldn't . . . It's hard to explain."

Skillet moves toward the wing and then stops. "Daisy Chain?" she asks.

"Hey there, Skillet."

Robin's name is a thunderous *clap-clap*. The girls are chanting it. She thinks about how she and Daisy Chain could never just talk about their feelings—how they kept missing each other, one of them entering stage left just as the other exited stage right. How they kept accidentally hurting each other because they were hurting.

"Let me guess—you want me to stall?" Skillet asks.

Robin nods her head.

Once Skillet starts talking again—this time with a very long-winded story about poor Adele, who will be beyond embarrassed after the assembly—Robin whispers, with anger in her voice, "So who are you now?"

Daisy Chain steps closer again, so that Robin can feel the tickle of Daisy's breath mingling with hers. *"All the world's a stage, and all the men and women merely players. They have their exits and their entrances; And one man in his time plays many parts."*

"That's not an answer," Robin says. Now she is practically yelling. She wonders if the audience can hear her, but she does not actually care. Nothing matters but this moment. Daisy Chain's words in the forest echo in her ears. *Don't waste your love on somebody, who doesn't value it.* God, Robin hates Shakespeare.

"That's what I'm trying to tell you," Daisy Chain says. She takes Robin's hands. Her skin is softer and thinner than the last time they touched, but her grip is still familiar. "No matter who I've been, I've always loved you."

On the stage, Skillet is throwing her hat into the air, and a few rows back, someone catches it. The girls cheer. Some of them cry. The auditorium is like a firework exploding in the night sky, so loud and electric that Robin finds herself crying too.

These girls are going to be okay.

Their futures stretch out before them like an open road.

"Okay," Robin says, but what she means is, *I love you too.* In a quick motion, she puts her hand out to Daisy Chain's chest and rips off her nametag.

Robin does not hear the rest of the opening remarks, or the string of colorful curses Skillet probably hurls at her after the assembly for leaving her in those bright spotlights alone again. She does not hear Little John's gasp of surprise, or how Wanda asks, *Wait, who was Daisy Chain again?*

She does not hear any of this because by the time the assembly ends, the two women, who were once girls, are already flying away on a red Aprilia RSV4 down a vacant road outside Nottingham, the wind filling in all the words they don't need to say.

THE END

ABOUT THE AUTHOR

DR. KELLY ANN JACOBSON IS THE author of many published books, including, most recently, her young adult novel *Tink and Wendy* (Three Rooms Press), winner of the 2021 *Foreword* Indies Gold Medal for Young Adult Fiction, and her contest-winning chapbook *An Inventory of Abandoned Things* (Split/Lip Press). Kelly's short fiction has been published in such places as *Boulevard, Best Small Fictions, Daily Science Fiction, Southern Humanities Review, The Texas Review,* and *Gargoyle.* Kelly received her PhD in fiction from Florida State University. She currently lives in Lynchburg, Virginia, where she is an assistant professor of English.

RECENT AND FORTHCOMING BOOKS FROM THREE ROOMS PRESS

Three Rooms Press | New York, NY | Current Catalog: www.threeroomspress.com

Three Rooms Press books are distributed by Publishers Group West: www.pgw.com